THE
NIGHT VISITORS

Also by Carol Goodman

The Lake of Dead Languages
The Seduction of Water
The Drowning Tree
The Ghost Orchid
The Sonnet Lover
The Night Villa
Arcadia Falls
River Road
The Widow's House
The Other Mother

CHILDREN'S AND YOUNG ADULT

Blythewood
Ravencliffe
Hawthorn
The Metropolitans

AS JULIET DARK

The Demon Lover
The Water Witch
The Angel Stone

AS LEE CARROLL (WITH LEE SLONIMSKY)

Black Swan Rising
The Watchtower
The Shape Stealer

Praise for Carol Goodman and *The Other Mother*

"Carol Goodman is, simply put, a stellar writer."
—Lisa Unger, *New York Times* bestselling author of *The Red Hunter*

"An atmospheric and harrowing tale, richly literary in complexity but ripe with all the crazed undertones, confusions, and forebodings inherent in the gothic genre. Recommend this riveting, du Maurier–like novel to fans of Jennifer McMahon."
—*Booklist* (starred review)

"This engrossing novel will keep readers eagerly turning the pages."
—*Publishers Weekly*

"An engaging read that will appeal to readers of Shari Lapena or Michelle Richmond."
—*Library Journal*

"In the spirit of du Maurier's *Rebecca* . . . A gothic thriller deliciously riddled with dark motives and shadowy paths."
—*Kirkus Reviews*

"[Goodman] offers puzzles and twists galore but still tells a human story."
—*Boston Globe*

"Goodman combines gripping suspense with strong characters and artistic themes. Those who read Anita Shreve or Jodi Picoult are likely to become fans."
—*Library Journal*

"Goodman specializes in atmospheric literary thrillers."
—*Denver Post*

THE
NIGHT VISITORS

A Novel

CAROL GOODMAN

WILLIAM MORROW

An Imprint of HarperCollins*Publishers*

P.S.™ is a trademark of HarperCollins Publishers.

THE NIGHT VISITORS. Copyright © 2019 by Carol Goodman. All rights reserved. Printed in the United States of America. No part of this book may be used or reproduced in any manner whatsoever without written permission except in the case of brief quotations embodied in critical articles and reviews. For information address HarperCollins Publishers, 195 Broadway, New York, NY 10007.

HarperCollins books may be purchased for educational, business, or sales promotional use. For information, please email the Special Markets Department at SPsales@harpercollins.com.

FIRST EDITION

Designed by Diahann Sturge

Library of Congress Cataloging-in-Publication Data has been applied for.

ISBN 978-0-06-285200-7 (paperback)
ISBN 978-0-06-288436-7 (hardcover library edition)

19 20 21 22 23   LSC   10 9 8 7 6 5 4 3 2 1

To the people of Family,
the true kindly ones

THE
NIGHT VISITORS

A name can change one's core identity:
"The Furies" thus became "The Kindly Ones,"
Athena ending senseless cruelty.

A name can change one's core identity.

Benevolence diverts from treachery;
and, shining like her crown, pure goodness wins.

A name can change one's core identity:
"The Furies" thus became "The Kindly Ones."

—Lee Slonimsky

CHAPTER ONE

Alice

OREN FALLS ASLEEP at last on the third bus. He's been fighting it since Newburgh, eyelids heavy as wet laundry, pried up again and again by sheer stubbornness. *Finally,* I think when he nods off. *If I have to answer one more of his questions I might lose it.*

Where are we going? he asked on the first bus.

Someplace safe, I answered.

He stared at me, even in the darkened bus his eyes shining with too much smart for his age, and then looked away as if embarrassed for me. An hour later he'd asked, as if there hadn't been miles of highway in between, *Where's it safe?*

There are places, I'd begun as if telling him a bedtime story, but then I'd had to rack my brain for what came next. All I could picture were candy houses and chicken-legged huts that hid witches. Those weren't the stories he liked best anyway. He preferred the book of myths from the library (it's still in his pack, racking up fines with every mile) about heroes who wrestle lions and behead snake-haired monsters.

There are places . . . I began again, trying to remember something from the book. *Remember when Orestes flees the Furies and he goes to some temple so the Furies can't hurt him there?*

It was the temple of Apollo at Delphi, Oren said, *and it's called a sanctuary.*

No one likes a smarty-pants, I countered. Since he found that mythology book he likes to show off how well he's learned all those Greek names. He'd liked Orestes right away because their names were alike. I'd tried to read around the parts that weren't really for kids, but he always knew if I skipped over something and later I saw him reading the story to himself, staring at the picture of the Furies with their snake hair and bat wings.

At the next bus stop he found the flyer for the hotline. It was called Sanctuary, as if Oren's saying the word had made it appear. I gave him a handful of change to buy a candy bar while I made the call. I didn't want him to hear the story I'd have to tell. But even with him across the waiting room, standing at the snacks counter, his shoulders hunched under the weight of his *Star Wars* backpack, he looked like he was listening.

The woman who answered the phone started to ask about my feelings, but I cut to the chase and told her that I'd left my husband and taken my son with me. *He hit me,* I said, *and he told me he'd kill me if I tried to leave. I have no place to go . . .*

My voice had stuttered to a choked end. Across the waiting room, Oren had turned to look at me as if he'd heard me. But that was impossible; he was too far away.

The woman's voice on the phone was telling me about a shelter in Kingston. Oren was walking across the waiting room. When he reached me he said, *It can't be a place anyone knows about.*

I rolled my eyes at him. Like I didn't know that. But I repeated his words into the phone anyway, trying to sound firm. The woman on the other end didn't say anything for a moment, and looking into Oren's eyes, I was suddenly more afraid than I'd been since we left.

I understand, the woman said at last, slowly, as if she were speaking to someone who might *not* understand. I recognized the social worker's "explaining" voice and felt a prickle of anger that surprised me. I'd thought that I was past caring what a bunch of morally sanctimonious social workers thought about me. *We can arrange for a safe house, one no one will know about. But you might have to stay tonight in the shelter.*

Oren shook his head as if he could hear what the woman said. Or as if he already knew I'd messed up.

It has to be tonight, I said.

Again the woman paused. In the background a cat meowed and a kettle whistled. I pictured a comfortable warm room—framed pictures on the walls, throw pillows on a couch, lamplight—and was suddenly swamped by so much anger I grew dizzy. Oren reached out a hand to steady me. The woman said something but I missed it. There was a roaring in my ears.

. . . give me the number there, she was saying. *I'll make a call and call you right back.*

I read her the number on the pay phone and then hung up. Oren handed me a cup of hot coffee and a doughnut. How had he gotten all that for a handful of change? Does he have money of his own he hasn't told me about? I slumped against the wall to wait, and Oren leaned next to me. *It will be all right,* I told him. *These places . . . they have a system.*

He nodded, jaw clenched. I touched his cheek and he flinched. I looked around to see if anyone had noticed, but the only other occupants of the station were a texting college student, the old woman behind the snacks counter, and a drunk passed out on a bench. When the phone rang I nearly jumped out of my skin.

I picked up the phone before it rang again. For a second all I heard was breathing and I had the horrible, crazy thought that it was *him.* But then the woman spoke in a breathless rush, as if she'd run somewhere fast. *Can you get the next bus for Kingston?*

I told you no shel— I began, but the woman cut me off.

At Kingston you'll get a bus to Delphi. Someone will meet you there, someone you can trust. Her name's Mattie—she's in her fifties, has short silvery hair, and she'll probably be wearing something purple. She'll take you to a safe house, a place no one knows about but us.

I looked down at Oren and he nodded.

Okay, I said. *We'll be there on the next bus.*

I hung up and knelt down to tell Oren where we were going, but he was already handing something to me: two tickets for the next bus for Kingston and two for Delphi, New York. *Look,* he said, *the town's got the same name as the place in the book.*

That was two hours and two buses ago. The last bus has taken us through steadily falling snow into mountains that loom on either side of the road. Oren had watched the swirling snow as if it were speaking to him. As if he were the one leading us here.

It's just a coincidence, I tell myself, *about the name. Lots of these little upstate towns have names like that: Athens, Utica, Troy.* Names that make you think of palm trees and marble, not crappy little crossroads with one 7-Eleven and a tattoo parlor.

I was relieved when Oren fell asleep. Not just because I was tired of his questions, but because I was afraid of what I might ask him—

How did you know where we were going? And how the hell did you get those tickets?

—and what I might do to get the answer out of him.

CHAPTER TWO

Mattie

I WAKE UP to the sound of a train whistle blowing. *Such a lonesome sound,* my mother used to say. I've never thought so. To me it always sounded like the siren call of faraway places. I used to lie in bed imagining where those tracks led. Out of these mountains, along the river, down to the city. Someday I'd answer that call and leave this place.

It takes me a moment to realize that it's my phone ringing that has woken me. And then another few moments to realize that I'm not that girl plotting her escape. I'm a woman on the wrong side of fifty, back where she started, with no way out but one.

The phone's plugged in on my nightstand. One of my young college interns showed me how to set it so only certain people can get through.

But what if someone who needs me has lost their phone and is calling from a phone booth? I asked.

She blinked at me like I was a relic of the last century and asked, *Do they even have those anymore?*

You ought to get out more, Doreen always tells me. *Come down to the city with me.*

It must be Doreen on the phone. She's the only one on the list of "favorites," aside from Sanctuary's number, that I'd programmed into the phone. When the college girl saw that puny list she hadn't been able to hide the pity in her eyes.

I reach for the phone, past pill bottles, paperbacks, and teacups—all my strategies to coax sleep—and manage to knock it over for my pains. I hear Dulcie stir, the vibration of the impact waking her. "It's okay, girl," I croon even though she can't hear me. "It's just Doreen riled up about something."

I swing my legs around onto the floor, the floorboards cold on my bare feet, and lean down to find the phone. The screen is lit up with Doreen's face (the college intern showed me how to do that too, taking a picture from Doreen's Facebook page of her protesting at the Women's March in January). Her mouth is open, midshout, which is kind of a joke because Doreen almost never shouts. She has the calmest voice of anyone I know. *She could talk anyone down,* the volunteers say. That's why she always takes the hotline for the midnight to six A.M. shift, those hours when the worst things happen. Men stumble home drunk from bars and women lock their guns away. Teenagers overdose and girls find themselves out on the road without a safe ride home—or take the wrong one. Which one of those terrible things has happened to make Doreen call me in the middle of the night?

I draw my finger across the screen to answer. "Hi, Doreen."

"Oh thank God, Mattie," she says in a breathless rush as if she'd been running. Doreen always sounds like that. She ran away from her abusive ex seventeen years ago, after he slammed her son's head up against the dining room wall, and sometimes I think she's still running. "I thought you'd let your phone die again."

"No, I just knocked it over. What is it? A bad call?"

Sometimes Doreen will call me because she's upset by a call. I don't mind. No one should have to sit alone in the night with the things we have to hear.

"A domestic violence case. Left home," she says, and my heart sinks. I let out a sigh and feel a pressure against my leg. Dulcie has picked up on my distress and come over to lean against me.

"With a child?" I ask, hoping the answer is no.

"A ten-year-old boy. She was in the Newburgh bus station. I offered the Kingston shelter but she said no. She said it had to be a place no one could find her."

"Oh," I say, reaching down to stroke Dulcie's soft head.

"I checked availability at St. Alban's and Sister Martine said they could take her," Doreen says, "but someone needs to pick her up at the bus station and take her there."

The sisters at St. Alban's are one of our best links on the domestic violence underground railroad. Their convent is on the river, gated, and guarded by a Mother Superior who would face down a dozen angry husbands come searching for their wayward women. It's a chilly place to wash up after you've left your home in the night, though: the nuns in their long black habits, the bare cells, the crucifixes on the walls. I think of that ten-year-old boy, of what he'll feel like in that cold gray place—

"I could call Frank," she says. I hear the hesitation in her voice. Has the woman told her something that makes Doreen think that it might not be a good idea to call our local chief of police—or has she just sensed that there might be some reason to keep the law out of it for now? Or maybe she's just uneasy saying Frank's name to me. Doreen has a theory that Frank Barnes has a crush on me. I've tried to tell her how wrong she is about that, but Doreen doesn't buy it.

"I'll pick them up and take them," I say, already getting up and reaching for the light switch. The weight against my leg slides away as the light floods the room. Doreen is saying something to me, something about the woman that had troubled her or something that the woman had reminded her of, but I don't catch it. I'm staring at the dog bed at the foot of the bed. I'd moved it there a couple of weeks ago because I kept tripping over Dulcie on my way to the bathroom. She's lying there now. Fast asleep.

THERE'S NO TIME to dwell on the phantom pressure on my leg. Diabetic nerve pain? Menopausal hot flash? The early-onset Alzheimer's that felled my mother by my age? More important, the woman and the boy will be arriving at the bus station in an hour. It's only a fifteen-minute drive from the house, but that's assuming the car starts and there's no ice to scrape off the windows and the roads are plowed. While I'm pulling on leggings and jeans, thermal top and sweater, I go to the window to look out. The view of my backyard is a gray-and-white blur of ominous lumps and dark encroaching forest. I can't tell if the snow in the yard is fresh or if the gray in the air is fog or falling snow. There's no back porch light to catch the falling flakes. *You should fix that,* I hear my mother's voice saying. *You're letting the place go to seed.*

You should mind your own business, I tell her right back. She's been dead for thirty-four years. When will her voice get out of my head?

Dulcie is up and shambling by my side by the time we reach the top of the stairs. One of these days we're going to topple ass-over-teakettle together down the steep slippery wooden steps and one of us will wind up in rehab. I'm not laying any bets on who'll survive the fall.

Downstairs, Dulcie heads straight for the back door to be let out as if it's morning. I don't like letting her out in the dark; the snow is deep out there and there are coyotes in the woods, but I don't have time to walk her, so unless I want to come home to a puddle, I'd better.

"Stay close," I tell her, as if she could still hear me, or would listen if she could. I step out with her and feel the sting of icy rain on my face. *Crap.* That won't make for easy driving.

I turn on the kettle and get out two thermoses from the drying rack. There's nothing but tea in my pantry and that won't do for mother or son. There's a box of donations in the trunk of my car, though, that I think had some hot chocolate in it. I should get the car started anyway.

I go out the front door and nearly slide right off the porch. I'll have to salt that. Avoiding the broken third step on the way down is tricky (*one of these days that will be the end of you,* I hear my mother helpfully point out) and the ground below is white with newly fallen snow. There's a good six inches on the car, all of it covered with a glaze of ice. The scraper's in the trunk, which is also sealed by ice. I use my fist to break through the ice over the front door and dig through six inches of powder to find another coating of ice over the door handle. As if the weather gods had decided to layer their efforts to thwart me.

It's not always about you, Mattea, says my mother's reproving voice.

I go back inside, grab the kettle, and bring it back out to deice the car. It takes three trips to get the door open and another two for the trunk. When I turn the key in the ignition I hear the exasperated mutter of the fifteen-year-old engine. "I know," I say, looking up at the religious medal hanging from the rearview mirror, "but there's a boy and his mother waiting for us at a bus station."

Whether from divine intervention or because the engine's finally warm enough, the car starts. I turn the rear and front defrosters on high and thank Anita Esteban, the migrant farmworker who gave me the Virgin of Guadalupe medal fourteen years ago. When I told Anita that I didn't believe in God she'd pressed the medal into my hand and told me that I should just say a prayer to whatever I *did* believe in. So I say my prayers to Anita Esteban, who left her drunk, no-good husband, raised three children on her own, went back to school, and earned a law degree. She's what I believe in.

I get the box of donations out of the trunk and bring it back to the kitchen, where I find enough hot cocoa to make up a thermos. I'll buy coffee at the Stewart's. There are Snickers bars in the box too, which I put in my pack. Of course the sisters will feed them, but their larder tends to the bland and healthy. That boy will need something sweet.

I'm closing up the box when I spot a bag of dog treats. I take out two Milk-Bones and turn toward Dulcie's bed . . . and see the open door. I feel my heart stutter: all this time I spent fussing with the car she's been outside in the cold. I open the screen door to find her standing withers deep in the snow, head down, steam shrouding her old grizzled head.

"Oh, girl!" I cry, grabbing her by the ruff and pulling her inside. "I'm so sorry."

Her hair is matted with ice. I wrap her in an old tattered beach towel, rubbing her dry, kneading balls of ice from her footpads. "Why didn't you bark?" I demand, when what I really mean is *How could I forget you?* I rub her until the ice has melted and she has stopped trembling. Then I use the same towel to wipe my own face.

Disgusting, I hear my mother say.

Yes, I agree, rubbing harder.

Then I look at my watch and see I've got ten minutes to make the fifteen-minute drive to the bus station. *That's what comes of flitting about in the middle of the night.* My mother is out in full force tonight. *Meddling in other people's business. Neglecting your own.*

Having almost killed my old dog, I have nothing to say in my own defense. So I grab my pack and go, turning the thermostat up a notch to keep poor Dulcie warm while I'm gone.

IT'S MOSTLY DOWNHILL from my house to town, something I appreciated as a kid when I needed to get away fast and could coast on my Schwinn from my driveway to the Stewart's without turning a pedal. Frank Barnes and I used to race down the hill, daring each other on. When I was seven and he was nine, I took the curve at the bottom too fast and wound up in the Esopus. I still have the piece of flannel Frank tore from his shirt to stanch the blood and the scar on my forehead as a reminder of my folly.

Coasting down the ice-slick road tonight, my wipers barely keeping up with the sleet and icy rain, has me praying to Anita, the Virgin of Guadalupe, Ganesh, and whatever pagan wood spirits haunt the lonely pines that stand guard around the little mountain hamlet of Delphi. I roll the window down and take deep gulps of cold, pine-scented air. The shock of the temperature steadies my hands on the wheel for the last hairpin curve before town and through deserted Main Street, past the boarded-up windows of Moore's Mercantile, where my mother bought me my school clothes every fall, and the Queen Anne Victorian that used to house my father's law offices but is now home to Sanctuary. There's a light on downstairs. Doreen's probably rearranging the food pantry and donation bins. *Every night like a goddamned house elf,* Muriel, the head of volunteer services, says. I'll check in with her after I drop off the mother and son at St. Alban's. Bring her a bear claw from Stewart's. Give her a chance to talk about the call.

The bus terminal shares a parking lot with Stewart's—the only place in town open. There's no bus there yet. Either it's late or I've missed it. But there's no boy and woman standing outside, waiting for me.

I park the car and turn it off, tempted to leave it running but afraid that someone will steal it. Some of the people who *do* get off the bus aren't the most savory—drug dealers running heroin from the city to the Catskills, gang members from Newburgh and Kingston, parolees from the prison over in Hudson.

You always think the worst of people, Doreen tells me.

It's what I used to say to my mother. *I'll stop when people stop confirming my worst suspicions of them,* she used to answer back.

Atefeh Sherazi is at the counter inside Stewart's. She smiles when she sees me come in. Doreen and I helped find her this job when she came to Sanctuary two years ago. She'd left her husband in New Jersey and taken the bus upstate with her two children. When I asked her if she was afraid her husband would follow her she said it was her brother she was worried about. He had brought her to America from Iran ten years ago by promising her an education and had instead brokered an arranged marriage. When her husband started hitting her she went to her brother, but he said that it was her fault she wasn't able to please her husband. *He'll kill me if he finds me,* Atefeh told us.

She'd stayed at St. Alban's until her application for Section 8 housing was approved and Roy Carver gave her this job. Now she's taking classes part-time at Ulster Community College, working toward the education she came here for.

"What are you doing out on a night like this, Ms. Lane?" she asks. I've asked her to call me Mattie many times to no avail.

"Picking up someone on the bus from Kingston. Has it come in yet?"

Atefeh shakes her head. "The driver called in half an hour ago to say he'd be late. Black ice on 28. He had to pull over and wait for the sand trucks. Can I get you some coffee while you're waiting? There's a fresh pot."

"I'll get it, Atefeh." I hold up my thermos and nod at the open biology textbook on the counter. "You keep studying."

I walk to the coffee counter at the back of the store and fill the thermos. Then I pour myself a cup, adding sugar and milk, to keep myself awake. I pick up a quart of milk, orange juice, butter, and then eye the pastries on the warming rack. The mother and son will be hungry when they get here.

While I'm deciding between bear claws and cinnamon rolls the bell over the door jangles. I look over to see if the bus has come, but it's only two guys in heavy camo gear getting out of a jacked-up plow truck, fake foam antlers strapped to the plow and a very real, very dead buck strapped to the roof. Their exhaust steam is billowing around my little Honda. I guess they're not worried about someone taking off with *their* ride. I turn back to my pastry selection and hear one of the hunters ask Atefeh for lottery tickets.

Like that's going to change your luck.

It's not that I have anything against hunters. I know enough families around here who rely on that meat, and the local hunting club always donates a venison roast for Sanctuary's community holiday supper. In fact one of the hunters, the older and heftier one, looks familiar. I think he's come into Sanctuary with donations a couple of times.

I glance back toward the men. The one I don't recognize, the younger, skinnier one, is staring at Atefeh's name tag.

"*Atefeh?* What kind of name is that?"

"It's Persian, sir. Here are your lottery tickets. Good luck to you and have a good night."

But the hunter isn't done. He turns to his friend. "Hey, Wayne, getta hold of this! Her name is Atefeh. Hey, why aren't you wearing your kebab doohickey?" He pokes his finger at Atefeh's head. I can see her flinch. Her shoulders have risen beneath her striped uniform as if she is bracing for a blow and fighting off the urge to flee at the same time.

Stand by the victim, I hear Doreen say. *Don't confront the attacker.* I move closer to the counter. "Is everything okay, Atefeh?" I ask, keeping my eyes on her.

Her eyes flick toward me and her shoulders lower a fraction. "Did you get everything you need, Ms. Lane?" she asks.

"Yes," I say, edging past the hunter.

"Hey," he says, "who said I was done?"

"Will there be anything else, sir?" Atefeh says with unfailing politeness.

"Yeah, I'll take a . . ." His eyes rove around the counter and then settle with undisguised glee on a baseball cap with an American flag on it. "I'll take one of those."

"Of course, sir," Atefeh says, removing the cap from the stand and ringing it up.

"No, wait . . ." He spins the stand and sticks his finger in at random. "I changed my mind. I'm not sure. Which one do you like?"

Atefeh stares at him wide-eyed. I move as close to her as I can with the counter between us so she knows I'm here for her. *Why aren't we supposed to confront the attacker?* I'd asked Doreen. *Because it will escalate the conflict and ultimately make things worse for the victim,* she'd replied. Doreen's always right about this stuff, but I feel like a pathetic wimp as Atefeh holds out a cap with a shaking hand.

"Oh, shoot," he says, looking straight at Atefeh and not the patriotic slogan on the cap. "I left my reading glasses at home. Could you read it for me?"

I've seen men like this before, men who have to make someone else feel small so that they don't. When he finally chooses one with a MAKE AMERICA GREAT AGAIN slogan on it, and pays in crumpled bills and a handful of linty change, Atefeh puts the cap in a bag.

"Uh-uh," Camo says, wagging his head with what can only

be described as a shit-eating grin on his face, "I bought it for you!" He looks back to see if his friend, who's paging through a *Field & Stream* magazine, gets the joke. "It's a present for Atefeh! Go ahead, put it on!"

Atefeh is looking down at the ugly polyester hat, her cheeks blotched red. I reach across the counter to touch her hand, but before I touch her she raises her eyes and meets the gaze of the hunter.

"Thank you very much for the present, sir, but I am not allowed to wear a hat at work. I will give it to my son, though, who loves American history and plays Little League."

It's a perfect response. Atefeh does not need me to fight her battles for her. Doreen was right—

"What's your son's name? Jihad?"

Afterward I will tell Doreen that I knew the coffee had cooled enough to make it perfectly safe, but the truth is that when I tip the cup toward Camo's groin I hope it will scald the grin right off his face and leave him sterile.

"Leave her alone!" I shout, as he howls at the pain. "And get the fuck out of here."

He glares at me, one fist curled protectively over his groin, and one cocked at his side. I put the pastry bag on the counter, slide my hand into my coat pocket, and curl my hand around my car keys, sliding the keys, teeth out, between my fingers.

I'm about to take my hand out of the pocket when the other hunter grabs his friend by the shoulders. "I think it's time we go, Jason. That stag on the roof isn't getting any sweeter while we stand here jawing."

"That bitch threw her coffee at me!" Jason complains, struggling—but not very hard—to get out of his friend's grasp.

"Yeah, well, that's what you get for being an asshole." The other hunter looks at me. There's a hint of a smile—and recognition—in his eyes; I've definitely met him before. "C'mon before the nice ladies call the cops on you."

"Well shit," Jason says, "I was just trying to be nice. Let's get out of here." He shrugs his friend's hands off and makes an exaggerated show of straightening his camo jacket as if it were an expensive suit, then manages to knock over the magazine rack on his way out.

His friend—Wayne—stops to pick up the magazines, but I hiss under my breath, "Just get your friend out of here."

He looks up at me. "He's not my friend; he's my dumbass brother-in-law." Then he looks back at Atefeh. "I apologize for my family, ma'am. Have a good night."

As soon as the door closes I turn back to Atefeh. She's shaking like a leaf. I move around the counter and put my arms around her. *Ask the victim if she's okay,* Doreen told us.

What a stupid question, I'd told her, *as if anyone is okay after being bullied and abused!*

"What an asshole!" I say now. I let loose a blue streak of curses that has Atefeh blushing through her tears. Then I help her clean up the coffee I "spilled."

"I'm so clumsy," I say, making Atefeh laugh.

By the time Atefeh's poured me a new cup of coffee the bus is pulling into the parking lot. "I'd better go," I say. "These two might not want anyone to see them."

"Let me know if I can help," Atefeh says, squeezing my hand. "And . . . thank you."

"Just don't tell Doreen," I say, hugging her. "I didn't exactly follow protocol."

It's only when I get out into the parking lot that I start to shake. It's not throwing the coffee that scares me—although if it had been hot I could have scarred Jason for life. It's the keys. I'd been ready to punch Jason in the face with a fistful of keys. I would have happily gouged his eyes out.

CHAPTER THREE

Alice

THE WOMAN STANDING in front of the convenience store, bareheaded in the icy rain, looks like one of those do-gooder old hippie types. Spiky gray hair, fuzzy shapeless poncho, heavy work boots. The poncho may well be purple but it's hard to tell in the weak fluorescent light of the store windows. She's holding a cup and a shopping bag.

"Is that her?" Oren asks, woken from his sleep by the shifting gears of the bus as it turned into the parking lot.

"Must be," I say. "She looks . . . okay."

"She looks like a social worker," Oren says, making it clear what he thinks of the profession.

"They're not all bad," I say. "Scott was nice, right?"

"Yeah," Oren says without much conviction. Scott, his last caseworker, *was* nice, but he hadn't been much help in the end. None of them are, really.

I get up to grab my pack from the overhead. Oren's already

got his *Star Wars* backpack shouldered. He'd slept with it crammed between his head and the window, one strap on his shoulder, his arms wrapped around it. When we left I'd given him five minutes to go back to his room and take only what he absolutely needed. I saw the library book sticking out the top when he met me at the door, but now I wonder what else he took—*money?*—that he's holding on to so tightly.

We're the only ones getting off the bus. I glance at the other passengers as we walk up the aisle—the college kid plugged into his earbuds, eyes closed, head nodding to tinny rap; a Latina woman with a baby whose eyes move over me without making contact; an old woman wrapped up in a scarf reading a book. No one who will remember a boy and his mother getting off in a nowhere town in the Catskills. Not even the driver turns to watch us make our way down the steps to the door. I have the creepy feeling that we are invisible. That once we step off this bus we will vanish from the known world, that the purple-shawled woman has been sent to lead us to the underworld like those snake-haired crones in Oren's book.

Sensing my hesitation, Oren stops at the steps down to the door and turns to look up at me, eyes wide and solemn. I open my mouth to tell him it's all right but he beats me to it. "It's okay," he says. "This is the right stop." The driver turns his head to us. He's wondering what's wrong with me that my son has to lead me off the bus—and he'll remember us now. I curse myself for hesitating.

"Of course it is. Thanks . . . honey." I remember at the last moment not to use Oren's name. I smile at the bus driver. "He's been studying the bus map since we planned this trip to Aunt Jean's."

"Good man," the driver says. "You take care of your mom, now."

Asshole, I think, giving Oren a little push to move him along and keep him from answering. He does anyway. "We take care of each other," he says.

The icy rain makes my eyes sting as we step off the bus onto the pavement, and I have to stop and wipe them. Oren takes my hand like I'm a goddamned invalid and leads me forward, out of the exhaust fumes. The woman is approaching, holding out a white paper bag. "You must be Alice and Oren," she says, looking first at me and then down at Oren. "I'm Mattie. I'd shake hands but I seem to have a bag full of bear claws. Do you think you could help me with those?" She holds the bag toward Oren.

"Are they real bear claws?"

The woman—Mattie—throws back her head and laughs. "Oh my, do I look like a bear hunter? Even if they *do* get in my garbage cans and make a stink, I consider the bears my friends."

"There are bears here?" Oren asks, eyes narrowing with suspicion.

"Why yes," Mattie says, "and coyotes and bobcats too. But the only kind of bear claws I eat are of the pastry variety. Here, why don't you try one?" She's still holding the bag out to him. Oren looks to me, as if I am the kind of mother who restricts his sweets intake. What a clever touch. I smile to show how much I appreciate it and he takes the bag from Mattie. He digs his hand in and takes out a glazed pastry as big as a man's fist. He holds it up to me.

"You take it," I say.

Oren takes an enormous bite, and Mattie looks up from him to me like she's waiting for me to say something, like I'm supposed to slaver all over her for some cheap pastries from Stewart's. That's what these do-gooders get off on. Still, I'd better keep on her good side until we're safely out of here. "Thanks," I say. "We had to leave too fast to pack any food."

"There will be something more substantial where you're going," she says.

"And where's that?" I ask. "It has to be someplace no one can find out where we are. Oren's father—"

"I understand," Mattie says. "Everyone in our network understands. Your whereabouts will be kept completely confidential. There's a convent fifteen miles from here."

"A convent?" I ask.

"The sisters are committed to protecting women and children. No one could be more confidential—most of them don't even talk!"

I think of the last time I was in a church and begin to shake. "I—I'm not religious."

"Me neither," Mattie says. She looks down at Oren, who has finished the bear claw and is licking icing off his fingers and studying me. "Let's get out of this sleet," Mattie says, turning toward her car, an old rusted-out Honda.

"Nuns are for orphans," Oren says, not budging. "And I'm no orphan."

Where on earth did he get that? Did some social worker threaten him with an orphanage? A swell of hatred for the profession overwhelms me and makes me want to tell this do-gooder with her sugary snacks to get lost. A convent! They'll probably try to convert us like the born-again foster parents I had one year.

I put my hand on Oren's shoulder. "The woman on the phone didn't say anything about a convent. We'll wait for the next bus and take our chances elsewhere."

Mattie gives me a level look and I can tell she sees right through me. I don't have the money for another bus and I don't have any idea where else we'd go. We're fresh out of chances. It makes me angry that she's so sure about me. Who is she to judge me? Now that we're closer I can see that her purple shawl is moth-eaten and there's an odor coming off her that smells like wet dog. She looks like she's getting ready to tell me to lump it, but then Oren pipes up.

"Couldn't we just stay with you? I bet that convent is far away and hard to get to in the snow."

Her brow creases. "We're not supposed to . . . ," she begins, but then she looks up at the sky. The driving sleet has changed to heavy wet snow as we've been talking, and it's sticking to the top of Oren's bare head and the black tarmac of the parking lot. I can see her thinking about the roads and wanting to get back to her nice, snug home. "I suppose if it's just for tonight. My house *is* closer . . ."

Oren grins and runs to the Honda. Mattie watches him go with a puzzled look on her face and then turns to me and offers me the cup of coffee she's holding. "He's one persuasive little guy," she says.

I nod and take a sip of the too-sweet coffee, turning away so I don't have to answer the question in her look. I imagine she's wondering, as I am, how Oren knew her house was closer than the convent.

WHILE WE WAIT for the windows to defog Mattie offers me more coffee from the thermos, explaining, "It's not sweetened." She must have seen me wince when I took a sip from the cup, which makes me feel guilty for turning my nose up at this woman's coffee when she's come out in the middle of the night to help us—but then angry at having to feel bad. That's what these do-gooders do, they make you feel like they're better than you.

"I'm fine," I say.

"Just help yourself if you want more," she says, settling the thermos in the well between our seats. "I'm afraid I develop a sweet tooth around this time of year. Starts at Halloween when I eat all the leftover candy, builds at Thanksgiving with all those pies, and reaches a peak when we do our Holiday Cookie Walk."

"What's that?" Oren asks sleepily from the backseat.

"Oh, that's a tradition around here. On the day before

Christmas everyone bakes up their favorite cookies. You buy a ticket at Sanctuary for a box and then you go house to house until your box is full. All the money goes to the local food bank. And there's hot cider and cocoa and skating on the pond. If you're still here next week I'll give you my box and you can collect the cookies and we'll split the booty. How's that sound?"

When there's no reply we both look back. Oren is slumped over his *Star Wars* pack, sticky mouth open.

"Poor lamb," Mattie says. "Have you traveled far?"

"From Newburgh," I say, remembering what I'd told the woman on the phone.

"We've got a donation center down there. Second Chances? My friend Ruth runs it."

Is she testing me? "We don't need to shop secondhand," I tell her.

"No, I can see that. The *Star Wars* pack is this season's. I bought one just like it at Target for my godson. The boy's jacket is new too. But your clothes"—she glances over at me, assessing my threadbare peacoat and worn jeans—"aren't."

"So?" I snap. "You're not exactly a fashion plate yourself."

She laughs so hard she starts coughing. When she recovers she says, "I like you, Alice. You've got fight in you. Just for the record, I wasn't criticizing. I was noticing you pay more attention to your son's clothing than your own. I bet you put him first in other things as well."

"So I've passed some kind of good mothering test with you?" I say, making my voice angrier than I feel so she doesn't guess how relieved I am. "Is that what I have to do to earn a meal and a bed for the night?"

"No," she says, all the laughter gone from her voice. "All you have to do for that is need it. You don't have to prove anything to me, but if you want to talk to me I'm here to listen."

"And if I don't?"

"That's all right too. I will assume you have a good reason to keep your and your son's location confidential."

"Oren's father hit him," I say suddenly. "And he hit me. He threatened to kill me if I took Oren away . . . I . . . I . . .'" I find it suddenly hard to talk. I feel as if Davis is in the car with us. *Lying cunt-faced bitch,* I hear him swear. *I'm coming for you.*

Although her eyes are on the road, Mattie must see me flinch. She lays a hand that feels like worn velvet on mine. "It's okay. You may hear his voice in your head but he can't hurt you anymore."

No, I think. *No, he can't.*

MATTIE'S HOUSE IS at the end of a long, wooded drive. I'm expecting some run-down shack or derelict mobile home, but it is instead an elegant Victorian with gingerbread trim and turrets and a wraparound porch.

"You own all this?" I ask, surprised.

"Me and the bank," she says, getting out.

I reach into the backseat to wake up Oren. He rubs his eyes, looking eight instead of ten, as if sleep has washed away the last two years of his life. If only it really could. As I watch, he remembers where we are, grasping his backpack and looking out the window warily.

"This lady's house seems okay," I tell him, "but if we don't like it here we can leave in the morning."

I wait for him to ask me how we're going to do that with no money and no car, but he only nods and gets out of the car. I get out and follow him up the ice-rutted path, watching my feet, so I bump into Oren when he stops in the middle of the path. He's staring up at the house, as surprised as I am to find ourselves at such a big fancy place.

"Do you live alone?" he asks Mattie, who's on the porch waiting for us.

Mattie looks surprised, but then she shakes her head and clucks her tongue. "I know what you're thinking: it's a crime for an old spinster like me to use up all this space."

Oren shakes his head. That's not what he meant. "Aren't there other kids here?"

I look at the house and notice now that although it's big and fancy it's also falling apart. Shutters hang crooked and the paint is faded and chipped. Plastic crates and black garbage bags—donations, I'm guessing—clutter up the porch. I've seen enough of these kinds of places in upstate New York to know what it looks like: a group foster home. That must be what Oren's picked up on. He thinks I've taken him to a foster home.

"It's okay," I tell him, laying my hand on his shoulder. He

flinches at my touch and fuck me if I don't immediately look up to see if the old woman has noticed. But she's looking at Oren, her face pinched and white.

"What do you mean?" she asks, all the treacly warmth gone from her voice. "It's just me and Dulcie here."

"Dulcie?" Oren asks.

"My old dog. Do you like dogs?"

He shrugs. Davis would never let him have a dog. But the old woman probably can't imagine a boy who doesn't love dogs. She turns and opens her front door—it's unlocked, I notice—and an old yellow Labrador comes limping out. She shambles down the porch steps, tail wagging, and butts her head up against Oren's chest. Oren stumbles back a jot so he's next to me, then steadies himself by putting his hand on the dog's head. After a second, he rubs the dog's ears. The dog lets out a sigh and then so does Oren.

"Good girl," Mattie says. "How 'bout we go inside and find her a treat."

Oren looks up at Mattie. "Are you sure there aren't any other kids here?" Something about the way he says it makes the hair stand up on the back of my neck. The old dog shifts her weight and leans against me.

"No," Mattie says. "No kids. I'm afraid I'm just an old spinster."

"What's a spinster?"

"Someone who talks too much while folks are standing cold and hungry on her doorstep. How 'bout we get inside where it's warm and I'll make us some eggs and pancakes?"

"With syrup?"

"And chocolate chips," she replies.

Oren nods and walks straight up the porch steps. He turns to see that I'm following. His face is tight, jaw rigid. A brave little soldier. It's like he's daring me not to follow him. For a second I think of turning around, getting back in the car, demanding that Mattie take us to that convent. How much worse can it be? But of course I don't. We both know I've come too far to turn back now.

CHAPTER FOUR

Mattie

BETWEEN THEM THEY eat half a dozen eggs and a dozen pancakes. It's a good thing I picked up milk and eggs and butter at Stewart's. Had I already been thinking of bringing them back here? Doreen will give me a talking-to, but it's just for this one night. I'll take them to St. Alban's tomorrow.

I load the pancakes with bananas, nuts, and chocolate chips and slather them with butter and maple syrup. The boy drinks a quart of milk and Alice finishes the thermos of coffee. I don't ask them any questions other than "More maple syrup?" and "Another glass of milk?" I'd meant it when I told Alice she didn't have to sing for their supper.

When the boy's eyes start to droop I hustle them both upstairs. I put them in the yellow room at the front of the house, my mother's old sewing room, though years ago I gave all the sewing stuff to a woman from Saugerties whose husband was serving a sentence for sexual assault. She'd used the supplies—along with a loan from the Delphi Rotary Club—to start a quilt shop and alterations business. She also runs quilting workshops at the domestic violence shelter where women use scraps of their old clothes to make "New Beginning" quilts. *Even if our lives have been torn apart,* she likes to say, *we can still use the pieces to make something beautiful.*

The only furniture left in the sewing room is the daybed where my mother used to take her afternoon naps. It's a trundle, so Alice and Oren can both sleep on it, but there's also a large walk-in closet with a futon. I point out the sleeping options, give them an armful of blankets and towels, and let them sort out who sleeps where.

The boy chooses the closet. *Victims of abuse,* I read in one of our training manuals, *sometimes like to be in rooms that have only one access point.* He tucks his backpack into the far corner, lays his head down, and is instantly asleep.

Alice kneels down to take off his shoes and coat. Beneath the coat he's wearing a *Star Wars* sweatshirt. Alice wrinkles her nose. "In case you're revising your opinion of my parenting skills, I'll have you know he's refused to take off this sweatshirt since we got it two months ago."

"My brother, Caleb, wore a Luke Skywalker T-shirt for three months straight after we saw the first movie. Here, give it to me and I'll wash it. I'll have it back to you before he wakes up in the morning."

She peels it off him and passes it to me, making a face, but I'm looking at Oren's arms. There's a bruise on his right forearm and one on his left biceps. She sees me looking, tilts up her chin, which is when I notice the marks on her throat. I could ask her about the abuse, but I sense that she's too tired to talk tonight so instead I say, "There's a clean nightgown if you'd like me to wash your clothes too," but she shakes her head. I imagine she's used to sleeping in her clothes. A nightgown makes you vulnerable. Before I go I turn on the night-light even though the overhead's still on. It casts a pattern of stars on the ceiling. I noticed the book of Greek myths sticking out of the backpack. I could tell Oren the stories of the constellations—

But they'll be gone tomorrow.

The convent will be the best place for them. The boy's going to need counseling. I saw the way he twitched when Alice touched him. And Alice will need job training. She looks like she's in her late twenties, so she would have been a teenager when she had Oren. I'm betting a teenage pregnancy followed by dropping out, a relationship with an older man, maybe a drug dealer, maybe a pimp . . . She wouldn't have had time for school. At least there aren't any track marks that I can see. I could get her into a vocational training program at Ulster Community College, far from the crime and drugs of Newburgh.

Downstairs, the kitchen looks like Boston after the Great Molasses Flood, but the smell of butter and maple syrup makes it worth it. I notice that Alice's peacoat has slipped off the kitchen chair. When I pick it up a piece of paper flutters out of the pocket. I bend down to pick it up. It's a bus ticket. I start to jam it back in her pocket when I notice the departure city stamped on it. It isn't Newburgh, as she told Doreen, it's Ridgewood, New Jersey. Well, Alice wouldn't be the first woman to come to Sanctuary who didn't tell the whole truth about where she came from. I'm a little surprised, though: Ridgewood is an affluent suburb. But it's none of my business. I tuck the ticket stub back in Alice's pocket.

I carry Oren's sweatshirt to the washing machine in the mudroom and turn on the machine. I add soap powder and throw in the towel I used to rub down Dulcie before—and check to make sure I haven't left her out again, but she's sleeping soundly in her dog bed. What will it be next, I wonder, forgetting to pay the bills? Wandering in my nightie down Main Street? Leaving the gas on? Even the decision to bring Alice and Oren back here is probably a sign that my judgment is slipping. And really, how can I think I'm fit to watch after an abused woman and child when I can't take care of my beloved old dog?

I pick up the sweatshirt and hold it to my face, inhaling its boy smell, as if it will smell of Caleb. It's just a coincidence that this boy is the same age that Caleb was when he died. Just a coincidence that they both love *Star Wars*. Just a coincidence that I felt that weight against my leg earlier tonight when I got the call—

I shiver, remembering that phantom pressure, so like the feeling of Caleb leaning against me on the couch when we watched Saturday morning cartoons or whenever my father yelled at him.

You'll never learn to stand on your own two feet if you're always running to your sister.

The shiver turns into full-out shaking. It's one thing to hear my mother's voice, another to hear my father's. I usually do a better job of drowning it out.

I stuff the sweatshirt into the half-full washer . . . and something clangs against the metal drum. I'm reluctant to search the boy's pockets but it could be some piece of electronics that will get destroyed in the wash. I reach my hand in and grasp cold metal. When I pull my hand out I see that I'm holding a six-inch bowie hunting knife stained with blood.

I put the knife down on top of the dryer carefully, as if it's a gun that might go off. The sweatshirt has already been sucked down under the churning soapy water. If there's blood on it it's too late to save it as—

What? *Evidence?*

Evidence of *what?*

Evidence of something that sweet ten-year-old boy did?

Or of something his mother did that he's protecting her from?

The situation is worse than Doreen or I thought. The question is what to do about it. I could confront Alice with the knife and try to convince her to go to the police and file an assault charge. Anything she or Oren did would most likely be considered self-defense. Oren's father would be put away in jail and they would be free to live their lives.

Until he got out. I've seen convicted offenders of abuse

serve as little as six months on aggravated assault charges. And what if Alice and Oren can't plead self-defense? What if Alice, tired of being hit and bullied, struck out first? It wouldn't be the first time a woman took a proactive stand against abuse and got convicted of assault. She could end up in jail and Oren could end up in his father's custody or foster care. And if it was Oren who stabbed his father . . . he could end up in juvenile detention and I know all too well what that can do to a kid.

All of these possibilities swirl through my head with the same murky force of the washer cycle, which has stalled because the tub is now half full and the lid is still open. I think about that boy upstairs—the first boy who's slept in this house since Caleb—and know what I have to do. I drop the knife into the water and close the lid.

THERE'S LITTLE CHANCE of sleep after that. I tackle the kitchen, cleaning up the pancake mess and moving on to the next layer of grime that's built up. Then I make up muffins for the morning. As the smell of baking wafts through the house, stirring memories, I sweep the downstairs, the fancy parlor that's now full of stacks of old clothes. I always take the donation bags home to wash the clothes and sort them by size and gender (although Doreen says that's very heteronormative of me). I find some jeans and T-shirts that I think will fit Oren and packages of unopened underwear and socks for both of them. I buy them at the dollar store in a wide variety of sizes. No one wants to wear hand-me-down underwear.

I keep the book donations in the dining room. Boxes of unsorted books on the Chippendale chairs and piles of sorted books on the long, polished mahogany table: romance novels with lurid covers, mystery novels with shadowy figures, dog-eared sci-fi novels with rockets and three-eyed aliens, horror novels with screaming faces. Doreen accuses me of reading all the books first and it's true that I do keep a pile for myself, but I also keep an eye out for books that we can sell to an antiquarian bookseller I know over in Hobart. I also like to monitor the distribution to our network of centers so the group foster homes get the good children's books, Horizon gets the good young adult, and the shelters have a wide selection of genres.

I remember seeing a book on constellations that I bet Oren will like, but it's not in the stacks of books on the table or in the boxes waiting for distribution. That's when I remember. It's not a donated book; it's a book my father owned.

The door to my father's study is at the end of the dining room and it's the only door in the house that locks. It's an old-fashioned lock that can be bolted from either side with a key that I keep in a Waterford bowl on the sideboard. I take it out now and turn it in the lock, the tumble of metal cylinders echoing in the pit of my stomach, the creak of the door feeble as my own step on the threshold.

Well? Are you coming in or not, mouse? my father would say when I hesitated in the doorway.

The taste of dust hits the back of my mouth like a hand reaching down my throat and I cough. There's only one lamp in the room, the heavy brass banker's lamp with the green glass shade. It's been so long since I've been in here that the bulb could well have burned out. I have to venture several feet in darkness from the wedge of light at the door to the lamp.

Caleb loved to play a game called Lava in which you pretended the floor was a boiling pit of magma that would instantly melt your flesh down to the bones. You had to navigate through the house by stepping from one piece of furniture to another. That's what it feels like to step from the wedge of light into darkness, like my flesh will turn to jelly, but I do it, reaching out to find the lamp . . .

Something cool brushes against my outstretched hand.

The one escape clause in Lava was the lifeline. You could toss a rope (we used the gold silk cord from one of my mother's bathrobes) to a stranded partner and he or she could walk it like a tightrope across the perilous lava field. That's what this feels like, even though I know it's just a draft of cold air from the uninsulated windows that need to be re-caulked.

I step across the dark expanse and reach for the lamp. My hand brushes against something and I hear a clear musical chime that reverberates in my chest. *It's only the scales,* I tell myself as I work my hand down from the smooth glass shade to the hard brass knob that turns the light on. The bulb crackles and flickers, threatens to go out, then steadies weakly into a pool of pale green light.

I haven't been in this room in months. Dust lies everywhere, like pond scum, coating the thick leather blotter, the desk, the glass-fronted bookcases, the cracked leather chair. I trail my finger in it as I come around the desk, tracing a spiral pattern like some Celtic charm against ghosts. I use my sleeve to wipe off the seat of the chair and sit down, the old leather creaking, and then I reach across the desk to still the glass scales that hang from the bronze statuette of Justice that sits at the center of my father's desk. She's part of a pen set representing the state seal of New York that was given to my father by the New York State Bar Association on the twenty-fifth anniversary of his judgeship. There's a plaque between her and another figure, Liberty: *Liberty and Justice,* my father would say when I sat in his lap and played with the scales, *you can't have one without the other.* Which confused me sometimes, because so often my father's brand of justice involved revoking some bit of liberty.

I turn away from the figures on the desk to look at the tall glass-fronted bookcase. My eyes immediately go to the seam in the wall behind the case where there was once a door, but I make myself focus on the case, trailing my hand over the dust-coated glass doors until I come to the fifth shelf from the floor. I rap the glass twice, giving any mice fair warning, and pull the glass door up.

The books are dustless behind the glass, their tooled leather spines as cool and clean as dried bones. I find what I'm looking for on the far right of the shelf, a tall slim book bound in blue the color of a summer night's sky with silver lettering the color of starlight. *An Astral Mythology: A Child's*

Guide to the Night Sky. It's an 1890 first edition of a transla-
tion of the third century B.C. writer Eratosthenes. According
to my antiquarian friend in Hobart it's worth several thousand dollars. I could have the roof fixed with the proceeds.
Or replace the windows. Or buy a new boiler for Sanctuary.

It will be perfect for the boy.

I get up to go, reaching for the lamp, and notice a pattern
in the dust—a random splatter of dots that might be the
footprints of mice or a new constellation in the night sky. *It's
all how you look at it,* my father would say. *Some people look
up at the night sky and see random scatter, others read stories
in the chaos. That's what I do when I adjudicate a case. I make
sense out of chaos.*

I turn the light off before I can start reading stories in the
dust and walk quickly out of the office, locking the door behind me. I go back into the kitchen and lay the book on the
table, then take the muffins out of the oven and put them to
cool on a metal rack beside the book. I can hear the thump
of the washing machine finishing its cycle, so I go into the
mudroom, pull out the sweatshirt and towel, put them in the
dryer, and then fish out the knife. It shines clean and cold in
the first rays of dawn coming in through the window. I slide
it under a pile of blankets stacked on the dryer.

Dulcie stirs and stands by the door. I let her out and step
outside for a moment. The storm has passed and the sky is
lightening in the east, an orange glow that reflects off the
newly fallen snow. There's nothing better than a clear morning after a snowstorm, and I am filled with an unaccustomed

sense of hope, of things beginning. I'll tell the boy I found his knife and ask him if I can keep it. For safekeeping, I'll say. I'll tell him that whatever he and his mother did to get away is their business. The only thing that matters is that they've gotten away.

I go back inside. Feed Dulcie. Put on the kettle. Turn on the radio. While the water is boiling I hear the muffled voice of the news announcer. One of the reasons I love this NPR station is that the newscasters speak in such subdued murmurs I can usually tune them out, but this morning a word snags my attention. Ridgewood. The town on Alice's bus ticket.

As I listen, sunlight swells over the window ledge above the kitchen sink, staining the pitted porcelain and scarred wooden counter a lurid blood orange. A body's been found in Ridgewood, New Jersey. A man in his thirties, stabbed to death in his home.

CHAPTER FIVE

Alice

I WAKE UP to the touch of a hand stroking my cheek. It's such a gentle touch, so tender, that I don't want it to ever stop. I keep my eyes closed, let myself slip back to sleep. I can feel a breath on my face, lips brushing my ear, then a whisper—

He's coming.

I open my eyes. I'm alone in the yellow room, sunlight warm on my face. That must be what I felt. Davis never touched me like that and Oren isn't here.

Oren isn't here.

I bolt upright, fully awake now, and tear into the little closet where he'd gone to sleep. No Oren. His backpack is gone too.

He's coming.

I hear the echo of that dream whisper. Had it been a warning? I step out into the hallway and hear the whisper again, only now it's coming from downstairs. I stand at the top of the stairs and listen, my heart skittering around in my chest like a hunted rabbit, and make out the singsongy murmur of the woman and then Oren. I can't hear what he's saying but I can tell by the happy lilt in his voice—when did I hear *that* last?—that he's all right. No one has come in the night to take him. And if Davis had—I put my hand on my chest to calm my heart—he wouldn't have left me sleeping. Besides, Davis isn't coming.

I walk back down the hall to find the bathroom. It's at the end of the hall and it's as big as my bedroom at home. It's got one of those old-fashioned tubs with creepy claw feet. No shower. I splash water on my face, pee, and then go exploring. That aw-shucks harmless-spinster crap is as good a cover as any for something dark and twisted inside. I knew a caseworker once—looked sweet as candy, cubicle full of cat pictures, dressed like your grammy—who was fired because she liked to pinch little boys' behinds when no one was looking.

She's left her bedroom door wide open, like she didn't have a stranger sleeping down the hall. Like she didn't lock her front door. Is she an idiot or one of those idealistic nuts? I listen for a second to the murmur of voices downstairs. I can tell by the excited rush of Oren's voice that he's embarked on one of his long stories. He's probably telling her the plot of all the *Star Wars* movies. *Good boy,* I think, as if Oren knows I need the distraction. And maybe he does, like he knew what town we were going to last night.

He's just smart, I tell myself, entering Mattie's sad spinster bedroom. Only one side of the bed is rumpled, a smelly old dog bed on the floor, a flannel nightgown tossed in a laundry basket. The night table is stacked with dog-eared paperbacks, mysteries mostly, the kind with teacups and cats on the covers where dotty old ladies solve crimes. I bet she sees herself as one of those Miss Marple types, coming to the rescue of stupid trashy girls like me.

There's also quite the assortment of pharmaceuticals. Ambien and Valium on the night table, and when I open the drawer—why, *hello!*—OxyContin. I wonder what ache those are for. I open the Oxy, tip out two tablets, and slip them in my pocket. As I put the bottle back I notice the framed picture. It's of a boy, about the same age as Oren, but with a terrible eighties haircut. Her son? Or the brother she mentioned earlier?

I help myself to a Valium and open more drawers, looking for something I could pawn. All I find is sad old-lady underwear, flannel nightgowns, turtlenecks and long johns from L.L.Bean and Lands' End. The only jewelry is cheap ethnic crap. The frame is silver, but I haven't sunk so low as to steal some kid's picture from a nightstand.

I walk back to the bathroom and wash down the Valium with a handful of water from the tap. Back in the hallway I open a few closed doors. There's a door at the end of the hallway that has been boarded over, which is creepy. In one of the group homes I lived in the older girls told a story about a foster mother who would lock kids up in the attic. She told Social Services that the kids ran away and boarded up the attic. When she moved out and a new family moved in they broke into the attic and found a mound of bones. The worst thing was that some of the bones had teeth marks on them that were too big to be made by mice. The story went that even after the bones were taken away the new family could hear knocking coming from the attic—those starving children banging on the floor for someone to let them out. Of course, then one of the girls would secretly make a big banging noise and all the little kids would jump.

The next door is a closet filled with moldy-smelling linens, and then a bedroom. This one is a child's room—a boy's room with a single bed, neatly made with a patchwork quilt and old-school *Star Wars* sheets. A bookcase filled with books about dogs and horses and Greek myths and astronomy. A mobile of the solar system, obviously handmade. There are plastic Day-Glo stars on the ceiling and a poster of the first *Star Wars* movie tacked to the wall. It could be Oren's room at home except that there's no computer, no video games, no sign that the boy who lived here once ever lived past the 1980s.

Which is even creepier than the boarded-over door.

What's even more creepy, though, is that of all the rooms I've been in so far, this one is by far the cleanest. Someone dusts it regularly.

OREN IS SITTING at the kitchen table in his newly washed *Star Wars* sweatshirt. When I walk in he looks up and breaks into a smile that cracks open my heart—or maybe it's the Valium kicking in.

"Mattie said I could go sledding after you came down. She's got a sled and there's a big hill where kids go. Can I?"

"Give your mom a chance to have her breakfast, kid," Mattie says, turning to look at me. In the morning light her face looks older than it did last night but also somehow prettier. Her silver hair catches the light and sparkles like tinsel, and her eyes look lavender against all the white snow out the window. "There's coffee," she tells me, nudging a chair out and pointing her chin at a Mr. Coffee on the counter.

"I'll get it!" Oren says, popping out of his chair like a jack-in-the-box. "Mattie made banana muffins too, with chocolate chips."

We'll both have diabetes if we stay here too long. But I smile back at Oren and take the muffin and coffee. He pours the milk in for me just the way I like it, makes a big deal of taking a muffin out of a basket and putting it on a china plate, sits back down for three seconds and pops back up to get me a napkin. He's wound up on sugar and nerves, trying so hard to please it sets my teeth on edge. Mattie sees it too.

"Kid," she says, "how are you with a shovel?"

Oren squints at her and says, "Depends on what kind of shovel." Like he's had experience with a multitude.

"A snow shovel. We got a foot last night and the Weather Channel says there's an even bigger storm on the way. The front path to the driveway and the one to the barn need digging out and my back just isn't up to it this morning. It would be a great help to me"—she looks at me—"if it's okay with your mom."

"I can do it, Alice," Oren says. "I've done our sidewalk in—"

"As long as you stay away from the road," I say, sneaking a look to see what Mattie's made of that *Alice*. "We should do something to pay back this nice lady for all she's done for us."

Mattie's face pinches like something pains her. I've stolen a little bit of her charity high. But then she nods and braces her hands on the table. "That's settled then," she says. I see her wince as she gets to her feet, and her first few steps across the kitchen are bow-legged and stiff. She's not kidding about her back. I feel a twinge of guilt for stealing her Oxy but then I remind myself that we've all got our pains.

Mattie picks up a newspaper from the counter and tosses it onto the table in front of me. "Help yourself to more coffee, Alice," she says. "I'll be back once I get Oren kitted out."

I take a sip of coffee and listen to them in the front hall. *These'll fit . . . Here, you'd better put on an extra pair of socks . . . Take this fleece . . . Try these boots . . .* She must have a whole assortment of boys' clothes, which I find a little creepy. Maybe it's just that she collects donations, but still, all the force-feeding us baked goods and giving us new clothes—and that boarded-over door upstairs—make me feel uneasy. Best we move on as soon as we can.

I take another sip of the coffee, which I have to admit is pretty good, and a bite of the muffin, which is *delicious,* and turn the paper around. A do-gooder liberal like Mattie, I'm expecting the *New York Times,* but it's a Kingston paper, folded open to the state and local crime report. I scan the page: a sexual assault in New Paltz, a drug bust in Newburgh, and there, at the bottom, a murder in northern New Jersey.

Ridgewood man found stabbed to death in his home. I read the two inches of print, the coffee rising in my throat. *Police are looking for a woman and ten-year-old boy for questioning.*

The words blur into gray sludge. I cover my eyes with one hand and breathe until the dizziness passes. When I open my eyes Mattie is standing in front of me, arms crossed over her chest, leaning against the counter.

"Is there anything you'd like to tell me, Alice?" she says, all sweet and butter-wouldn't-melt-in-her-mouth.

I shouldn't say anything, but I want to wipe the smug right off her face.

"Yes," I say. "I'm glad the bastard's dead."

CHAPTER SIX

Mattie

ALICE TELLS THE story against a sound track of metal scraping against ice. We can see Oren laboring with the shovel outside the window, a diminutive figure in a red parka, peaked blue hat, and too-big snow boots. We both keep our eyes on him as she talks, as if we're afraid he might vanish if we don't.

"I was really young when I met Davis," she begins. I've listened to hundreds of these stories over the years and they always begin the same. *I met a man. He seemed so nice. He treated me so special.* "He seemed so grown-up, and it felt cool that a man that age would pay attention to me. I never knew my father."

She pauses, takes a sip of coffee. I picture myself standing on the threshold of my father's study waiting for that imperious *Come!*

"So I guess I had daddy issues." She laughs. I smile. Say

nothing. Wait. "And Davis *was* cool. He's a musician—or at least he was until I got pregnant with Oren and he had to take a day job. I guess that's when things started going bad—not that I regret having Oren for a second; he's the best thing in my life, you know . . . or maybe you don't. Do you have kids?"

I'm familiar enough with this tactic of deflecting attention not to answer the question. "I can see how you feel about Oren. He's a great kid."

Most mothers, you tell them their kids are great, they beam right back at you. But Alice seems to shrink into herself a little more and hunch over her coffee cup, as if she resents my pointing this out. There's something off about these two. Him calling her Alice, for instance. Not that plenty of kids, especially only children, don't try out their parents' first names, but there was the way she looked up at me when he said it, like she was wondering what I made of it. I can sense that same hesitation now, like she's checking out what I think of each thing she says, whether I'm buying it. Well, I'm not going to give her that. I stay quiet, and after a moment's pause she goes on. "He's so smart it's scary sometimes. Davis says he gets it from him, but he's way smarter than Davis. And Davis knows it. It started making him . . . *jealous.* Isn't that weird? A parent being jealous of his own child."

"Depends on the parent," I say, trying not to be drawn in. My mother quips back, *Depends on the child.*

"Well, *I* thought it was weird. It made him really hard on

Oren. He was always prodding him, trying to prove he was better—than his own kid! When I objected he'd say I was too soft on him, that he'd grow up a sissy. Then when Oren would come to my defense Davis would say I'd poisoned Oren against him."

"Come to your defense how?" I ask, not willing to let that slide past.

"When Davis hit me." She holds up her chin as if I'm going to challenge her. "Oren would try to stop him." She pulls up her shirtsleeve and shows me a line of white ridges on her forearm. Burn marks. "He started punishing me when Oren was at school. I tried not to let Oren see them but there's not much that gets past him. He stopped going to school—and he *liked* school. He'd pretend to be sick, and when Davis made him go anyway he'd sneak back. Aren't you going to ask me why I didn't leave?"

"I imagine it's because you had no place to go," I say.

All the muscles in Alice's face harden as if I'd struck her. She's trying not to cry, I realize. "No, I didn't," she says defiantly. "I grew up in the foster system, so I don't have anyone. But even if I did, Davis said he'd kill me if I tried to leave him."

No matter how often I have heard some variation on this threat, I am still amazed by the possessiveness of the abuser who tells a woman ten times a day that she's worthless but still won't let her go. Amazed, but not surprised. Nor am I surprised to learn that Alice grew up in foster care. She has the wariness I've seen in dozens of kids in the system, as if the ground beneath their feet's not steady. Which it usually isn't. If we had more time I'd ask her about that, but we have only as long as it will take Oren to finish shoveling and he's already gotten to the driveway and started on the path to the barn. So instead I ask, "What happened yesterday?"

She hastily wipes her face, although no tear has fallen. As she speaks her voice rises in pitch, but whether because she's nervous or lying I can't tell. "I tried to leave. Davis was going into the city for some gig. He was supposed to be out of the house all day, but he came home because he'd forgotten something. Oren and I were all packed to go. He . . . tried to strangle me . . ." She touches her hand to the marks on her throat. ". . . and Oren got in between us . . . and . . . something snapped. I just couldn't take it anymore. I picked up a knife and stabbed him. I—I didn't even know if he was dead. I just grabbed Oren's hand and we ran. We waited in the bus station for the next bus . . . well, you know the rest."

Do I? I wonder. She's rushed through the story. Maybe because it's too painful to talk about, but I think there's something else. "Where'd you get the knife?"

"What? What does that matter?"

"The police will ask you, so I'm asking you now."

She turns white at the mention of the police. "I grabbed it off the kitchen counter. I'd been using it to cut up some apples earlier."

I let her sit with that for a minute. Then I get up, go into the mudroom, and retrieve the bowie knife from under the blankets. I bring it back into the kitchen and lay it down on the kitchen table in front of her. "I don't know about you, but I don't generally pare my apples with a hunting knife."

"Where'd you get that?" she asks in a hushed whisper. As if she's afraid that Oren will hear her.

"It was in Oren's sweatshirt pocket. It had blood on it."

She stares at it for a long moment and then looks up at me. "It doesn't now."

"No," I concede. "It slipped into the washer. No blood, no fingerprints. Nothing to prove who was holding that knife. But it wasn't you, was it? It was Oren who stabbed his father."

She glares at me with such anger and hatred that I'm sure I must be wrong. *This* is someone who could kill a man; not that sweet boy outside. Or maybe I just want to be wrong. I want to take it all back—*why must you poke your nose where it doesn't belong?*—but she's nodding now, wiping away a tear.

"He did it to protect me," she says. "He didn't know what he was doing."

"Why didn't you go to the police and tell them that? Or at least call 911?"

"And let them take Oren? You know they would, even if I told them he was protecting me. They'd put him in juvenile detention. Can you imagine that sweet, smart boy in one of those places?" She says it like she knows what she's talking about. Like maybe she spent some time in one herself. She wouldn't be the first foster kid to end up in detention. "It would ruin his life."

I can't say I disagree with her, but I make myself ask, "And what kind of life are you going to have on the run?"

She shakes her head and begins to cry. "If you're going to call the police just give us a head start and we'll clear out."

And go where? I wonder, picturing Alice and Oren thumbing a ride on the road, taking a lift from who knows who. "No," I say. "I can help you. Give me a day and I'll make arrangements. I can find a place that will be safe for you and Oren." She's crying harder, so I add, "You can trust me." But she knows that. We both know I made up my mind to help them when I tossed that knife in the washer.

THE FACT IS I've helped people who were wanted by the law before. Parents who were defying court-ordered custody arrangements that they believed put their children at risk, women who had struck out against violent partners, teenagers who had run away from abusive parents. Doreen and I had an agreement that when these cases came up I would handle them without involving Sanctuary, so that we wouldn't give the local police department an excuse to shut us down. I'm going to need help, though, finding a safe place for Alice and Oren. They can't stay long at St. Alban's—but there is someone at St. Alban's who can help.

I take Alice into the parlor and tell her to choose from the piles of clothing whatever she and Oren need. She doesn't ask me where we're going, for which I'm grateful. The boy won't be so easy. I go outside and find him crouched on the newly shoveled path. He's carved a straight-edged tunnel from the porch steps to the driveway, and then from the driveway to the barn, piling the snow in neat walls on either side. Now he's scooping a shallow niche out of the snow wall. He takes something out of his pocket and places it inside the niche. When I step closer I see it's a plastic action figure of Han Solo.

"Ah," I say, "Han Solo frozen in carbonite ice in Cloud City. Are you sure you want to leave him there?"

He nods and stands up. "Luke and Leia and Chewbacca are on the way to rescue him."

"And R2-D2 and C-3PO, don't forget," I say, reminding myself to grab the figure before we leave. "You did a good job on the path."

He shrugs, trying not to look too pleased. "It was easy. Can we go sledding now?"

I'm about to tell him no, we've got more important things to do, but then I think of all the promises he's seen broken. "Absolutely. I know a great hill. Go pick out a sled. There are a couple in the barn." I point across the yard to the barn and watch him tear up the newly shoveled path. Does he *know* his father is dead? Does he even remember stabbing him? I hope the moment has been absorbed into some fantastical story of bravery and valor, of heroes and villains. He saved the princess from the evil Darth Vader. Maybe in his version he also saves Darth Vader.

WHEN OREN SEES the extra pack his mother's carrying he looks once at me and then away. He's silent for the drive into town, staring out the window at the snow-covered pines and then Main Street, where people are out shoveling their sidewalks. Delphi almost looks cheerful and bright with everything trimmed in new-fallen snow. Even the shabby Sanctuary office looks pretty nice. Doreen's put up some Christmas lights and cleaned up the donation piles on the porch, something she usually does when she's anxious. Last night's call must have brought up some ugly stuff for her; I'll stop there on my way back to visit with her and tell her that I've sent mother and son safely on their way. I won't tell her about the knife or the dead man in Ridgewood. She thinks they came from Newburgh, so if she hears the story on the news hopefully she won't connect it to them.

It's another fifteen miles to St. Alban's. When we pass through the black iron gates Oren sits up straighter, craning his neck to read the sign, then glares at me. "I thought you said you wouldn't take us to the convent," he says.

"You won't have to stay here long. Sister Martine is going to find you a safe place to go," I say. "She has the best resources," I add in a lower voice to Alice, but she's looking out the window, her face closed.

"They've also got the best sledding hill," I say in a high, artificial voice that makes me cringe. "See?"

We've made the turn and can now see the convent, an imposing brick building that looks like a hospital—or a juvenile detention institution. Which it *was:* during the nineteenth century and well into the twentieth it was St. Alban's Home for Wayward Girls and Fallen Women, where girls pregnant out of wedlock or deemed "promiscuous" were sent. Sister Martine will still take in pregnant teenagers, but now St. Alban's is also a shelter for victims of domestic violence and their families and a temporary residence for at-risk youth.

I roll down the window to let in the shouts of children sledding down the long hill to the river, hoping that the sound will banish the austerity of the building. Oren is watching the children with equal parts wariness and longing. Then he looks toward the convent and seems to freeze. "I don't want to go in there."

"You don't have to," I say quickly. "You can go sledding. Your mom and I will just have a quick talk with Sister Martine."

Alice looks toward me. "I don't want to leave Oren by himself," she says.

I sigh. The whole point of coming here was for Sister Martine to meet Alice and Oren. She will be more likely to help if she sees them. Especially Oren. No one could resist those large brown eyes, the quick, smart spark of him. A spark that has gone out at the sight of the convent and the thought of being separated from his mother.

"How about this," I say. "You two go sledding and I'll go in and have a talk with Sister Martine. Then we'll both come out to talk to you."

Oren's eyes flick from me to Alice, waiting for what she says, but Alice looks back at him and asks, "How does that sound, buddy?"

"Only if you go on the sled with me."

Alice groans. "Okay, but just the one time. I'll get soaked."

"Twice," Oren demands.

I see the hint of a smile on Alice's face as she concedes. What a relief it must be to be tussling over minor rights and favors after what they've been through.

"That's settled then," I say, feeling like a weight's been lifted from my shoulders. But then I look back at the massive building and feel every brick of it settle squarely on my chest. For a moment I'd forgotten that I still had to go inside.

OREN'S EXCITED TO show Alice the sled he's picked out. To my surprise he didn't pick one of the bright plastic sleds I bought a couple of years ago for Atefeh's kids. He'd gone to the back of the barn and dug out Caleb's old Flexible Flyer—an antique even when Caleb used it; it had been mine first. It still has the nick in the wooden crosspiece from when Caleb and I crashed into an apple tree sledding at Hanson's Orchard. I still have the scar on my right forearm, which I'd thrown over Caleb's face to protect him from the impact.

You could have gotten the boy killed, my mother had scolded when we came back. The sled had vanished into the back of the barn. I'm surprised Oren was able to find it and a little alarmed that he'd gone exploring so far back in the barn. There are dangerous things in there—mowing scythes, old tractor parts, ice picks, pulleys, and hooks. What had I been thinking, to let him go in alone? *I really am losing it,* I think as I wiggle the crosspiece to see that it still moves the rails. They creak but still work. They are remarkably free of rust.

"Cool," Oren says when I show him how to steer with the rope attached to the crosspiece. Alice is looking at the sled more dubiously.

"Have fun," I say. "And be careful. That sled goes pretty fast."

Oren is already running toward the hill, dragging the sled behind him. It bumps over the snow-covered lawn, and for a moment I see the shadow of another boy riding on the sled, me pulling it, laughing at Caleb's cries to go faster. I blink and brace myself against the car at the sudden wash of vertigo.

"Are you all right?" Alice asks.

"Just tired," I say. "I didn't get much sleep last night. You go and have fun. I'll talk to Sister Martine and we'll come out to see you in a bit. Maybe by then Oren won't mind coming inside to warm up."

Alice shakes her head and looks toward the convent. "Once he's decided a place is bad there's no getting him to change his mind."

"I understand," I say. I watch Alice follow Oren. I do understand. I too once promised myself that I would never set foot inside St. Alban's again.

IT'S NOT THAT St. Alban's is a bad place; only that it's a place people come to when nowhere else will have them. The very stones have absorbed the fear and sadness of the last resort, though the building itself is quite beautiful. I step through the wide oak doors and into the shadowed vestibule, where the marble floor is splashed with blue, red, and green lozenges of light. The air smells of incense and lemon wax. Someone is playing a piano somewhere.

Although it's warmer in here, my skin has broken out into gooseflesh and I have to remind myself that I'm a grown woman (*a grown-ass woman*, as Doreen is fond of saying) with a home, not a scared girl with no place else to go. I stamp my feet to shake the snow from my boots—or maybe to announce my entrance. Either way, the noise fails to wake up the nun napping in the glass-fronted booth by the door. She's probably deaf. Many of the old ones are. And they're all old; not many young recruits these days. I wonder how long Sister Martine will be able to keep St. Alban's going. I imagine the diocese is keeping its eye on this riverfront property.

As I walk past the drowsing nun I feel like Psyche sneaking past drugged Cerberus. It's the boy, I think as I walk the long hall to Sister Martine's office, who's put me in mind of mythology—all those stories my father read to me and I read to Caleb. It would have been fun to look at the stars with Oren and talk about the heroes and their adventures, but we won't do that now. Once I explain the situation, Sister Martine will want them to leave immediately. She will know a safe place to send them; by tomorrow they'll be across the border in Canada. I stop in the middle of the hallway, swamped by an overwhelming sense of loss. *Don't be selfish,* I hear my mother say, *you know the right thing to do.*

Do I? I wonder as I force my feet the rest of the way down the hall. I knock on the door before I can change my mind.

"Come!" a gruff voice calls from inside. For a moment I picture my father behind the door and I can't move, but then I hear a querulous voice add, "Or don't! It's all the same to me."

I adjust my lapel so my pink I STAND WITH PLANNED PARENTHOOD button is visible and open the door. Sister Martine looks up from the stack of folders on her desk, blue eyes peering over reading glasses that have slipped to the end of her long aquiline nose. She looks like a bird of prey scanning the horizon for lunch. But when she sees it's me, her face fans into a multitude of fine lines, like an origami flower unfolding.

"Mattea," she croons, making of my full name a song. "It's been too long."

She begins to stand up but I hurry closer to stop her. The walker she's been using since she broke her hip last year sits in the corner as if it's been sent there for being bad. Sister Martine braces herself against the desk with one hand, knuckles down, and reaches for me with the other. She squeezes my shoulder with surprising strength and then stands straight to look me in the eye. It startles me to realize we're the same height; I always picture her towering above me.

"You look tired," she says. "You haven't been sleeping."

"You should talk," I counter, taking in the bruised-looking skin under her eyes and the thermos of coffee and towering stack of folders on the desk. One night, when I was staying here, I tried to slip out. I had to go past Sister Martine's office, which I didn't think was a problem since it was three A.M. As I crept past I saw a light and looked in. She was at her desk, stockinged feet up, wimple discarded, hard at work. That was decades ago, but I'm pretty sure she keeps the same hours now. "Tell me you haven't been up all night," I add.

"Only time I can get some work done without interruption." She pats the stack of files. "I have to keep up with all my children."

Brown folders and blue folders; I'm familiar with the system. Each brown folder represents an unwed mother who came to St. Alban's to wait out her pregnancy. Each blue folder represents a baby born here. Sometimes a woman has two folders: a brown and a blue one. These are the women who were born here and then show up years later to have their own baby. *That's often the only way I find out what happened to the children who left from here,* Sister Martine told me once.

She pats my cheek as if I were one of her children (which, in a way, I am) and looks into my face. I feel split open by her gaze. To avert it I tap the pin on my lapel. "Look what you get when you donate to Planned Parenthood these days."

She screws up her face into a scowl, then flips up the collar of her habit to reveal an identical pink pin. "No kidding."

I burst out laughing, the first time I've really laughed since I don't know when. Sister Martine could always make me laugh. When she caught me trying to run away that night she told me to go ahead. *What?* she'd asked in a perfect Jewish inflection. *I should worry you're going to get knocked up?*

"Did you contribute in your own name?" I ask.

"Of course not. I contributed in the name of our new vice president and gave his address. But I helped myself to a pin when I drove one of my girls over to the center in Pough-keepsie."

"You drove a girl to Planned Parenthood?" I can't disguise the surprise in my voice. I know Sister Martine has unusual views for a nun, but taking a girl for an abortion would probably get her excommunicated. "For . . . ?"

"An STD test and to be fitted for a diaphragm. But please don't tell Doreen. The last time she tweeted about me and I got in trouble with the archbishop."

"I bet," I say, grinning back at her. I notice that her hand on my shoulder is trembling and help her back into her chair, pulling another chair close. I asked her once years ago how she could remain with the church when she disagreed with its position on birth control and abortion. She told me that her beliefs were between her and God and that they were both content that she was in the place she could do the most good. *And what more could I pray for,* she'd asked, *other than world peace, an end to hunger, and a new water boiler for the convent, than to find the place where I can do the most good?*

When I've got her settled I sit back in my own chair and see she's studying me. "You've brought someone for me, haven't you?"

I lift my chin toward the window behind her, which faces the river and the long hill that slopes down to its banks. Right now it also affords a view of children sledding and pummeling one another with snowballs, and a troop of nuns and pregnant teenagers snowshoeing. I spot Alice pulling Oren on the Flexible Flyer to the rim of the hill.

"The woman in the peacoat with the boy in red—Alice and Oren. They came in on the bus last night. He's got bruises on his arms; she has marks on her throat."

"They could go to Mulberry House in Kingston," she says, smiling as Alice gives Oren a push and then jumps on the back of the sled. We can hear their high, excited whoops as they careen down the hill. "It's a safe place."

By "safe place" she means that the location is kept secret. Even most of our volunteers don't know where it is.

"Men have found it before," I say.

Sister Martine doesn't argue with that. Over the years children have told their fathers where they are. Women have told their sisters-in-law, who have told their brothers. Men have come to the shelter and demanded to be let in. And because the men have come, the police have come too.

"Are you afraid that the man who hurt them will find them?" she asks.

I shake my head. Then I tell her about the knife, the blood, and the news of the dead man in Ridgewood. She listens to it all with no sign of shock or judgment. Doreen might be the best at talking people down, but Sister Martine is the best listener I've ever met. I've told her things I've never told anyone else.

"Do you believe it was the boy who stabbed his father?" she asks when I finish.

"I don't know," I say. "If I asked the boy I think he would tell me."

"But you don't want to ask the boy." She looks back out the

window where Oren is pulling his sled up the hill, laughing as Alice throws a snowball at him. "Because whichever one did it, the end result will be that one of them gets sent away. Still, I worry that if we hide them, they will have to live with that guilt between them forever."

"The guilt of killing an abusive man?" I ask.

"The guilt of killing a parent," she replies, turning now to me. "No one should have to live with that."

I avoid her eyes and look out the window myself. "They'll have each other. Isn't that what matters most?"

When I look back at Sister Martine she holds my gaze for a long moment. It's hard keeping my eyes level with that blue stare, as blinding as the light reflecting off the snow. But I do, and after a long pause she gives one curt nod. "I'll make a few calls, set up a place up north. Bring them to me tomorrow."

I'm about to tell her that they've got their stuff and can stay here tonight; she above anyone will understand why I can't have the boy a second night. But before I can, I see something that freezes the words in my throat. A police car has pulled into the driveway.

CHAPTER SEVEN

Alice

OREN SEES THE policeman before I do. We're climbing back up the hill, both of us soaked from our many falls in the snow (and the snowballs Oren has slipped down my collar). But I don't feel cold. I would go up and down this hill with Oren forever to keep that open look on his face, one I haven't seen in months.

But then he freezes. The blood drains from his face and his features go sharp the way they do when he's scared, like he's drawn into himself to make a smaller target. I follow his gaze up the hill and see a dark figure silhouetted against the sky. For a moment I think it's Davis, come back from the dead to punish us for thinking we could get away from him. *I'd follow you to the ends of the earth,* he told me once. I'd thought it was romantic, until I recognized it for the threat it was.

But then the figure turns and I see the uniform and that

the man is bulkier and fairer than Davis. He's turning because someone has called his name. *Frank*. A figure in a
purple poncho is wading across the snow, arms flapping
like a big-ass bird trying to take off. It's Mattie, hailing the
policeman like he's her best friend. She must have called
him to turn us in.

Oren tugs at my sleeve. "Come on," he says. "Mattie's trying to distract him so we can get away."

As if. It's more likely she's trying to save her own skin. But
I don't need to tell Oren that. We *do* need to get away.

Oren pulls me toward the hedge that borders the sledding
hill. I'd barely noticed it before, but Oren leads us straight
to an opening in the dense, prickly wall and through it into
a path bordered by more tall hedges. "It's a maze!" Oren
shouts, the color back in his face. He loves mazes. After we
read the story about Theseus and the Minotaur he begged
for a puzzle book with mazes he could solve. This is like his
daydream come to life. "This is the perfect place to hide!
C'mon." He drops the sled and my hand and takes the right-
hand turn.

I follow, hissing at him, *"Slow down!"* I don't want to shout
in case the policeman and Mattie hear us. I especially don't
want to call Oren's name.

Oren looks over his shoulder and laughs before rounding
another corner. *Shit.* I run to catch up, stumbling through
the shin-deep snow. He's turning our flight into a game. And
whose fault is that? For months I've done the same thing.
Let's pretend we're planning a trip! I'd said when I got the

bus schedules. *Let's make it a secret.* And then the one I feel worst about now: *Let's be extra nice to your dad.*

I'd seen the look of hurt on Oren's face after that one, as if I were telling him it was his fault when Davis hit him. After all, that was what Davis told him. *Why do you have to go and make me so mad? Are you trying to work on my last nerve? Didn't I tell you last time that this is what would happen? Aren't you listening to me? Are you deaf or just stupid? Do you want me to hit you?*

When I turn the next corner Oren is gone. My mouth floods with acid. He's run away from me. All these weeks of telling him to be nice to Daddy, to tiptoe around Davis's moods, so we could stay safe long enough to get away, what Oren has heard is that I blame *him* for the things Davis does. I have again and again failed to keep him safe. And now he's taken his revenge by stranding me in this stupid maze like I'm the father in that horrible movie that Davis let him watch one night that gave him nightmares for a month.

A spark of anger flares in my chest. *After all I've done for him, to be lumped together with Davis . . .* but then I see the footprints in the snow. Little-boy feet splayed out like a duck's. *Duckfoot,* Davis called him. He's just playing a game with me. I still feel that ember of anger at my core, but I tamp it down. Better he still wants to play games.

As I follow the tracks of his booted feet I remember another game we used to play. Oren called it Tin Can. It began on a snow day when we were stuck inside. I made us grilled cheese sandwiches and Campbell's tomato soup for lunch,

Oren helping me pour the condensed soup from the can and then washing it out for recycling. He said his teacher had shown him how you could make a telephone out of two cans tied together with string. Sound traveled along the string because of vibrations. When I looked skeptical he insisted we try it.

I found another can amid Davis's empties, used a screwdriver to punch holes in their bottoms, and tied them together with a length of heavy twine from Davis's toolbox. *You have to make the string taut,* Oren told me. I stood in the kitchen and Oren took the can all the way down to the last bedroom. The house was what was called a shotgun shack, so he could go a long way without turning any corners. *Look away so you can't cheat and read my lips,* he'd shouted. Which made me smile, because if I could hear him without the phone, what was the point of the phone anyway? But I turned to the wall, pressed the can to my ear, and waited.

Can I tell you a secret? Oren's voice was a whisper in my ear, but it was as if he were standing right beside me. *Over and out. That means you can talk now. You have to answer my question.*

I moved the can from my ear to my lips and whispered, *Yes, you can tell me anything.* I moved the can back to my ear before remembering I had to say "over and out," but Oren was already talking, a slow, steady murmur that traveled the length of the house and then traveled down my spine to settle into the pit of my stomach. They're still there now, all those whispered words, all the awful things that Davis had done to him—the taunts, the threats, the slaps. They're what led to my being here now in a ridiculous maze (why would nuns have a maze anyway?) following tracks in the snow—

Only the tracks have abruptly stopped. I am standing looking at an untouched square of white snow surrounding a statue of a woman holding up snow-covered arms as if remarking on the emptiness of the space around her. I check to see if Oren is hiding behind the statue but he is not. I look back at the tracks I was following but my tracks have covered Oren's. As if I've wiped them out.

I choke back a sob. I'm being ridiculous. There has to be an explanation—

And I know what it is. In that horrible movie the little boy leads his crazy father into the maze and then walks backward in his own footprints to trick him. That's what Oren has done to me. He's tricked me and abandoned me.

I sink down into the snow, my back against the statue's stone base, and try to get my breathing under control. That boy poured his secrets into my ear and I did nothing. *He could be making it up,* I thought. *No one will believe you,* I told myself. Especially the last thing Oren had said. He couldn't have known *that.* But the truth was I was afraid of what Davis would do if I told anyone. I put my own safety before Oren's.

I cry until the tears freeze on my face, until I am so cold I might as well become another statue at the feet of the stone saint.

And what good will that do?

The voice—a boy's voice—is so close that I snap open my eyes, sure it is Oren come back for me. But I'm alone. I notice, though, something I hadn't noticed before. Across from the opening in the hedge I came through there's another opening. And there are footprints there. I get up to look. They're the same boot prints. The same duckfooted gait. Oren. Somehow he crossed the expanse of the square and went out the other opening without making a footprint in the square. Did he jump onto the base of the statue? Or sweep the prints away? Maybe the wind blew them away.

I wipe the tears from my face and follow the footprints back through the maze. When I finally exit I find Oren standing to the side of the opening, the sled by his side, looking up at the top of the hill. Mattie is still talking to the policeman, flapping her arms around like an agitated goose. The policeman's watching her, arms crossed over his broad chest. At last he turns away from her and heads to his cruiser.

"It's okay," Oren says, looking back at me. "Mattie told him a story to get rid of him."

I don't ask how he knows that. I kneel down and turn him around to look at me, my hands digging into his narrow, frail shoulders. "Don't ever run away from me like that again," I cry, my voice coming out angrier than I meant it to. "You scared me half to death."

His eyes get wide the way they would when Davis yelled at him. "I just wanted to show you I could take care of myself," he says in a small scared whisper. "Didn't you see how I doubled back like that boy in the movie?"

"Don't make things up," I say, shaking him just a little. I'm not the same as Davis, it's just that when he makes things up it scares me. Like the thing he'd said that day into the can. "I saw your tracks leading out the other way."

"What other way?" Oren asks, the tears spilling now, his mouth an O of hurt. "I came back the same way."

But that can't be. No more than Oren could have known what he told me through the tin can. I'd believed all the things he said that Davis had done to him. But after he'd listed them all he said, *It won't stop there. If we don't leave he'll kill both of us.*

CHAPTER EIGHT

Mattie

I'LL GO SPEAK with him," Sister Martine says, getting to her feet. "You go out the back door and get the boy and his mother away. I'll call you later to arrange a meeting place."

This would be a fine plan if Sister Martine could walk at a regular pace, but despite her best efforts (and some very un-nun-like muttering), by the time we get to the front door the officer has already gotten out of his cruiser and is walking toward the rim of the sledding hill.

There's no way Sister Martine is going across that snow. I tell her I'll call her later and wade into the drifts, calling Frank's name. Because of course that's who it is. Frank Barnes, Delphi's chief of police. The last man I want to talk to right now.

On the plus side I don't have to worry about how ridiculous I look. Frank crosses his arms over his chest and watches me wade through the snow. He could come to me, but he's not going to make this any easier. For him I'll always be the spoiled brat who grew up in the big house on the hill. Judge Lane's daughter.

The Little Judge, he'd call me when I accused him of cheating at Monopoly or when I'd balk at some quasi-criminal prank he'd dreamed up, like sneaking into the courthouse at night or dressing up the statue of George Washington in women's clothing. For a police chief's son he had remarkably little respect for the law, which I'd always attributed to a contrary streak in his nature. Most things about Frank have changed since we were kids playing pranks—except for that contrary streak. He's happy to stand and let me make a fool of myself bleating like a stray lamb stuck out in the snow.

I have the urge to give him the finger and turn around, but just past Frank's bulky shape (he's put on weight this winter, but then so have I) I spy a flash of Oren's red jacket and blue cap on the hill. If Frank sees Oren and Alice he'll know they're not local. He'll want to talk to them, and then he might connect them to that mother and son on the run from New Jersey.

"Yoo-hoo!" I call, hating myself for sounding like the dotty old spinster everyone thinks I am. But sometimes it's better to play the harmless old lady. "Frank Barnes! Just who I wanted to talk to. Do you have a minute? Or are you out here looking to ticket speeding sledders?"

He doesn't crack a smile. "I don't know, Mattie, are you planning to sled? If you sled the way you drive I may have to."

I force myself to laugh as I traverse the last few feet between us. Frank has pulled me over for speeding half a dozen times over the years and once for an illegal U-turn on Main Street at three in the morning. I've accused him of lying in wait for me in various alleys and lay-bys throughout the county. "Oh, I think my sledding days are behind me. I'd probably break a hip." Out of the corner of my eye I see Oren pulling his mother toward the hedge maze. Clever boy. If they can hide in there until I get rid of Frank we'll be okay.

"I think you're made of stronger stuff than that, Mattie. What are *you* doing out here?"

"Just dropping off some donations." I glance back at the building so I don't have to meet Frank's eyes. We've known each other since we were kids. Our fathers were friends—the judge and the chief of police—and we used to play while our fathers jawed on the front porch of my father's law offices. One of the games we'd play was Three Truths and a Lie. Frank always knew what my lie was. "And having a chat with Sister Martine. Is that who you're here to see?"

"I'm looking for a woman and boy gone missing from northern New Jersey," he says. "I thought they might have landed here. Unless they turned up at Sanctuary."

"A woman and boy?" I echo. "How old's the boy? There was a woman with a three-year-old in two days ago who needed help applying for food stamps." This is true so I give Frank a steady look, daring him to accuse me of making up indigent women and children.

Frank meets my gaze, unsoftened by my good works. "This boy's older. Ten. The woman's in her early thirties. They were spotted getting on a bus in Kingston."

"What'd they do?" I ask, absorbing the notion that Alice is older than she looks. "Knock over a Stewart's?"

"I'm just looking for them. They could be in trouble. Have you seen them?"

I shake my head. "Believe it or not, I'm not aware of every runaway woman and child in the Catskills and Hudson Valley."

"So if I check Sanctuary's log for last night I won't find a record of a call from a woman on the run?"

"You'll need a warrant to see those logs," I say, bristling. Frank knows full well that he needs a warrant, but he enjoys piquing me on this point. "Unless we believe a caller presents a danger to himself or others, those calls are confidential."

He shifts his weight, looks away, scanning the sledders for any strange ten-year-old boys, then brings his hand to rest on his hip near his holster. Letting me know what he's got backing up his point of view. "What if I told you that woman and child were in danger? Would you tell me if you'd been in contact with them?"

I notice he doesn't threaten me with breaking the law by concealing Alice and Oren's location. He knows that won't sway me, that I'm more likely to talk if I think I'm protecting them. And it *does* give me pause. Frank might be a bit officious, he might throw his weight around like most men, and our history predisposes him against me, but he's not a bad man. If he thinks Alice and Oren are in danger . . . but then I recall that the man who threatened Alice and Oren is dead.

"Of course if I thought a client was in danger I'd do whatever was necessary to keep him or her safe," I answer, holding Frank's gaze steadily. We both know this to be true.

Frank gives me a thin-lipped smile. "Always the judge's daughter, eh, Mattie?" My carefully evasive wording hasn't gotten past him.

I know I should laugh it off, but I can't help thinking about the other time he said the same thing to me. The remembrance makes me mad. And as Doreen has often pointed out, I don't have a filter when I'm mad. "Always the police chief's son," I answer back, "snooping into other people's business."

Frank's face flushes red as if I'd slapped him. I'd like to take the words back, not only because they sound like something my mother would say, but because it's thanks to Frank's father's snooping that I'm alive. I start to apologize but he cuts me off. "What did you want to talk to me about?"

I'd almost forgotten saying that and for a moment my mind is completely blank. But then I think of something. "There were some rednecks giving Atefeh a hard time last night in Stewart's. Some hunters—Jason and Wayne—in a souped-up plow truck."

Frank nods. "That would be Wayne Marshall," he says. "You don't remember him? He was in school with us, a year ahead of me."

I shake my head, ignoring the implied criticism that I was too stuck-up to take notice of most of the locals.

"Yeah. He lived downstate for a while, divorced, moved back here to take care of his mother when she had cancer.

He works for the DEP now and does some snow plowing on the side."

"Wow," I say. "Do you know his shoe size too?"

He scowls. "It's my job to know what people are like. Wayne's a nice guy. *He* was giving Atefeh a hard time?"

"No," I admit. "It was Jason, who Wayne said was his—"

"Dumbass brother-in-law. Yeah, I know him. He *is* a dumbass. And a racist homophobe. Half the reason I think Wayne sticks around is to keep an eye on his sister and her kids. You can't pick your family, can you?"

For a moment this sentence hovers in the air between us. We're both thinking, I imagine, just how little we would have chosen our own families. Except for Caleb. I would always choose Caleb.

Frank narrows his eyes at me, suspicious cop again. "What were you doing at Stewart's last night?"

"You caught me," I say, holding my hands up. "I was jonesing for a bear claw."

He holds my gaze for a long moment, but before he can challenge me someone calls his name. We both look toward the convent and see the unlikely sight of Sister Martine making her way through the snow, the aluminum prow of her walker breaching the drifts like an arctic dogsled. Frank sighs. "I'd better stop her before she breaks something. But seriously, Mattie, if you know the whereabouts of this woman and boy you should tell me. There are things about this case you don't understand . . ." He looks like there's more that he wants to say but either he's afraid Sister Martine is going to fall or there's information he's not willing to share with me, and he storms off without another word. I watch him take Sister Martine's arm and steer her back toward the convent. I can count on Sister Martine to keep him distracted long enough to get Alice and Oren out of here.

I look down the hill and see that Oren and Alice have come out of the maze. I hold up my hand, fingers splayed wide. Then I point to the lower drive, which won't be visible from Sister Martine's office. Will they understand that I want them to meet me there in five minutes? When Oren holds up his hand in the same gesture I'm pretty sure he does.

I walk back to the car, keeping an eye out for Frank and going over our conversation in my head. I shouldn't have let him get me ruffled, but even when we were kids playing on the porch of my father's law offices, he could rile me up just by looking at me cross-eyed. I shouldn't have told him about being in Stewart's last night, but if he warns that idiot away from Atefeh it will be worth it. It occurs to me, though, that I should stop at Stewart's and ask Atefeh not to mention that I was meeting the bus last night. I hate asking her to lie, but she of all people will understand. I've just got to keep Alice and Oren hidden for one night and then they'll be out of my hands. Which is probably for the best. There was something about Frank's face when he told me that I didn't understand the case that makes me think it will be better for everyone when Alice and Oren are gone.

CHAPTER NINE

Alice

IT'S USELESS TRYING to get Oren to admit that he came out by another path. "Maybe you didn't realize it was a different way," I suggest as we wait on the lower drive for Mattie.

"Duh-uh. Didn't you hear what I just said? I walked backward in my own tracks."

Duh. That's what Davis would say when he was pointing out how stupid I was. How I just didn't get it. "Well, I know what I saw," I say. I'm keeping my eye on the drive for Mattie's car, standing in front of Oren as if that will protect him if the cop comes back. "There were footprints leading out of the maze on a different path."

"Well, Jesus, Alice, I guess there couldn't have been anyone else in the maze."

The voice is so much like Davis's that I spin around to stare behind me, sure that Davis has somehow shown up to taunt me. *Yeah, Jesus, Alice, how could you be so stupid to believe that I'd die of that pathetic little stab wound? Like I'm ever going to let you take my boy away from me.* But there's just Oren standing there, his face purple with rage. Somehow it's scarier to know that hateful voice came out of this little boy.

"Please don't speak to me in that tone," I say, trying to keep my voice calm.

"You called me a liar!"

"I didn't call you a liar." Davis always accused me of calling him a liar when I confronted him with a discrepancy, like why were there only two beers left in the six-pack if he drank only two or why did work call to ask where he was if he was *at* work. "I just thought you might have gotten mixed up."

"You're the one who's mixed up, stupid-face! Just because you followed someone else's footprints—"

"They were the same boots!" I cry, pointing at his boots. "And the same duckfooted prints."

His face turns the color of a bruise. I'd forgotten how much he hated when Davis made fun of him for splaying out his feet. "I am not a duckfoot! I am not!" Then he hits me.

It's the teeniest, lamest punch on the arm but it knocks the wind right out of me. "Oh great," I say, cradling my arm. "So now *you're* hitting me. Just like your father."

He gives me a hateful look that hurts much worse than the punch and then takes off straight up the road, dragging the sled behind him, his oversized boots slapping the pavement like big angry duck feet. I've said the very worst thing I could have said to him, but I'm not sorry. He's being a little shit, and if no one stops him he *will* grow up to be just like Davis. A spoiled little boy in a man's body always blaming someone else for his problems. Let him see how far he gets on his own or how he'll like it if that cop gets him first.

I'd forgotten about the cop.

"Oren!" I call. "Come back. I didn't mean it."

But Oren speeds up, stamping in the puddles from the melting snow, the sled bouncing behind him. I run after him, but he's gotten a head start and I'm soon out of breath. That's what I get for taking up smoking again. "Or-ren!" It comes out in a wheeze, hoarse and ugly.

I know that Oren's taking his anger at his father out on me because I'm *safe*. I won't hit him back. But I'm tired of being the safe one. Look where it's gotten us: homeless, on the run, waiting on the charity of nuns and social workers. It's time I took charge. *Time I taught the boy a lesson*. I'm only inches from Oren, reaching out for his arm, when I hear the words in my head. Davis's words in Davis's voice. I'm the one who has become just like Davis.

My hand is already on Oren's arm, fingers curling around his skinny biceps. I only want to stop him to tell him I'm sorry, but he jerks forward at my touch and I tighten my grip to keep him from falling—

I hear the pop as his shoulder dislocates and then the scream of pain, and Oren falls howling to the ground. I fall beside him, trying to cradle him in my arms, repeating "I'm sorry, I'm sorry" and then "Let me see, let me fix it." But he scoots away from me. I hear a car pull up and footsteps approaching. This is it. The police have gotten us. For a moment I'm almost grateful. This will all be taken out of my hands. *Oren* will be taken out of my hands. And maybe that is for the best. Because clearly I don't know what the fuck I am doing.

But when I look up I see it's not the cop; it's Mattie. "What happened?" she cries, kneeling beside Oren. The little shit huddles against her like he needs her protection from me.

"Nothing. We had a fight and he was running away. I was afraid he was going to run into that cop. I was just trying to stop him."

Mattie isn't paying attention to my litany of excuses—how fast they trip off my tongue! I have learned a thing or two from Davis. She's inspecting Oren's arm, peeling off his jacket, wrapping her large capable hands around his shoulder and biceps. "Do you know what this reminds me of?" she asks in such a calm voice that Oren is startled out of his hysterics.

"Wh-what?" he blubbers.

"The time that Luke lost his hand in the lightsaber fight with Darth Vader."

What a weird thing to say—and is she actually comparing me to Darth Vader?—but it delights Oren. "Am I going to lose my hand?" he asks, eyes popping.

"Nah," she says, "but if you *could* choose between a cyber hand and your regular hand, which would you choose?"

While Oren is pondering this Mattie pops his shoulder back into the joint. Oren emits a sharp cry and his eyes flutter like he might faint. I feel like I might as well. But then his eyes get big and he gives Mattie an appreciative look. "Hey, you fixed it!"

"Yep," Mattie says, "good as new. It's going to smart for a while though." She looks at me for the first time, those wintry lilac eyes as cold as the December sky. "We'd better get him back to the house and put some ice on it. Get some Children's Tylenol in him as well."

"We're going back to your house?" I ask. "I thought—"

"Change of plans. Sister Martine is making arrangements to move you tomorrow."

"But won't that cop check on your house after seeing you here? Isn't there any other place we can go?" The last place I want to go is back to that creepy old house with this bitch looking at me like I'm a child abuser. Like she knows the first thing about dealing with a kid.

Although she *did* know how to fix a dislocated shoulder. I wonder where she learned that.

She gives me a nasty look. "Sorry. My spare vacation house is being redecorated. And I don't want to involve any-one else in . . . *this*." She says *this* like she's talking about a turd she found on her carpet. "As for the police, I can take care of Frank Barnes. If he comes by I'll keep him out."

Frank? So she *is* chums with the police. I'm liking this less and less. "Take us to a motel," I say. "We can stay there until the nun's ready to move us."

Mattie's mouth goes hard. Before she can say anything Oren whimpers, "I want to go to Mattie's house. My arm hurts . . . and . . . and . . ." He's working himself up to a full-out tantrum and I'm afraid he's going to come out with some ugly accusation against me, but instead he sobs out, ". . . and I left my Han Solo there!"

"That you did, kid," Mattie says, smiling down at Oren. The smile's gone when she lifts her face to me. "It's one night, Alice. It'll be the best thing for the boy."

What can I say to that? I shrug. "Sure. Why not?" I get up and offer my hand to Oren, but he cowers against Mattie. He's not going to let me live this down quickly. I shrug again. "Have it your way," I say, and get in the backseat of the car.

Mattie helps Oren to the car. He's really hamming it up, limping like it was his leg I hurt and not just his arm. When Mattie goes to put him in the back with me he says he wants to sit in the front. Mattie acquiesces but makes sure Oren buckles up.

No one talks on the ride back to town. Mattie turns on the radio, which is tuned to NPR—big surprise. Oren doesn't even ask to change the station, which he does whenever I'm listening to a talk show. He's on his best behavior now. I've seen him act this way with me after Davis has gone after him. *Sure he's an angel with you, the kid's a great actor. He's a little shit with me.* I'd always thought it was a pathetic ploy to shift the blame onto a child, but now that I'm on the receiving end I can kind of see what Davis meant. The kid *is* a great actor. How long before he convinces someone that *I'm* the monster? How long before he convinces me?

Suddenly the idea of being alone with Oren on the run—cooped up in crappy halfway houses, living off the charity of nuns and social workers, then winding up in some shitty Section 8 housing—seems unbearable. But what other choice do I have?

It's then I remember Social Worker Scott. The only male social worker ever assigned to Oren, and the one decent one who seemed to really like Oren—and like me. In fact, it became obvious that he *liked* me liked me. So much so that Davis was jealous, said Scott was just hanging around because he wanted to screw me. That was what the last fight was about. When Davis came home and caught Oren and me getting ready to leave he accused me of running away with Scott.

Now I wish we *had* been. Although he tried to pretend otherwise, it was clear that Scott came from money. He'd gone to a fancy college upstate and always had the newest iPhone. He drove a Volvo. We wouldn't have had to take the crappy bus with Scott; he'd have taken us to Canada in his Volvo.

Maybe he still would.

Although I ditched my cell phone, I know Scott's phone number. I memorized it because I was always afraid to put it in my Contacts in case Davis looked through them.

Just as I'm thinking this Mattie pulls into the Stewart's where she picked us up last night. "I'm going to get some Children's Tylenol and an ice pack for Oren's arm," she says, barely glancing back in my direction.

"Can you get me another one of those bear claws, Mattie?" Oren asks in a pathetic little whimper.

"Sure, kid," she says. Then, deigning to look back at me, "Do you need anything, Alice?"

"I'm good," I say. "And no more bear claws for Oren, please. He had three cavities at his last checkup." There. How's that for good parenting?

"Oh, I think just this once, to take his mind off his arm." She gives Oren a sugary smile that turns to a warning scowl when she turns to me.

"Sure," I mutter under my breath as she gets out of the car, "you're not the one who'll have to pay the dentist's bill."

"I only had two cavities," Oren says as soon as Mattie's out of the car. "The third was just a 'spot' we were going to watch until my next checkup."

I'm tempted to tell him that eating bear claws is the surest way to turn a spot into a cavity, but I don't have time to argue. This might be my only chance to call Scott. "I'm sorry about your arm, buddy, but look, I just have to go run a real quick errand while Mattie's in the Stewart's."

He spins around and looks at me suspiciously. "You just told Mattie you didn't need anything."

"I need a girl thing I didn't want to have to tell Mattie about," I lie. When Oren makes a face I add, "I'm just going to pop into that CVS down the street. I'll be back in a second. Okay, honey?"

He shrugs and faces the front of the car. "It's a free country."

He's clearly not ready to let me off the hook yet. I don't have time to win him back right now, though. "Just stay put," I say, and get out of the car. "And lock the doors," I add before closing the door.

I hear the clunk of the locks as I jog away from the car—

and then they clunk a second and a third time. He's messing with me, but that's okay. He'll forgive me eventually. He has to. And he'll be happy when he sees Scott. He likes Scott and Scott likes me. He thinks I'm a "good caretaker." And Scott will be a good role model for Oren. I should have thought of calling him sooner, if only to tell him that we're okay.

When I get to the CVS I have a moment of panic because there's no pay phone, but then the cashier tells me there's a "courtesy phone" back by the pharmacy for people calling their doctors. *How civilized,* I think, walking down the aisles of mouthwash and brightly colored bottles of cough syrup, *maybe living in the country isn't so bad.* Maybe Scott can help us settle in some little town like this. He said once that he wanted to live in the country. I said I'd be bored stiff, but that was because when I got stuck in a foster home in the country it was always worse because we couldn't go anywhere. But that would be different now: I'd have a car, for one thing, and for another boring doesn't sound so bad.

The phone is next to the prescription pickup counter, where an old man is asking a million questions about the drugs he's getting. The pharmacist, an Indian lady, keeps smiling and repeating the same damn thing over and over again. I stand with my back to them so they won't see my face and punch in Scott's number, praying that he'll answer. Scott's one of those rich kids who's so used to smartphones that he texts everything instead of calling. I picture the number showing up with an unfamiliar upstate area code. He'll think it's some telemarketer . . . and then I hear a muffled voice, almost inaudible over the background sound of traffic, say hello.

"Scott!" I cry. "It's me. Alice."

There's a pause and I'm afraid he's going to hang up. What has he heard? Have the police questioned him? Then I hear a laugh. "Alice. I figured it was just a matter of time before you called."

The plastic receiver slips greasily from my fingers. The Indian pharmacist and the old man look up when it clanks against the counter. I jam it back into the cradle and turn around, the drugstore spinning queasily around me, all those brightly colored bottles smearing into a multicolored mess like the time Oren ate too many Skittles and threw up.

I stumble from the store and find my way back to the Stewart's. Oren must have fallen asleep and slid down in his seat because I can't see him. I run the last few yards to the car only to find it empty. I spin around in the parking lot searching for Oren's red jacket, his *Star Wars* pack, his blue cap, but I see only Mattie coming out of the store carrying a tray of hot drinks and a plastic bag.

"Where's Oren?" I demand.

Mattie looks at me as if I've lost it. "Isn't he in the car with you?"

I spin around again and the whole parking lot revolves. The world has been turned on its head. Davis is alive and I've lost Oren.

CHAPTER TEN

Mattie

ALICE IS HYSTERICAL. I've been worried about her since that scene back at the convent, wondering if it's really safe to leave her alone with the boy—and what do I do but go and leave her alone with the boy! Has he run off, or has she done something to him while I was in Stewart's? I'd spent longer than I meant to inside, trying to reassure Atefeh and doing the opposite. She's scared, now that I've brought her to Frank's attention, that she'll get deported. I can't seem to do anything right today.

This is what comes of sticking your nose in other people's business.

Not now, I practically say out loud, which is just what Alice needs to hear: me talking to myself. She's already stomped through Stewart's, looked in the restroom, and cross-examined Atefeh as if she thought she was holding Oren in the broom closet.

"Did you see him come in here?" I ask Alice for the second time.

"No," she says, her eyes darting back and forth, looking anywhere but at me. "I—I didn't see where he went. I—I just closed my eyes for a second and fell asleep. When I woke up he wasn't in the car."

She's lying. I can tell by the way her eyes shift up to the left, a *tell* Doreen taught me about. "Were you fighting?" I ask.

"NO! I just told you, I was asleep . . . Fuck this! We have to find him." Her eyes get big and she looks at me. "Unless you took him? Did you decide that I wasn't good enough to take care of him and take him away?"

I ignore the fact that I *have* been wondering if Alice is able to take care of Oren and practice one of the techniques we learn in counseling instead: reflect back what you hear the client saying. "Why would I think that?" I ask. "Are you worried that you're not able to take care of Oren?"

Like many of the techniques we learn in counseling, this one doesn't fly so well on the ground. Alice looks like she'd like to smack me. I automatically shift my right foot back so I can pivot away from the blow if she does. Out of the corner of my eye I can see Atefeh tense behind the counter. Loud angry voices are triggering for her.

Looking at Alice, I consider what Frank said: *There are things about this case you don't understand.* I'm beginning to think he's right. I've made the mistake I caution my interns not to make: I've made assumptions. I've assumed that Alice is the victim because she's the woman. But what if she's the abuser? What if *she* killed her husband and fled with Oren because he's a witness to her crime? I recall how Oren flinched when Alice touched his arm last night—and then this morning she grabbed him so hard she dislocated his shoulder.

I've made a terrible mistake. I should call Frank immediately, but if I give any indication that's what I'm going to do, Alice will bolt. Then Frank won't be able to question her. I have to keep her calm—and I have to find Oren.

"I bet he just went exploring," I say with a calm I don't feel. "Oren's an adventurous boy. Let's take a walk through the village. We can stop by Sanctuary and get one of my colleagues to help—"

"I don't want any more of you people involved," she cuts in.

"All our volunteers are pledged to confidentiality"—*unless the client presents a threat to self or others,* I think but don't add—"and it'll just be Doreen, who talked to you last night on the phone." I'm hoping that Doreen will be there. I can park Alice with her and call Frank.

"But what if he comes back here looking for me?" she objects, but in a much weaker voice. I can tell that she's running out of steam.

"Atefeh will keep an eye out for him. Won't you, Atefeh?"

Atefeh nods eagerly, obviously relieved that the yelling has stopped. "That I will," she says. "And I bet Ms. Lane is right. The boy has gone adventuring. My little boy is always running off, scaring me half to death, but he always comes back."

Alice gives Atefeh a tight nod and then turns to me. "Shouldn't we split up? We'll cover more ground."

I was afraid she would suggest this. "You don't know the town," I say. "I know the places a boy would hide."

She gives me a strange look. "Is that because you had a little brother?"

Although I've prepared myself for a physical blow, I am completely unprepared for this. "How did you know about Caleb?" I demand.

Alice flinches as if I'm the one who's out of control. "I—I saw his picture—and you have a lot of boy stuff in the house. What happened to him?"

"We're wasting time," I say. "Let's start walking toward Sanctuary."

I walk out quickly, not caring for the moment if she follows me or not. It's been years since anyone asked me about Caleb and it feels like a violation. There's something wrong about this woman . . . something . . .

And then it hits me. The picture of Caleb she said she saw. The only picture I have of Caleb is in my bedroom. What was this woman doing in my bedroom?

ALICE IS RIGHT that the reason I know where a boy would hide is because of Caleb. He was always running away.

He likes the attention, my mother would say when I called. But the summer I came back to stay, when Caleb was ten, it seemed to me that what he wanted was to disappear. No doubt it was because of the tension at home, which was

worse than ever that summer. My father was always locked
in his study poring over old case files, my mother scrubbing
the kitchen floor until her knuckles bled. To get Caleb away
I'd take him into town for an ice cream at Stewart's, and
when I turned around he would be gone. It scared me half
to death the first time it happened; I thought he'd been kidnapped by a pervert trucker passing through town. I kept
picturing his body discarded and broken at the bottom of a
ravine—so I'd headed first for water.

As I do now. There's a path that leads from the back of
the Stewart's parking lot down to the creek and a little swimming hole—the hollow, we called it, growing up. I'm scanning the path for footprints when Alice comes up behind
me. "There!" she says, her voice sharp and hysterical. She
points at the snow at the edge of the parking lot. "Those
are Oren's prints. The boots you gave him have that pattern
on the sole and he splays his feet like that . . ." Her voice
catches. She *does* love him, I think, but then I've seen people
do the worst hurt to the people they love.

"So did Caleb," I say, stepping off the asphalt into the
snow. "My mother made him wear braces until he was ten."

"The doctor said that doesn't work," Alice says, following
me onto the wooded path.

"Your doctor is right," I say. "But there was no telling my
mother that. She liked things that she could control, things
she could *shape*. Fastening those straps made her feel like
she had Caleb in her control."

"She sounds like a piece of work."

The path is narrow, so we're walking single file (*Indian file,* I grew up calling it, but Doreen has informed me the term is no longer politically correct) and Alice can't see the grin on my face. *A piece of work* doesn't begin to cover it. "She had her own bad history," I say, and then I think that this might be a way to draw Alice out. "It's not uncommon for victims of abuse to become abusers. It's the only model they know—"

"Why would Oren come down here?" Alice cuts in. Clearly she doesn't want to hear the cycle-of-abuse speech. "How would he know this path is here?"

"Maybe he saw another kid going down here," I say, even though it's clear that Oren's are the only footprints in the snow. "This is kind of a local kids' hangout. In summer it's a swimming hole; during the year teenagers come here to smoke and make out." I can hear my voice waver on the last part and I'm glad Alice can't see my face. This isn't just the place where I'd find Caleb; it was also the place that Frank and I used to meet.

"In this weather? Jeez, I thought it was bad in the group homes but at least we had a rec lounge."

I'm surprised Alice offers this clue into her upbringing. Maybe she does want to talk about the cycle of abuse. I should follow it, draw her out, but we've come to the bottom of the hollow. The pool is frozen over, a perfect circle of ice surrounded by low overhanging pine and fir branches. I've been thinking about Caleb so much that I can almost picture him here. I can see him crouched by the edge of the pool, hiding one of his toys in the roots of an old hemlock.

What are you doing here, buddy? I'd asked, squatting down beside him in the dirt.

Luke is hiding from the stormtroopers, he'd said. He'd placed the little action figure of Luke in a hollow that had been scooped out between the roots. There was a green Yoda already there. We'd just seen the third *Star Wars* movie and I'd bought the action figures for him at a garage sale. They were secondhand, the paint chipped on Luke's tunic and one of Yoda's ears broken off.

Well, I'm here to report that the coast is clear and it's safe to return to the ship.

I still remember how he'd looked up at me, his face full of trust . . . and then I'm remembering another face. Frank's. The last night we met here. Instead of trust, though, he'd looked at me as if he knew I was lying to him. Which I was.

"Could he have fallen through the ice?" Alice says, shaking my arm.

"There aren't any cracks in the ice," I say, staring at the frozen pond. Though the snow *is* disturbed below my feet: flaked with moss and soil as if someone has been digging here. I step over the place in the snow where the roots of the tree are showing, remembering Caleb's trusting face looking up at me. *Let's take Luke and Yoda home, buddy.*

Just Luke, Caleb had answered. *Yoda lives here. We have to leave him here in case Luke needs to come back for help.*

I'd meant to come back later and rescue Yoda before some other kid took him, but I'd had a fight with my father that night and gone back to the city without finding Yoda or even saying goodbye to Caleb. He'd been so angry when my mother told him I was leaving that he'd run away the next morning before I left.

Okay, I'd shouted into the woods around our house, *have it your way.*

I shake my head of the memory and am glad to see a clue to the present-day missing child's whereabouts. "Look—I see footprints going back up on the other side." I walk briskly up the slope, ignoring Alice's wheezing behind me. She's a smoker, I guess, although I haven't seen her light up since she's been here. She must try not to smoke around Oren. I give her credit for that, but it's got to be hard going without, especially given all the tension she's under right now. She probably snuck off to have a smoke while I was in Stewart's.

When we get to the top of the hollow we're in the cemetery. I check the Lane family mausoleum with its niche where Caleb liked to hide. I pause only a moment beside the statue of the woman with the bowed head that marks Caleb's grave, but Alice notices the name on the stone anyway. "Crap, is that your brother? He was only—"

"Ten," I say.

"How did he die?" she asks, her voice hushed. As usual when people ask me how Caleb died, I can hear beneath the shock and pity a hint of prurient curiosity. *How could you*

*have been so unlucky and stupid to lose a ten-year-old boy?
Tell me so I can be sure I never make the same mistake.*

"Carbon monoxide poisoning," I reply. "There was a leak while they were all asleep—my mother and father and Caleb. I was out . . ."

"That's awful," she says, and then, maybe realizing she and Oren are staying in the same house where it happened, "What causes . . . ?"

"A faulty furnace," I reply, turning to her with my mouth stretched into a rictus grin. "But don't worry. I had the furnace replaced afterward."

I leave her gaping at Caleb's grave and head across the cemetery toward Main Street, where I dodge a snow plow with obnoxious fake antlers on its hood. I climb the sagging, rotten steps of Sanctuary. When my father's law offices were in this building he used to sit out here on the wide, elegant porch drinking bourbon and smoking cigars with his cronies—Hank Barnes, Frank's father and the town chief of police before him; Maynard Clay, who owned most of the land in the county; Sam Abbott, the county medical examiner; Carl Shapiro, district circuit judge in Albany— and jawing about the sorry state of the world and *kids today* and permissive parents. All of those men are dead now, but I can still catch a whiff of bourbon and cigars and hear the old men's querulous smug voices.

Now the porch is home to a sagging old sofa and bins of toys. The toys are there for kids to play with while their parents are inside filling out forms for food stamps, complaining about their spouses, or just taking a much-needed break. And when I open the front door the intern at the front desk—Arianna or Andrea or something like that—looks up at me and says, "Oh good, Doreen's looking for you. Did you let your phone run down again? There's a kid upstairs with her who says he's staying with you?"

The upward lilt in Alana's—that's it—voice could be millennial speech or incredulity that I've violated Sanctuary's protocol and taken a client home. I don't care. I cross the wide-planked floor in three assertive strides and lean over the counter to speak in Alana's ear. "There's a woman right behind me who is looking for her son. Tell her he's fine and that Mattie's gone to get him. Sit her down and give her some forms to fill out."

"Wh-which forms?" Alana asks, her kohl-rimmed eyes bugging out. Another volunteer, a young college student from Bard, looks up from the food pantry.

"Myers-Briggs personality tests for all I care. Just keep her busy."

Alana smiles. The interns all love drama. She's smart too, despite the multiple piercings, millennial speak, and name that sounds like a yoga pose; she'll figure out a way to detain Alice.

I open the door that says STAFF ONLY. As I'm closing it I hear the front door open and Alice's voice demanding where that woman Mattie Lane's gotten to. I take the stairs two at a time. I should have just enough time to call Frank from the office phone (Alana is right; I did forget to charge my phone last night) and then Doreen will help me keep Alice and Oren here until Frank arrives. It's for the best. Alice is clearly not stable. If Oren *did* stab his father and he's tried as a juvenile, I can testify at his hearing. The juvenile detention centers aren't as bad as they used to be. Doreen and I could make sure he ends up at one of the better ones, and Doreen will help me keep track of Oren in the system. Just because I'm turning him in to the police does *not* mean I am giving up on him. If I'd told Frank my suspicions about what was going on in my own home thirty-four years ago, Caleb might still be alive.

When I reach the top of the stairs I hear Oren's voice. He's happily telling a story about Luke Skywalker's training as a Jedi. When I round the corner I find Oren sitting at Doreen's overflowing desk, a plate of cookies and a glass of milk perched precariously amid casework files and training manuals. When Doreen looks up my heart swells. She's in her late fifties with dark bags under her eyes, gray in her dark curly hair, and a stain on her faded sweater, but to me she looks beautiful. How did I ever think I could do all this without her?

"Here's Mattie now," she says in a bright, calm voice. Only I would hear the strain beneath its surface. "I told you she'd be here soon—sooner if she'd learn to charge her phone."

Oren laughs—*he's fine, he's fine, he's fine*—and holds up his hand. He's grasping a green toy in his fist. "Oh good, now we can go back to your house. We need to rescue Han Solo from the ice caves and I found someone who can help." He waggles the toy in his hand.

As I walk toward him I feel as if I'm floating two feet off the floor. The toy in his hand is so old the green paint has flaked away and one of its long ears has chipped off. But I recognize it. A late-1970s-model Yoda. The same one that Caleb buried in the hollow thirty-four years ago.

CHAPTER ELEVEN

Alice

THE BOHO CHICK with the pretentious name at the front desk
tries to tell me that Mattie's gone to find Oren, but I can tell
she's lying. Her eyes slide over toward a door with a STAFF
ONLY sign on it and she might as well be pointing to where
Mattie is. She pushes a clipboard with some forms on it toward me, but I ignore her and head toward the door.

"Hey!" Boho calls.

A bearded guy wearing a THIS IS WHAT A FEMINIST LOOKS
LIKE T-shirt comes around from the desk and gets in between me and the closed door. "Can I help you?" he asks.
His breath smells like ramen noodles; there's even some
stuck in his beard. He reminds me of Scott, always trying
to help, always putting his nose where he shouldn't. Like
going around to the house to check on me and Oren. That's
what must have happened. Scott went to the house and
found Davis injured and mad as hell that Oren and I had

gotten away. Knowing Scott, he would have tried to help, and knowing Davis—

That's why Davis has Scott's phone. It's not Davis whose body the police found at the house; it's Scott's.

The room spins and I feel faint. Ramen guy reaches out a hand to steady me but I bat it away.

"You can get the hell out of my way," I say, angry at this guy for looking like Scott when Scott is dead, "so I can get my son and get out of here."

The Scott look-alike holds up both hands. "I can hear that you're angry . . ."

"Can you, asshole? I'm so glad your ears are working. What about your feet? Can they walk your skinny ass out of my way?"

Fake Scott blinks at me. He's not used to being talked to like this. He must be new to the job. He probably grew up in a nice house where nobody yelled and went to a nice college where everybody talked about "safe spaces." Like Scott. Well, there are no *safe spaces* in this world. Certainly this place isn't, for all it's called Sanctuary.

I lean closer to Fake Scott and shout right into his ramen-stinking beard. "GET THE FUCK OUT OF MY FACE!!!" He's so startled he jumps, and I use that moment to push past him and open the door, behind which I find a flight of stairs. I can hear Oren's voice coming from above. I take the stairs two at a time, my heart pounding. Oren's voice sounds happy, but I know that he's able to pretend to be happy when he's not. I've taught him that, after all.

I find Oren sitting cross-legged on the floor with Mattie and another woman. He's got a toy Yoda in one hand and a Luke in the other. The Luke toy I recognize, but the Yoda's unfamiliar. He lost his Yoda before Thanksgiving when he left it in his cubby at school and someone took it. He looks really happy, not faking-it happy. And Mattie is glowing. The other woman—a skinny librarian type with dark curly hair—looks a little more reserved. She's the only one who looks up when I come in.

"You must be Alice," she says, getting stiffly to her feet. "We talked on the phone last night."

"Yeah," I say. "Doreen, right? Thanks for your help and all, but we gotta go." I hold out my hand for Oren and he looks up at me.

"Look who I found," he says, holding up the Yoda. "Remember I said he had gone back to Dagobah? He was waiting for me in the swamp all along!"

He's beaming at me, not mad anymore. It's like finding his lost toy—or one like it—has made up for everything that happened.

"That's great, buddy. Let's pack up your things now. We've bothered these nice ladies long enough." I'm trying to calculate how much time we have. The number from the pharmacy would have shown up on Scott's phone just now. And even if it didn't, all Davis would have to do is call back to find out that I'd called from a CVS in Delphi, New York. He could be driving here right now . . . in fact, he sounded like he was already on the road.

I look at Mattie and see her wipe her eyes. What's gotten into her? Doreen is also giving her a strange look, but then she looks back at me. "No bother at all. It was a treat to take a break from all this boring paperwork"—she waves her hand at a very messy desk—"but I did have time to look up a shelter west of here in Oneonta."

"How far is that?" I ask. "Can we take a bus there?"

"It's about an hour more on the same bus you were on. I think there's one leaving at four thirty."

"Sister Martine has already made arrangements to have them moved tomorrow," Mattie says. Her voice is strange—flat somehow—and she keeps her eyes on Oren and that silly green Yoda toy.

"I think we'd better leave before that," I say. "We've taken up enough of your time. Only . . ." I feel sick when I realize what I've got to ask. "I—I don't have the bus fare."

"We can get you a voucher for the trip," Doreen says. "Can't we, Mattie?"

Mattie tears her eyes away from Oren and blinks at Doreen. What's wrong with her? She looks like she's high.

Before she can answer, Oren chimes in. "I don't think the buses are running anymore. On account of the storm."

"What storm?" I say, but when I look out the window I see what he means. Curdled gray clouds are massing over the mountains to the west.

"We *are* supposed to get a storm tonight," Doreen says, putting on a pair of glasses that dangle from a beaded chain around her neck. "A nor'easter. Let me call Trailways."

She takes out a cell phone and taps at the screen. While she's doing that Mattie leans toward Oren. "Tell me again how you found Yoda."

Really? I want to demand. *That's what you want to know while we're running for our lives? When Davis could be driving up the Thruway right now?*

"I told you," Oren says, his voice edging toward impatience. "I used the Force."

I roll my eyes. Ever since we watched those movies that's been Oren's explanation for everything. How did you get away from those bullies? *I used the Force to distract them.* How did Davis's beer bottles all explode in the cooler? *I used the Force to break them so he wouldn't get drunk again.*

Mattie seems to be taking him seriously, though. "And how does that feel?" she asks. "When you use the Force?"

Oh, for God's sake. I go over to the window, where Doreen is listening to her phone. I hear Oren's answer, though. "Sometimes I just feel like a . . . tingle and things . . . happen. Or sometimes I hear a voice."

I feel a tingle myself, but it's only the chill leaking in through the old wooden window casements. It's gotten colder since this morning. The thought of getting on a bus and heading west into those mountains, under that leaden sky, makes me want to crawl into a hole.

"Did you hear a voice telling you where this Yoda was?" Mattie asks.

My ears prick at the question. Is she asking Oren if he hears voices? Does she think he's psycho? I look down at the cluttered desk, at the titles of the books stacked there. *Mental Health First Aid USA. Choosing to Live: How to Defeat Suicide Through Cognitive Therapy.* These women have been trained to detect mental illness. They probably spend all their free time just hoping to make a juicy diagnosis. Does Mattie think that Oren is crazy?

"Yes, I heard—" Oren begins.

"Oren has a very active imagination," I cut in. "He likes to pretend, don't you, baby?"

"I'm not a baby," he says, annoyed. Davis used to use that nickname for him.

"Well, he was right about the buses," Doreen says, putting down her phone. I'm relieved I've distracted Oren from telling Mattie about his imaginary friends. All we need now is for her to get it into her head that he's crazy and try to have him put away. "Trailways has suspended service for the rest of the day and there's a weather alert for Ulster, Greene, and Delaware Counties. High winds and accumulations up to twenty-four inches."

"Wow!" Oren says, his eyes lighting up. "That's a lot of snow to shovel. We'd better get back to your house now, Mattie."

"We have an arrangement with the Best Western in Kingston," Doreen says. "We can put you up there for the night."

"That'll be a lonely, cold place in a storm, Dory," Mattie says. "I can keep them one more night."

Doreen frowns. "Maybe Alice and Oren would like to go

down to the food pantry and pick up some supplies," she says in a pinched voice.

"We could use some more pancake mix," Oren says, getting up. He tucks the Yoda in his coat pocket and shoulders his backpack. "And chocolate chips."

Mattie grins at him. "See if you can get us some canned beans and tomatoes. I'll make you my four-alarm chili for dinner."

Oren smiles back at her and then turns to me. "Make it three-alarm. Alice doesn't like it too spicy." He reaches out to take my hand and something melts in me. He's excited at the idea of hunkering down for a big storm in a big old house full of good food. This is why we were leaving Davis: so we could take pleasure in ordinary things again without the fear of his tantrums hovering over us.

I take Oren's hand and squeeze it. "Sure, buddy, let's stock up. We'll get on the road tomorrow."

What choice do we have? I tell myself that if Davis does make it up here, he only knows we were at the CVS. He doesn't know where Mattie lives. How would he ever find us way out in the woods? I tell myself that and try to believe it.

CHAPTER TWELVE

Mattie

AS SOON AS Alice and Oren go downstairs I turn to Doreen. "I know what you're going to say. We never take a client home. It's not good for us and not good for the client and it never ends well. That's what we teach our volunteers."

"Oh good, I thought you'd forgotten all the training protocols," she says sharply. "I thought I had to dig up the manuals."

"But you and I both know there are exceptions."

"That's not fair," she says, a quaver in her voice. "That was different."

"It was different because I was pretty sure if I didn't take you home that night you would have killed yourself," I say.

Doreen is right. It's not fair to bring up that night sixteen years ago, when I found Doreen drinking herself to death at the Reservoir Inn out by Route 28. She'd just found out that she'd lost custody of her eleven-year-old son, Gavin, to her ex-husband, Roy, even though Doreen had testified in court that Roy had hit her multiple times (and Gavin once, which was all it took for Doreen to finally leave). The fact that Doreen had two DUIs, no job, and a twelve-year-old misdemeanor for marijuana possession worked against her, and Roy—bank manager and upstanding citizen of Rensselaer, remarried with a stay-at-home mom ten years younger than Doreen—had looked like the more stable parent. Doreen had been given every other weekend visitation and alternating Christmases.

"I told Gavin he'd never have to go back there," she'd said—or slurred, rather. "How am I supposed to tell him that he has to because Mommy's a pothead and a drunk?"

I told her she could re-sue for custody, that I would help her. I told her Sanctuary could help her find a job—heck, she could come work for Sanctuary. She'd been volunteering there since she'd landed in the Kingston shelter a year ago. I told her that even if she saw Gavin only every other week she could still be a positive force in his life.

She listened to everything I had to say and thanked me. She went on to thank me for all I'd done for her over the last year and asked me to thank Frank Barnes, who had intervened six months before when Roy showed up to take Gavin back and had testified as a character witness at the custody hearing. She asked me to thank Kate Rubin, who had represented her at the hearing pro bono. She asked me to thank all the volunteers at Sanctuary.

"Shit, Doreen," I said. "You're either making your Academy Award acceptance speech or you're planning to off yourself. Which is it?"

Doreen is fond of saying in our suicide awareness training sessions that this is *not* the way you're supposed to ask someone if they're planning to kill themselves. You're supposed to reflect back the "invitations" they have provided (*I hear that you're feeling hopeless and you've expressed a lot of negative feelings about yourself . . .*) and then ask them directly, "Are you thinking about suicide?" You're not supposed to say, "You're not thinking about doing anything stupid, are you?" Or make cracks about the Academy Awards. But what I said that night worked. First she nearly fell off her barstool laughing (a testament less to my wit than to how many Jack Daniel's shots she'd knocked back), and then she started crying, and then she admitted she had a stash of Vicodin from her last root canal back in her rented room and was thinking of washing it down with some vodka.

Protocol would have suggested I keep her talking and then, if I still thought she was a suicide risk, call one of the suicide intervention services available in the county. Instead I drove her home to my place and we sat up the rest of the night eating popcorn and talking. I told her about the year I spent in JD when I was fourteen and I told her about Caleb. I told her the truth about what happened the night my family died. She was the first—and last—person I ever told the whole story. Sometime around dawn, when we were both falling asleep on the big couch in the parlor, I asked her if she was still thinking of killing herself, and she said, "No, I think you're a bigger suicide risk than I am. I'll stick around as long as you need me." We made a pact then that if either of us was ever thinking about killing herself she'd tell the other first.

"Are you telling me," I ask her now, "that it was a mistake to take you home that night?"

"No," she admits. "You saved my life. But I worry about this woman and boy—"

"There's nothing wrong with the boy," I snap.

"Noooo—" She draws out the word. "He's a sweetheart. Smart as a whip. He reminds me of Gavin . . ."

Her voice trails off and I see that there are tears in her eyes. *Of course,* I think, Oren's brought it all back up for her. The way her son changed in the following years. The problems in school, the drugs, rehab, juvenile detention, and then rehab again. She hasn't heard from him in over a year.

"You wouldn't want Alice to lose him," I say. "You wouldn't want Oren to end up in JD."

It's not fair to use the threat of JD, a threat my parents held over my—and later Caleb's—head all my life. It's not fair but I can see right away that it works. She shakes her head. "No, no, of course not. But let me call Frank. You'll all be in danger if the father comes looking for them."

"He won't," I say quickly, relieved that Doreen hasn't heard about the dead man in New Jersey—or if she has she hasn't connected him to Alice and Oren. "He doesn't know where they are."

Doreen looks skeptical. "You know how many times we've had a woman call her ex and tell them exactly where they are."

"She doesn't have a cell phone," I say. "And it's only for one night. Where else are they going to go?" I look out the window and see that it has begun to snow. Heavy feathery flakes fill the air with silver light. When I look back at Doreen I see that silver light showing up every line and shadow on her face. I wonder when she last slept. "You should take the night off," I add. "Let Alana and the Bard student man the phones."

"I could come back with you," Doreen offers.

I don't want her there, I realize. I want Oren to myself. I want him to tell me about that voice he heard, the one that told him where to find Yoda.

"I think you should go home and get some sleep," I say. "We'll talk in the morning. Okay?"

Doreen nods, her eyes on the falling snow. "Sure," she says, "just . . ."

"I know," I say, already turning away, anxious to beat the storm back to the house. "I'll be careful."

I pick up my poncho from the floor. When I turn back Doreen is still standing at the window, a dark silhouette against the swirling snow, looking as insubstantial and spectral as the ghost I'm seeking.

CHAPTER THIRTEEN

Alice

ALL THE WAY back, through the heavy snow, Mattie listens uncomplaining to the long complicated game Oren has dreamed up. It's something to do with Yoda and Luke having to save Han Solo from the ice caves before Darth Vader gets him. From what I remember of the movie this isn't exactly what happens, but it's not unusual for Oren to make up his own story. Scott said that Oren was "working through" his issues by playacting these stories, that Darth Vader stood in for Davis. Sometimes I'm Princess Leia, but today he's decided that Mattie is the older Princess Leia from the new *Star Wars* movie and I'm Rey, the kick-ass heroine. That's okay with me. There have been whole afternoons when I had to pretend to be Chewbacca.

The truth is I'm grateful for Oren's distraction. There's no opportunity for me to talk to Mattie, to come clean about Davis. She'd definitely call the police, which is what we should do. Since Davis isn't dead there's less of a chance that Oren will end up in juvie for just a stab wound. It's Davis who will go to jail for killing Scott.

And Oren? Where will Oren go?

"Alice? Earth to Alice. I'm talking to you!"

I turn back to look at Oren. He's waggling the green Yoda at me.

"What?" I ask.

"Weren't you listening to me?" Annoyance is seeping back into his voice. I see Mattie flick her eyes toward me, suspicion and distrust etched on her face. She hasn't trusted me since I pulled Oren's arm back at the convent.

"I *was* listening, buddy," I say, making sure my voice is extra loving and patient. "Luke and Yoda have to save Han Solo from the ice caves while Princess Leia and Rey are marshalling the resistance."

"But didn't you hear what I said about Darth Vader?" He kicks the back of my seat for emphasis.

I swallow a curse. "What about Darth Vader? I thought the Emperor killed him."

"No! He was just pretending to be dead. He's alive and he's coming for Luke and Leia. He's already killed Lando."

Something icy crawls down my spine. *It's just a story*, I tell myself. Oren has no way of knowing about my phone call with Davis. "It's all right," I say automatically. "Darth Vader doesn't know where Luke and Leia and Rey are and their location is . . . cloaked. Look"—I point out the window—

"you think that's snow? It's really a cloaking device hiding Luke and Leia and Rey's location."

I'm proud of myself for coming up with this colorful solution, but Mattie is staring at me and Oren looks dubious. He peers out the window as if trying to make out enemy Death Stars through the swirling snow. Mattie is watching him in the rearview mirror. We're both, I realize, waiting for his verdict.

"I don't know if it will cloak us," he says finally, "but I bet it will slow him down."

Mattie grins, but I feel the ice spread from my spine into my gut. "No one at Sanctuary would tell anyone where we are," I say to Mattie, "would they?"

"Of course not," Mattie says with a prissy little cluck of her tongue. "That's the first thing we teach our volunteers. Everything about the client is confidential. Don't worry. We're safe as houses."

"Safe as houses," Oren repeats to himself, obviously pleased with the phrase. "Safe as houses." As he says it a second time, Mattie's house looms out of the snow as if he has made it appear by magic. The way he made those tickets to Delphi appear. The way he made those footsteps appear in the maze. *The kid's creepy,* Davis said to me once. It had shocked me that a father would talk about his son like that, but I've caught myself thinking the same thing sometimes.

When I look out the rear window the road has vanished, as if the snow has swallowed up the rest of the world and all that's left is this old house. I briefly wish that Oren and I had stayed at the convent or that Best Western. But it's too late now.

The moment Mattie stops the car Oren jumps out. He runs toward the house, kicking at the new-fallen snow, which is already filling in the path he shoveled earlier. *How much more snow is going to fall? I wonder. How will we ever get out of here?*

"Is there anything you want to tell me, Alice?" Mattie asks.

"What do you mean?" I snap back too quickly. She sounded so much like Davis for a moment. She's staring at me with those unnerving lavender eyes as if she could see right through me.

"It's just you seem nervous."

"I'm homeless and on the run with a ten-year-old boy. Who wouldn't be nervous?"

"But the man you were running from is dead," she says.

I stare at her. Does *she* know that Davis isn't dead? Did that policeman tell her something? Did he tell her something about *me*? But if she knew the truth about either me or Davis she would have turned me in already. Oren and I would be sitting at the police station back in town.

"You know that's not the only man I'm running from," I answer finally. "Or have you already told the police that we're here? You seemed pretty chummy with that cop."

She laughs, which seems to surprise her as much as me. "Trust me," she says, "he's no chum of mine." And then, putting her hand on my shoulder, "I didn't tell him you were here, Alice. I know what it's like to lose a child. I wouldn't do that to you."

She holds my gaze for a long moment and I start to relax. Then something hits the window hard behind me. I jump and swivel around as Mattie powers down the window to reveal Oren, his face red from the cold, his eyes strangely excited. "He's gone!" he shouts, his voice high and shrill in my ear.

"Who?" I cry, grabbing his arm. "Did you see someone? Who was it?"

He winces at my touch—I've grabbed the same arm I dislocated before—and looks past me toward Mattie. "Han Solo. He's gone! Someone's taken him."

CHAPTER FOURTEEN

Mattie

OREN INSISTS ON dragging me down the snow-filled path to the place where Han Solo *isn't*. There's the little scooped-out niche where he placed the action figure and it is, indeed, empty. I remember thinking that I should take the toy before we left because I wasn't planning on bringing Oren and Alice back here. But did I? I surreptitiously check my pockets but find only cough-drop wrappers and balled-up tissues. I search my memory as well but find only a similar assortment of detritus. "Maybe he fell down," I suggest.

Oren drops to his knees and sweeps the loose snow. "I already looked," he says. "Somebody took him." He looks up at me accusingly.

"Not me, buddy," I say, hoping that it's not a lie.

"Then it was somebody *else*," Oren says, his voice quirking up at the end.

"Somebody else who did what?" Alice asks. She's taken

her time following us from the car—maybe to collect her thoughts. She'd looked rattled by my question and then she'd jumped like a nervous cat when Oren smacked the window. She'd jumped the way a woman with a history of being hit jumps.

"Somebody took Han Solo!" Oren cries. "Was it you, Alice?"

"The action figure Oren left here is gone," I explain.

Alice sighs. "I've told you not to leave your toys outside." And then to me, "He's always leaving them places around the neighborhood."

"That's how you play the game, dummy!" Oren punctuates the sentence by kicking Alice's leg.

"What have I said about calling people dummy?" Alice snaps back. I can see how this is going to escalate.

"Hey," I say. "We're all going to be frozen like Han Solo in the ice caves if we stand around here much longer. Why don't we look for him in the house?"

"You think he's inside?" Oren asks, eyeing me slyly, as if he suspects that I've hidden him somewhere. *And who knows?* I think a little hysterically. *Maybe I have and I've just forgotten because I have early-onset Alzheimer's like my mother.*

"Well," I say, "maybe the Rebel Alliance rescued him and he's in hiding."

"Yeah," Oren says, his face lighting up. He takes Yoda out of his pocket. "Let's go find him, Yoda, before Darth Vader does." He runs down the path and up the porch steps, pounding so hard I fear he's going to crash through the rotting floorboards. How many years has it been since anyone entered this house with that kind of eagerness? When was the last time I felt this lift in my heart?

I turn to Alice to see if she is sharing my delight in Oren's enthusiasm, but she looks pale and drawn. "*Did* you take his toy and hide it?" she asks with an accusatory tone that makes me feel like I'm twelve again and have been caught dressing up the town statue of George Washington (Frank's plans hadn't taken into account that people would recognize the clothes we used).

"No," I say, "but don't worry. I think I know where there's a spare Han Solo."

Alice doesn't look relieved. In fact, she looks sick. "Then who the fuck took it?"

ALICE STOMPS OFF as soon as we're inside. I can hear her prowling the perimeter of the ground floor like an angry house cat. I leave her to it and go look for Oren, finding him in the kitchen petting Dulcie and talking softly in her ear. Or rather, Yoda is talking in her ear.

"Hey, buddy," I say, taking the milk out of the bag, "before we start your game how 'bout helping me restock our provisions and getting dinner on."

Oren holds Yoda to his ear and cocks his head as if listening to the wise green gnome. The gesture is so like Caleb that I pause by the open refrigerator door, the cold lapping at my legs, and hear Caleb's voice: *Better batten down the hatches, Leia, the enemy forces are on their way.* All those mock battles Caleb waged . . . why didn't I stop to wonder what he was really trying to tell me?

"What does Yoda have to say?" I ask.

"He says we're safe for now and we need to keep up our strength. Rey is securing the perimeter so it's a good time to eat."

"Rey? Oh . . ." He means Alice. It must be a character from the new movies, which I haven't had the heart to see. "Yes, I'll get the chili started. I like mine with home fries. You could start peeling the potatoes . . . only . . ." I stop, remembering his injured arm.

"I can do it," he says, hopping to his feet. "My mom taught me."

"That's not what I was worried about," I say, getting an ice pack out of the freezer. "I'm thinking about your arm. How's it feel?"

"Fine," he declares, holding it up over his head. "Good as new. Besides, it's my left arm. I peel with my right."

"Okay," I say warily. Abused children learn to deny their pain. I study Oren's face for any sign of discomfort but he looks . . . *happy*. I put the ice pack on his shoulder. "If it starts to hurt, you stop, okay?"

I help him get positioned with the ice pack draped over his left shoulder, a paper bag on the floor, and a colander on the table for the peeled potatoes. I'd rather he took it easy, but I can see how eager he is to help. "I bet you're a big help to your mom."

"I guess." He shrugs modestly. "When she was feeling poorly I tried to help out."

"Does she feel poorly often?" I ask, sitting beside him and picking up a potato to peel.

Oren looks at my hands and makes hesitant swipes, dislodging snail-shell curls the size of my fingernail. I suspect he's never peeled a potato in his life.

"Yeah, she used to feel bad a lot of the time, especially after she and Dad went out. She'd say she had a headache and needed the blinds down and sometimes she'd throw up."

Drinking? I wonder. *Or drugs?* "Oh my," I say. "That doesn't sound fun. Did she go see a doctor?"

"She went to a hospital," he says, flailing at the potato with more determination.

So rehab.

"Then she came back . . . hey, are you going to use those beans?" He points his peeler to the two cans of pinto beans on the counter. I've seen this kind of diversion tactic before. The topic of his mother is off the table.

"I was going to, unless you don't like beans," I say, letting it go.

"Oh, I like them, I just wanted to use the cans after. We can make a phone. That way we can talk to each other if we get separated."

"Good idea, buddy." I get up and dump the two cans of beans in a big pot. I add canned tomatoes and a pound of frozen chopped meat, thinking through what Oren's told me. If Alice was away in rehab he must be afraid of her leaving him again. "Don't worry," I say as I rinse the two cans. "We won't get separated. No one's going anywhere in this storm."

Oren looks out the window above the kitchen table. The snow is coming down fast and hard now, the wind blowing gusts that completely obliterate the world outside. Drifts are mounding up along the bottom sills and condensation is creeping across the panes. It feels as if we are slowly being sealed off from the outside world. "I guess no one could get here either," Oren says.

"Not unless they had four-wheel drive and a snow plow."

"My dad has a pickup truck."

So it's his father he's worried about, which means he doesn't know his father is dead. Would it be better if he did? Before I can decide, Alice bursts into the kitchen. "Do you know that half the windows on the first floor don't lock?"

"Is that so?" I ask in my calm counselor's voice. Her pupils are dilated and she's white as a ghost. Is she high? Did she disappear in town to score a fix? "I bet more than half of them don't even open. It's an old house, Alice. Wood swells. Metal rusts. Things break." *Shit happens,* I'm tempted to add. "The last thing I'm worried about is locking the windows. We're in the country. Folks don't even lock their doors."

"Well, *folks* are stupid," she retorts.

"Mattie says no one can get here through the storm," Oren tells her. "Not unless they have four-wheel drive and a plow."

"So I suppose no serial killers or rapists have those?" she snaps back.

I raise my brows and cut my eyes over to Oren. The

kitchen, which had felt warm and cozy a moment ago, suddenly feels cramped and airless. I listen to the furnace roaring below in the basement, the ticking of the water flowing through the old pipes, and the creak of the old house's joints in the gusting wind. "No one's coming up that road in this," I say with more certainty than I feel. The fact is I'm beginning to worry that no one *could* make it up the hill. What if we need help? What if Alice OD's? "What we *do* need to worry about, though, is losing power. I'm going to go check on flashlights and candles and wood for the stove. Why don't you sit down, Alice, and help Oren peel potatoes. We'd better get dinner on while we've still got power."

I hand Alice my peeler and she looks at me like she'd like to use it to gouge out my eye. Maybe I should have thought of a different chore for her. But then she sits down and begins swiping at a potato with shaking hands. She's even worse at it than Oren. I leave them, hoping Alice doesn't cut herself, and remind myself to check for first-aid supplies.

I find candles and flashlights in the dining room sideboard along with the first-aid kit. I check the kit for Narcan. I picked up the nasal spray when I did a drug awareness course in Kingston last fall. *What have I gotten myself into?* I sit down on the one chair without books on it. Seeing Oren with that stupid Yoda really rattled me. I was sure it was the same one Caleb buried thirty-four years ago. It had seemed like a sign—

Christ, I sound like one of the new age interns! A sign of what? That Oren is somehow in communication with Caleb?

Have I brought Oren back here so he can *contact* Caleb? And what purpose would that serve? What would I say to Caleb after all these years?

And what would he say to me?

Of all the stupid reasons for bringing this woman and boy into my home—misguided charity, anger at Frank, making amends, liberal guilt, my problems with authority—this supernatural hoo-ha is the craziest. And the most pathetic.

It's time you began thinking clearly and taking responsibility for your actions.

My father's voice this time, so clear that I look toward his study door, expecting to find it open and him standing in the doorway. But of course the door is locked. As I told Alice, wood swells, metal rusts, things break. I've gleefully let this house rot around me, but I've carefully oiled and preserved the lock on my father's study door. I keep it locked from the outside. *To keep people out,* I tell myself, but sometimes I wonder if it's to keep something locked in.

I listen to the house. The furnace roars, the pipes tick, the joints groan . . . and two voices murmur in the kitchen. I get up, fish the key out of its crystal bowl, and open the study door. I shut it behind me and use the key to lock the door from the inside, then cross to my father's desk and sit down in his chair. In front of me is the seal of New York pen set with its figures of Justice and Liberty. I reach into one of Justice's scales and retrieve a small key that I use to open the bottom drawer. Inside, resting on a stack of file folders stamped with the same figures of Justice and Liberty that stand on my father's desk, is my father's Winchester revolver, which he inherited from his father.

I hesitate. Doreen would be appalled to know I even *have* a gun in the house, let alone that I'm thinking of taking it out of the only locked room. With a child spending the night. But then, if I need it . . .

I pick up the gun, startling at the coldness of it, and check that the safety's on and put it in my cardigan pocket. I close the drawer and lock it.

Before I stand I notice the pattern in the dust on the top of the desk. This morning the mouse tracks looked like a random spattering of stars, but now they've become a constellation. A constellation I recognize.

CHAPTER FIFTEEN

Alice

OREN IS WORKING away at the potatoes like he's spent his whole childhood doing hard labor. "Hey," I say, "this is like that old movie we watched where those guys in the army had to peel sacks of potatoes when they did something wrong."

"KP duty," Oren says without looking up. "But Mattie isn't punishing me; I'm just pitching in, like you said about shoveling the path this morning."

"Sure," I say, annoyed that he's come to her defense. Why does he like her so much? "I was just worried about your arm. Does it feel okay? I'm sorry about before . . . I was just trying to keep you from running up the drive where that cop could see you."

"It's okay," he says, shrugging. "It feels fine now. Look, Mattie gave me an ice pack."

"And you're okay about staying here tonight?" I ask, as if we had any choice.

"Yeah, I like it here. It feels like a family lives here."

Like ours didn't. Like this crazy-ass spinster living in a falling-down old house is more like a family than Davis and me. "Yeah, *the Addams family*," I say. I start to hum the theme song to the show, which we watched on Nick at Nite, but Oren glares at me.

"Don't do that. Mattie might hear you and she'll think we're making fun of her house."

I roll my eyes. "Come on. How much can she really care about this house when she keeps it like this? The place is a mess." I lean forward and lower my voice to a conspiratorial whisper. "I found mouse poop."

Oren wrinkles his nose.

"Yeah," I go on, "and stacks of newspapers from, like, the eighties. You know what? I think Mattie might be a hoarder." This was another show we sometimes watched, but only because Davis liked it. He liked to make fun of the people on the show because he thought they were such sad sacks compared to him.

Oren shakes his head. "She collects all this stuff to give to people," he says.

So that's why he thinks Mattie is so great. Because she's a do-gooder. "Yeah? Then why does she keep her dead brother's room just the way he left it, huh?"

Oren looks up. I've finally gotten his attention, but maybe this wasn't the best way to get it. I was telling the truth when I told Mattie that Oren has a really active imagination. After watching that scary movie about the crazy dad in the big hotel, Oren was spooked about bathtubs because of one of the scenes. He refused to take a bath for a month, until he smelled so bad Davis started calling him Stinky. I'd convinced him to get in the tub only by agreeing to sit in the bathroom with him, which Davis teased him about mercilessly.

And then there was the "poltergeist" that started taking things, after we watched *that* movie. First it was little stuff like some change Davis left on the counter or Davis's socks or the can opener or the TV remote. *They're here!* Oren would say in a creepy, singsongy voice whenever something went missing. At first it made Davis laugh, but then bigger stuff went missing, like bills from Davis's wallet and a bottle of Jim Beam. That's when Davis started blaming Oren and threatening to give him a *whupping* if he didn't put the stuff back.

Oren kept up the story even after Davis took a belt to him. *It's the poltergeist, Dad!* he cried over and over.

Then why does it only take my shit? Davis demanded with every swing of his belt.

The next day the belt was gone. Davis tore the house apart looking for it. I locked Oren and myself in the bathroom. When I asked Oren if he knew where the belt was he looked at me like Han Solo looks at Lando when Lando turns him over to Jabba the Hutt. *I told you, it's the poltergeist. He takes stuff from people he's mad at.*

I told Oren there was never going to be any peace until he just admitted to Davis that he'd taken the stuff.

That would make the poltergeist really mad, Oren said, *unless . . .*

Unless what, buddy?

Unless it knows we're doing it for a good reason, like it's part of a plan.

What kind of a plan? I'd asked, feeling the cold from the bathroom tiles travel up my spine.

A plan to get out of here. To go away. The poltergeist told me that Davis is just going to keep hitting us. It's just going to get worse.

We could tell a social worker, I'd said. *Scott could help.*

Oren had considered it. He liked Scott. *Would they let me stay with you?* he asked. When I didn't answer right away he said, *Because I really, really want to stay with you, Alice.*

The ice creeping through my veins melted then. *And I really want to stay with you, buddy,* I said, and I meant it. *We'll leave. I'll start saving money tomorrow. We'll take a bus upstate somewhere. There are shelters that take in women and kids up there. We'll figure it out.*

You promise?

I looked down at him, a little boy crouched on the bathroom floor clutching a Luke Skywalker in one hand and a Chewbacca in the other, and realized he was the first person who'd ever really needed me. *Yeah,* I said, *I promise.*

The next day all the lost stuff came back. Loose change, dirty socks, beer bottles, and Davis's belt, all in a big pile on the living room floor. Not the missing cash, though. I found

that in my purse: a roll of bills that added up to $316. I hid
the money in a tampon box under the sink and got a Trailways bus schedule that day. I started saving my tips from
the diner instead of using them to buy books and toys for
Oren. I looked up shelters and domestic abuse services. Ulster County seemed to have the most services and it felt . . .
familiar. My adoptive parents had lived up there. I remembered them talking about the orphanage where they got me
like it was someplace nearby. And after they died when I was
seven, I was placed in a group home not far from where they
had lived. Never mind that I didn't like it then; now it would
be a good place for me and Oren. I kept my promise and the
poltergeist stayed away.

Oren already seems to know about the dead kid. "She
keeps it that way because she wants him to stay," he says.

"Wants *who* to stay?" I ask, the potato peeler slipping in
my hand and nicking my thumb.

"Caleb."

"Did Mattie tell you that?" I ask, pressing a napkin to my
thumb to stem the blood flow.

"No," Oren says. "Caleb did."

My whole body twitches. I grab him by both arms and he
yelps. The ice pack balanced on his shoulder slides to the
floor with a wet thump. "Don't you start this again," I say,
keeping my voice low so Mattie won't hear us.

"Ow!" he cries, but low, like he doesn't want Mattie to
hear either. "You're hurting my arm."

"Your arm was good enough for peeling potatoes for Mattie," I spit back. "And we had a deal. You promised that if we left the poltergeist would go away."

"Caleb's not a poltergeist," he says in that prissy tone he gets when he thinks I'm not smart enough to understand something. "He's a ghost. That's different. He wants to tell Mattie something. That's why Mattie brought us back instead of taking us to the police. She thinks that Caleb will be able to tell her through me."

I let him go and lean back, staring at him. "Did she tell you that?"

Oren stares at me like I've lost it. "No," he snaps. "I told you—"

"Yeah, yeah, *Caleb* told you." I picture Mattie sitting on the floor with Oren at Sanctuary, asking him if he heard voices. I thought she had gotten it into her head that Oren was psycho, but now it occurs to me that she wanted to know because she thinks Oren is some kind of medium who's going to communicate with her dead brother.

"Hey, buddy." I make my voice gentle. "You know it's all a game, right? You don't really hear that boy's voice, do you?"

He shakes his head. "I don't hear Caleb's voice."

I let out my breath. Oren's not crazy. *He's a* pleaser, Scott told me once. *He's learned to anticipate the needs of adults around him and come up with ways to meet or deflect them.* He's picked up on Mattie's need to communicate with her dead brother and he's trying to help her because he's grateful to her for taking us in. Well, I'm not going to let her take advantage of him.

"Of course you don't, buddy." I hold out my arms and he collapses into them. I feel a swell of protectiveness rise up in me, burning off the chill of the house. We'll be okay. One more night in this batty old house and we'll hit the road. Just Oren and me. We don't need anyone else.

He murmurs something against my shoulder that I can't make out. "What's that, buddy?" I ask, holding him at arm's length.

"I said I don't need to hear Caleb's voice. He sends me messages."

The chill creeps back up my spine. "What kind of messages?" I ask.

"Like finding Yoda," he says, "and the marks on the windows." He points behind me and I turn around. The bottom half of the window is fogged over and there are, indeed, dots drawn in the mist. Who knows how long they've been there. Mattie certainly hasn't cleaned these windows in years.

"Those look pretty random," I say, peering closer at the window.

"They're not. The same pattern is on all the windows." He's pointing to the window over the sink. I get up to look at it more closely. Above the mist I can just make out an old red barn and below, yes, the pattern does look the same. "It means something to Caleb. I haven't figured it out yet. I think it might be . . ."

I don't hear the rest of Oren's sentence. There's something moving in the snow—a blurry shape. At first I think it's a dog or a deer, but then the snow lets up for a moment and I make out the figure of a man. Then it disappears in another gust of snow. Or it's gone inside the barn.

"I've got to get something from the barn," I tell Oren hurriedly. "You stay here."

I'm up before Oren can stop me. Before I leave the kitchen I slip a carving knife into my coat pocket. No one is taking Oren away from me.

CHAPTER SIXTEEN

Mattie

IT WAS THE first constellation my father taught me. Other kids learned the Big Dipper or Orion; I learned to find Virgo, the Maiden, who looked like a limp rag doll, with a kite-shaped face, sprawled out across the sky.

That's the sign we both were born under, my father told me. *People call her Virgo now, but the ancients called her Justice.*

I lean forward to reach the constellation globe on the corner of the desk and spin it, my fingers tracing the raised glass bumps that mark the stars. The creak of the chair releases the odor of leather and pipe tobacco, and I can feel the itchy tweed of my father's jacket sleeve brushing against my bare arm as he guides my hand along the pattern of stars. *Follow the arc in Arcturus and speed on to Spica,* he'd say. I feel the same little thrill the words gave me then, as if he were launching me into space, just as the maiden Justice flew up to the sky because she grew disgusted with the injustice she saw on Earth. *She remains in the sky,* my father would say, *looking down and judging all that we do. Remember that, mouse, we're all responsible for our actions. There's no running away from justice.* Then he would touch the scales on the figure of Justice, which would chime together like a clock tolling the hour.

When I find her constellation on the globe, I trace the pattern from her feet to her head and along her outstretched arms to the ear of grain she grasps in her left hand—the *spica* that gives the brightest star its name. Then I look down at the pattern in the dust. It is the same configuration. But how can that be? Could the globe, which used to be lit from inside by a bulb that burned out years ago, have cast the pattern onto the desk somehow? Or did I unconsciously draw the pattern when I came in last night? Just because I don't remember doing it doesn't mean I didn't. If I could forget to let Dulcie back in the house I could forget drawing a pattern in the dust. My mother used to forget she'd bought milk and go to the store for another quart. When I came home from graduate school the summer Caleb was ten there'd been four quarts in the refrigerator, all souring. Is that what's happening to me? My mother was only in her late fifties when it began. I'm fifty-nine.

And is fearing that any worse than believing the alternative: that Caleb drew the pattern, that he did it as a message to me?

He knew what the constellation meant as well as I did. He was raised by the same father, who grew even more obsessed with the idea of justice as he aged. Always a severe judge, he'd gotten stricter as he perceived the world growing more chaotic around him. *Kids doing drugs, parents not caring—someone has to show these kids that actions have consequences.* The sentences he passed became harsher. Kids brought in for shoplifting, fighting in school, or smoking a joint were sent to JD. When I was fourteen and got caught making out with Frank Barnes in the back of his father's car, I got sent too. *What would it look like if I didn't treat my own daughter the way I treated everyone else?* he'd asked, refusing to recuse himself from the case. Frank, sixteen, was also accused of stealing his father's car and was sent to a boot camp.

When Caleb started acting up the summer he was ten I heard my father telling him the story of the constellation too and reminding him—as he'd often reminded me—that we can never escape justice. At night I saw Caleb lying in his bed staring up at the constellation on his ceiling. But why would he call for justice now? And more important: What kind of justice can I give him after all these years?

I get up from the desk abruptly. The gun clanks heavily against my leg, the metal cold through my thin cardigan.

The only real justice, I once heard my mother say, *is seeing the ones responsible dead in the ground.* It was the summer before they all died. She and my father had been arguing—they were always fighting that summer. She'd already started losing her mind and it made her snappish and paranoid, especially with my father.

That's not justice, Celeste, my father had replied with weary patience, *that's vengeance.*

Is that what Caleb would want? Vengeance?

I take the gun out of my cardigan pocket, check again that the safety's on, and put it in the snugger pocket of my pants, where I can feel it pressing cold against my hipbone. I can't keep it on me, but I can keep it somewhere closer than this locked room.

I look down at the pattern in the dust once more. Now that I've identified the constellation it's impossible not to see it, but as Doreen is wont to say, *to a hammer everything looks like a nail.* Maybe to a judge's daughter everything looks like a question of justice.

Or to my mother's daughter, a question of vengeance.

I LISTEN FOR Oren and Alice as I go up the stairs. They're still in the kitchen, talking softly, peeling potatoes. I need to put the gun away before I join them. I have the feeling that Oren's sure to notice that I have it on me if I go in there with it, and I don't like the idea of the gun being anywhere near him.

When I enter my room I pause on the threshold to see if I can feel that Alice has been in there—and then dismiss that idea as ridiculous. As ridiculous as thinking Oren would know I have the gun on me. As ridiculous as the idea that Caleb is leaving me messages written in the dust. You can't *feel* that a person's been in a room. When I look at my night table, though, I'm pretty sure that the framed photograph of

Caleb has been moved. I sit down on the edge of my bed and look into his face, the face of a ten-year-old boy who would never see eleven. He hated that school picture. His hair is recently cut and he's wearing a collared shirt, striped tie, and a jacket that's too big for him, all purchased at the Delphi Department Store by my mother, who insisted he dress up for picture day even though by the eighties no one did that anymore. He would have felt stupid and embarrassed in clothes that clearly marked him as the late-in-life child of too-old parents. *A change-of-life baby,* I once heard one of the women in town call him. *A mistake,* she might as well have said.

Still, Caleb is smiling. An infectious grin that defies the stupid clothes and the missing front tooth (from a fall two weeks before) and the whispers that he must have heard all his life. This is not the face of a boy who would want vengeance for his death.

But then, maybe by the time he died, two months after this picture was taken, he wasn't the same boy.

I put the picture down and a pill bottle falls to the floor with a rattle. *Crap. Of course.* I pick it up and look at the label. Valium, prescribed for back spasms. I take it only when the pain is so bad it keeps me up, and I always count them so I don't forget and take too many. And so I know how many I've got in case . . .

In case of what? Doreen would ask. We both know that suicide risks (*People with suicidal thoughts,* Doreen would correct me, *we don't name the person for their disease*) count their pills. They like to know they've got an exit plan.

Last night I counted fourteen. There are thirteen now.

Alice.

I check the other pills on the night table and the ones in the drawer. There are two OxyContin missing from the bottle in the drawer. So I was right to suspect drug use. The only thing that surprises me is the modesty of her drug raid; most addicts wouldn't have been able to resist pocketing the whole supply.

I sigh. This is the woman I was going to let Oren go off with. I should call Frank right now . . . only my cell phone is in my coat pocket downstairs, dead. I pull out the charger from the wall and stuff it in my cardigan pocket—and feel the gun in my jeans pocket. Right. That's why I'm here. I take out the gun and place it in the night table drawer . . . right where Alice found the pills and is likely to come back looking for more. Nope. That's not the right place for it. But what is? I look around my room—at the dusty piles of books on top of the dressers, at the threadbare flannel nightgown hanging from the bedpost, at the half-rumpled bed—and see it as Alice must have: the abode of an aging spinster. So where would an aging spinster hide a gun?

In her bed, of course, where no one but her goes. I slide the revolver between mattress and box spring (checking one more time that the safety is on) and smooth down the blankets and quilt over the edge of the bed. If someone comes in the night I'll be able to reach it quickly. It makes sense to have it up here, I tell myself. Why didn't I think of that before?

You know why. My mother's voice.

Ignoring it, I get up and leave my room, closing the door behind me. I wish I had a key to lock it, but my father refused to put locks on any doors but his study, and since the house became mine I have lived here alone and so never saw a need.

I stop in Caleb's room before going downstairs. I don't pause. I don't stand on the threshold, gazing at my dead brother's room, which is what Alice probably thinks I do. I don't keep his room the way it was as some kind of memorial for me to sit and wallow in. I keep it this way because I can't bear to throw out his things. On the morning I wake up and can, I will.

What I can do now is give away his collection of *Star Wars* action figures. Oren has given me that much. I take down the metal *Star Wars* lunch box from the bookshelf and sit on the bed. I pass my hand over its rusty surface, but only because it's dusty, not because I'm remembering taking Caleb to the Target in Kingston and buying it for him. My mother had bought him a horrid plaid satchel that looked like something a thirty-five-year-old accountant would use.

Thanks, Matt, he'd said. *I've already ditched two of those plaid ones.*

I lift my eyes from the lunch box to wipe them and catch a glimpse of scattered prints in the mist on the window. It looks creepily as if someone had pressed his or her hands to the window to get out. I get up, still holding the lunch box, and go to take a closer look.

It's the same pattern of spots that's drawn on the dust on my father's desk. Virgo, the Maiden—

Justice.

A gust of snow hits the pane with the dry rattle of ice pellets. I look up past the misted-over part toward the back-yard, which has all been swallowed by the snow. The only landmark I can make out is the barn, the door to which is open.

Crap. Oren must have left it that way when he got the sled out. I should go close it before the snow drifts inside.

And that's when I see a figure making its way across the snow toward the barn. A slim figure in a peacoat. What the hell is Alice doing out there?

I turn to go and see I've still got the lunch box in my hands. I might as well take out the action figures for Oren. I put the box down on the bed and open it.

The box is empty. All of Caleb's toys—Luke and Leia, Chewbacca and Han Solo, Darth Vader, R2-D2, C-3PO, and some assorted Wookiees—they're all gone.

CHAPTER SEVENTEEN

Alice

THE MINUTE I step outside I realize this is probably not such a good idea. It's snowing really hard, and not the soft pretty flakes like before; this is like having buckets of ice pellets thrown in your face. I duck my head down to keep the ice out of my eyes, and when I do look up I see I'm heading right past the barn into the woods.

I remember one of the foster parents I lived with telling us kids a story about a boy who went out to check on the cows during a blizzard and got lost between the house and the barn. His parents found him frozen to death in a drift not two feet from his own back door. The story was supposed to be about how hard it was in the olden days and how good we had it now. Like we were lucky to have a washing machine to use when it was our turn to do the enormous bags of dirty laundry, which included our foster father's gross stained boxers. Or we should be thankful we didn't have to haul coal from the cellar to heat the stove. As if Lisa (that was that foster mother's name, I remember now) had grown up as a pioneer, when really she came from suburban Long Island and had bought this old broken-down farm because she had some hippie idea of living in a commune. Only she and her alcoholic deadbeat husband (*Travis,* I recall, *Travis and Lisa*) couldn't make a go of it, so they took in foster kids for the state subsidy and cheap labor.

The story about the frozen boy was also supposed to keep us from running away. It gave the younger kids nightmares. At night when the branches knocked on the windows the little kids said it was the frozen boy trying to get in.

And now that could be me. When I turn around to go back to the house I can't see it. It's like the storm has blown the house away, leaving me out here to turn into the scary ghost that knocks on the window. Always on the outside trying to get in—

I bump right into the fucking barn.

Couldn't hit the broad side of a barn, Davis would say when I tried to throw a ball for Oren. But at least my failed attempts would make him come out and toss the ball around with Oren for a while. For half an hour we were a real family. Father and son, tossing a ball on the front lawn while Mom watches on.

Stupid. Like that made a family any more than pretending Travis and Lisa were going to be real parents.

I feel my way around the corner of the barn to the door— and suddenly I remember why I'm out here and it seems like the stupidest thing I've ever done. If there's someone in the barn what am I going to do about it? I feel for the knife in my pocket and grip the handle. If it's Davis in there do I have the nerve to kill him? When it came down to it back in New Jersey, I froze. I let Oren do it. What kind of mother does that? If I had any true maternal instincts wouldn't I have protected Oren?

I bet Mattie would have. She's got the whole mom thing down, with her pancakes and make-believe games. You can see Oren's already crazy about her. The way he's glommed on to her . . . well, it's the way I glommed on to each new foster parent. Every time, I'd think, *Wow! This is going to be the one!* I'd fallen especially hard for Lisa because she had the whole earth-mother-granola vibe and talked about our being a family. But then it turned out she just wanted a bunch of kids to do her laundry and haul manure for her "organic" garden.

The barn door is open about six inches. I sidle in, careful not to jostle the door. Stepping into the dark from the blinding snowstorm, I can't make out anything right away. It's not completely dark, though. What's left of the day is filtering in through gaps between the slatted walls and holes in the roof.

As my eyes adjust, I can see that like the rest of Mattie's property, the barn's falling apart. And it's full of junk. There are stacks of cardboard cartons splitting at the seams, old rusty farm equipment standing around like dinosaur skeletons, the carcass of an old rusted-out Chevy pickup truck that Davis would give his eyeteeth for, and, hanging from the ceiling in the middle of the barn, a huge iron hook that looks like something from a slasher movie. That's where the stupid teenage girl who went exploring (that's me) would find a dead body hanging—

Something stirs behind the truck. I grip the knife handle in my pocket and take a step forward. "Davis?" I call. "Is that you?" Like he'd answer if it were. I take another step, my eyes on the shadows behind the truck. There's a ray of light coming from a hole in the roof. It's hard to take my eyes off it, but I try to look in the shadows instead. "Hey, I'm sorry we ran like that. Oren was so scared—he thought he killed you. He'll be so glad to know he didn't. You know he didn't mean anything by it. He was just trying to keep you from doing something you'd be sorry about later . . ." As I step around the front of the truck something moves. I pull the knife out of my pocket and lunge for it, stepping into the beam of light. Something hits my head and I bring up my arm to protect myself, cowering against the next blow, already pleading for him to stop—

But all that comes is a cascade of feathers. It was only a bird: I watch as it flies up to land on a long chain that runs the length of the barn and sets that goddamned hook to swaying. The sound the hook makes is awful, like a puppy dying, but even worse is the smell that comes off it. It smells like . . . rot and blood. It smells like death. Maybe it was where the farmers slaughtered their cows and hung them up to bleed out. Like Travis did with a deer one time. *Ugh.*

I prowl the length of the barn, stomping my feet to shake off the cold and disrupting a family of mice from their home in a filing cabinet, but find no human intruder. Nothing valuable or pawnable either. Aside from the rusting farm equipment, the barn seems mostly full of paper. File folders, fat bound documents with big state seals on their covers, and like a century's worth of old newspapers. These have blown around and plastered the whole barn. I pick up one and read the date: August 17, 1953.

Whoa. That's old even for Mattie. Hoarding must run in the family. I pick up one of the legal documents and check out the judge's name. *The Honorable Matthew T. Lane.* I bet that was Mattie's father. No wonder they had this big old house; he was a judge.

Something moves behind me and I spin around, my heart in my throat, picturing Davis. But it's only a stack of newspapers sliding down from the top of the filing cabinet. I must have jarred it when I opened the drawer. The avalanche of papers reaches my feet, one paper lapping up over the toe of my boot like an overfriendly lapdog. I reach down and pick it up. It's a Poughkeepsie paper, yellow, from the eighties. On the front is a picture of an old man in a judge's robes, looking smug and pleased with himself the way judges do, like he's won an award for something or he just sent some lowlife scum to juvie because she stole a couple of dollars from her cheap-ass foster parents. I recognize that look—and I recognize that face. He looks just like Mattie.

I start to kick the paper away—I don't need to read about

how great Mattie's family was—but then I catch a bit of the caption. "Respected judge dies . . ."

I snatch up the paper and read the story.

> **Judge Matthew T. Lane was found dead in his home in Delphi, New York, along with his wife and ten-year-old son. Police suspect accidental carbon monoxide poisoning. The only remaining family member, Judge Lane's 25-year-old daughter, Mattea Lane, discovered the bodies when she came home—**

"If you wanted some reading material there's plenty in the house."

I nearly piss my pants, she startles me so bad. Mattie is standing not three feet from me, arms folded over her ample chest, with that same smug look on her face as her father's.

I toss the newspaper onto the pile at my feet. "I thought I saw someone out here and I came to check it out. A bunch of newspapers fell over and I was just picking them up."

My hand itches to grab the knife, but if I do Mattie could say I was threatening her, so I don't. Mattie smirks and looks around the barn. "Because you wanted to leave things neat?"

"Yeah, it's a mess in here. A fire hazard. You really should clear it out . . . and what the hell is that hook for? It looks like something out of a horror movie."

She gives me a look like I'm an idiot, the way that Lisa used to look at me when I didn't know something about living in the country. *City kid,* she'd call me, even though I'd spent most of my childhood in foster homes in upstate New York. "It's a hay pulley that was used for lifting hay bales into the loft," Mattie says, then she points at the knife I laid on the filing cabinet. "Did you scare off the intruder with that?"

"There wasn't anyone out here, but they could have gotten away before I reached the barn." I suddenly remember that Oren's alone in the house.

Mattie must realize the same thing. "Let's get back," she says, reaching past me to pick up the knife. "We shouldn't leave Oren alone." She puts the knife in the pocket of her baggy old cardigan, like she's used to carrying weapons in there, and turns around. But then her eyes snag on the newspaper I let drop to the floor and she flinches like someone's hit her. She walks out of the barn quick then, like she doesn't even have to check on whether I'm following her.

I hurry to catch up with her, stopping only to pick up the newspaper and stuff it in my coat pocket. Mattie's a pretty cool customer. I'd like to know what made her flinch like that.

CHAPTER EIGHTEEN

Mattie

I DON'T STOP until I reach the back door. Why *that* newspaper, out of all the trash out there? (*My archives*, my father
called them.) I didn't even read the local papers after my
family died. But they came to the house anyway—the judge
subscribed to four daily papers—and at some point after
I'd let them stack up on the front porch, one of the well-
meaning church ladies who came by to straighten up after
the tragedy must have decided they belonged in the old barn
with the other junk.

Unless Alice was snooping around trying to find out more
about me. To blackmail me or commit identity theft. One
of our volunteers, a sweet man getting his MSW in Albany,
gave his credit card to a woman to buy groceries. Big surprise, he had more than a thousand dollars in fraudulent
charges on his next statement. What had seemed to bother
him the most was the frivolous nature of the charges—an

Xbox at Best Buy, a case of beer from the Beverage Barn—as if the poor didn't want the same things everyone else did.

I turn to watch Alice making her way across the snow, bare head bowed, arms wrapped around her skinny chest, face pinched and intent. Her hair is plastered against her head and without its soft fall around her face she looks much older than I first took her for. Early thirties, Frank had said. More like mid-thirties, I'd say now. She's not the poor teenage mother I'd first taken her for and sympathized with. How much else about her have I missed?

She looks up when she reaches the shelter of the porch, and there's so much anger and resentment in her eyes that I flinch. I've seen that look before in abused women, that look that doesn't just expect the next blow but says, *I know I deserve it.* But I've never gotten used to it, or liked how it made me feel, that little split-second flicker of *Maybe you do.*

Most of the people who come before my bench have done something to get themselves there, my father used to say. *You're not doing them any favors by feeling sorry for them and not holding them accountable.*

"What?" Alice demands like a surly teenager. "What are you waiting for?"

"You," I say. "I wanted to make sure you made it."

"You should have gone right in to check on Oren. He doesn't like being alone." She pushes past me into the mudroom and then stops, listening to something. I close the door behind me and listen too. It's Oren, talking, but to whom?

Alice rushes into the kitchen and I follow, my hand on the

knife. When I reach the kitchen, though, I see that except for Dulcie, who's sleeping under the table, Oren is alone. He's standing at the stove stirring the chili with one hand and holding one of the empty tin cans to his ear with the other. A six-inch-tall shaggy figure stands on the counter.

"Who are you talking to?" Alice demands.

Oren rolls his eyes and holds up the empty tin can. "I'm listening to orders from the rebel base and relaying them to Chewbacca, of course. Who were *you* talking to out in the barn?"

Alice blanches like he's caught her at something. *Was* there someone out there? Maybe an accomplice I don't know about? "No one. There was no one out there. Hey, didn't you lose your Chewbacca?"

"This is one of Caleb's," Oren answers. Hearing Caleb's name drop so casually out of his mouth gives me a chill.

"Where'd you find it?" Alice asks.

When he doesn't answer right away I suggest, as gently as I can, "Maybe you found them in the *Star Wars* lunch box upstairs. I don't mind, buddy. I was going to give them to you anyway."

Oren shakes his head. "That's not where I found him. He showed up right here in the kitchen to remind me to stir the chili. It was going to burn otherwise, Mattie."

"Toys don't just show up out of nowhere," Alice says, an edge in her voice as if Oren has made this claim before. "Did you go into that boy's room and take his toys?"

"It really doesn't matter," I interject quickly. She has some nerve attacking Oren for stealing when she's been in my medications. "As I said, I was going to give him all the toys in that lunch box—"

"Why?" Alice asks, wheeling on me. "So Oren could use them to speak to your dead brother?"

I'm so flabbergasted that I don't know what to say. Where in the world did Alice get that idea? Before I can think of an answer Alice is at me, shoving her face in mine, spit flying from her hard little mouth. "I heard you asking him if he heard voices. What kind of a social worker takes advantage of a child's fantasy world to feed her own neuroses? That's sick! I'm going to report you to the Department of Social Services."

It shouldn't, but this makes me laugh. It's a bad habit of mine, laughing when I'm nervous. "Really? Are you going to report yourself at the same time? Are you going to turn yourself and Oren in while you're at it and watch Oren end up in juvie?"

Alice's face turns as bright red as the chili Oren is stirring. "Don't you dare threaten me with that! You fucking—"

"Stop it!" Oren shoves himself in between us. He drops the tin can but holds on to the wooden spoon, and gobs of hot chili fly off and hit Alice in the face. She lets out a horrible shriek and lunges for Oren's hand, but he backs up, brandishing the spoon like a weapon.

"You little shit!" Alice screams.

His eyes widen and his face goes white. "You . . . you . . ." The words sputter out of his lips. "You are NOT my mother!" Then he flings the spoon at Alice and runs from the kitchen.

Alice is so startled by the blow, which has spread chili across her face and hair, that she stands there frozen for a long moment. Then she turns to me, her face streaked with red sauce, her eyes stricken. "This is your fucking fault," she spits at me, before she turns and leaves the kitchen, calling Oren's name as she goes.

I listen to her voice as it travels upstairs. But what I'm hearing is Oren's words.

You are not my mother.

It's a thing that kids have screamed at their rightful parents for generations. I said it to my own mother in this very kitchen.

Good. Who'd want a hateful girl like you for a daughter? she'd responded.

But the way Alice looked when he said it has made something click in my head. A lot of things, actually. The way Oren flinched when Alice touched him. The fact that he always calls her Alice. The fact that, now that I think about it, they don't look all that much alike. Oren has dark, curly hair and brown eyes. Alice is fair with washed-out blue eyes.

I reach into my coat pocket, find my phone, and then take out the charger from my cardigan pocket. I plug the phone into an outlet next to the stove, then pick up the spoon and tin can from the floor. As I'm picking up the tin can I hear something—a murmuring like the sound you hear when you press a conch shell to your ear. Before I can question why I'm doing it, I lift the can and hold it to my ear—

"Matt?"

I drop the can like it's on fire. There were only two people who ever called me Matt and one of them is dead.

I'm reaching to pick up the can again when my real phone buzzes to life on the counter. I look at it and see that I have a text message on the screen from Doreen:

> Called Dept. of Child Welfare. Alice isn't Oren's mother. Not even stepmother. She's the next-door neighbor who babysits. The father

The text is cut off there. I have to swipe it to get the rest of the message, but my hands are too damp and shaking (*Was that Caleb's voice?*). I take two steps to reach the mudroom to grab a towel from the top of the dryer . . . and hear something behind me at the back door.

It's the doorknob turning.

Above the doorknob, in the plate-glass window silhouetted against the static gray of the snow, is a hooded figure.

I reach beneath the pile of towels for the bowie knife. As my hand curls around the handle, the lights go out.

CHAPTER NINETEEN

Alice

I HEAR OREN running up the stairs and follow him, but when I get to the top he's nowhere to be seen and all the doors in the long hallway are closed. He's hiding from me. I could be mad but that's on me. I taught him to play hide-and-seek. It was our first game together when he started hanging around my back porch.

Our porches were next to each other. In the summer I sat out there to smoke after my shift at the diner. Davis would come out and offer me a beer. Oren would play with his toys. Han Solo and Luke and Leia, that was all he talked about. I told him I thought *Star Wars* was cool, even though I wasn't really into all that spaceship and lightsaber stuff. But it was nice to have company and Davis—Davis had this slow smile that made you feel like you were something special, and I didn't have anyone else in my life who made me feel like that. So maybe at first I was nice to the kid because I liked

Davis, which is ironic because by the end I was just staying with Davis because of Oren. But back then I wanted to spend some time alone with Davis, so I told Oren that I'd play hide-and-seek with him.

"Yeah," Davis said, winking at me, "you go hide, son. We'll come looking for you."

Oren had looked at his father doubtfully, but then he'd turned to me and handed me one of his grimy little toys. A plastic dog with its tail broken off. "This is Chewbacca," he told me. "He'll help you look for me. I'll leave clues that you can follow but you have to count to a hundred before you come looking so I have time to hide good."

"We'll give you plenty of time, sport, now . . . *scram!*" Davis had lunged forward and shouted in a scary growl that made Oren yelp and my heart skip a beat. But then Oren was laughing as he ran and I figured that was just how they played. What did I know about how fathers played with their kids? The foster parents I lived with never had time for that "nonsense"; even Travis and Lisa, who gave us big speeches about being a "family," always had another chore we had to do when we asked to play games. So I laughed too and started counting, but Davis started calling out random numbers to mess me up and then he pulled out a joint and we sat out there smoking and drinking. When we did get around to going inside and looking for Oren we saw that he'd set up this whole elaborate game for us to find him. He'd left his toys with goofy messages taped to them, like "Look someplace stinky," which turned out to be in Davis's Nikes, where we found another toy with another message—"Look someplace sweet," which meant the sugar bowl.

That's what he's done now. I see the Wookiee standing on the windowsill on the landing with a Post-it note stuck to its feet.

I turn the Wookiee over and read the note.

"Find me where the hunter stalks the hare."

Well, crap, Oren's gotten a little more sophisticated since "Look someplace stinky." This clue probably has something to do with the mythology book or that constellation book Mattie gave him. Could he have read it so fast? Maybe. I forget how smart he is sometimes. *Scary smart,* Davis used to say.

If it's stars, then I know where he's hiding. Caleb's room, with the stars on the ceiling. Plus if Oren did take the *Star Wars* toys he's probably looking for more. I'll give him a few more minutes to sit and stew, though. There's something else I need to read.

I take the newspaper out of my pocket and glance down the stairs to check for Mattie, glad there's only this one staircase up, no back stairs like in some old houses. But there's no one there. Mattie's probably in the kitchen calling that cop. Maybe that's not a bad idea. If that figure I saw was Davis . . . but no, there was no one in the barn and it's snowing too hard for Davis—or that cop—to get out here.

I unfold the old newspaper and read the rest of the story about how Mattie's family died.

Judge Matthew T. Lane was found dead in his home in Delphi, New York, along with his wife and ten-year-old son. Police suspect accidental carbon monoxide poisoning. The only remaining family member, Judge Lane's 25-year-old daughter, Mattea Lane, discovered the bodies when she came home in the morning after being forced to spend the night at a friend's house because of a blizzard. When she entered the house she smelled gas. She found the judge in his study, unconscious and unresponsive. Mrs. Lane, née Celeste Van Allen, was found dead in her bedroom. Ten-year-old Caleb Lane was not at first discovered, leading to the conjecture that he had escaped his parents' fate, but after an exhaustive search of the house and grounds, Chief Henry Barnes discovered the body of the boy outside in the barn, where he had apparently died of hypothermia and exposure to the elements.

Froze to death, I think, remembering the boy in that story Travis and Lisa had told us. Mattie didn't mention that detail. *My parents and brother died of carbon monoxide poisoning,* she'd said, not *My parents died of carbon monoxide poisoning and my brother froze to death trying to get the hell out of this batshit-crazy house.*

A gust of ice pellets hits the window, making me jump. There's more to the story, but I've read enough. I fold up the newspaper and tuck it in my pocket. Then I walk down the hall to the boy's room. It's easy to tell which one it is, because it's got a pattern of plastic stars on the door—a pattern just like the one that showed up on the window downstairs. I consider knocking, but I'm afraid Oren will just crawl under the bed, so instead I open the door slowly.

At first I'm so dazzled that I'm not sure what I'm seeing. Pinpricks of light dance around the darkened room. It's like the star show I took Oren to see at the planetarium. He had begged to go because it was called "Star Wars." I thought he'd be bored when he found out it wasn't like the movie, but he liked it so much we stayed straight through three showings, hunkering down in our seats so they wouldn't kick us out between shows.

"Oren?" I call quietly, scanning the room. It's hard to make out anything through this crazy light show, which I realize is coming from a lamp on the night table. A constellation projector lamp. Oren asked for one at Christmas but it was too expensive. He must have been over the moon when he found this one.

I move cautiously across the room, expecting Oren to jump out at me any minute. But there's nothing really to hide behind. The only place he could be is under the bed.

I walk slowly to the night table, offering up my bare and vulnerable ankles. "I wonder where Oren can be," I say, mock-serious. "It's too bad he's not here to tell me the names of all these stars. Hmm . . . I think that one's called Rumplepotomi Doofus. And that group over there must be the Three Stooges."

I think I hear a tiny giggle from under the bed.

"And that must be the constellation of Snuffleupagus." This time I hear a definite snort. "And this one, under the sign of the bed, must be—" I drop to my knees and grab under the bed, ready to pull out a giggling boy, but instead my hands close on dust balls. I sweep the space, finding only one small plastic figure, a miniature R2-D2 with a Post-it note that says: "These are not the droids you're looking for. Look inside the house inside the house."

What the—

I flatten myself on the floor to look under the bed for a trapdoor, somewhere Oren could be hiding, but just as I do all the lights go out. Followed, two heartbeats later, by a scream from downstairs.

CHAPTER TWENTY

Mattie

WHOEVER IS COMING in must be startled by the lights going out because he freezes. His hesitation gives me the advantage: I'm in the dark, but there's still a little light left in the sky so I can see him—or at least the shape of him. A man, definitely, with a baseball cap under a hood. His face is in shadow. I can make out the gun in his hand perfectly well and an inch of bare skin between coat cuff and gloved hand. Although I'm flattened against the wall I've angled myself, with my dominant foot back, in exactly the right defensive posture we learned in self-defense class, so when I swing my right arm forward I bring my leg with it, adding force to the blow I aim at his wrist.

The knife sinks deep into flesh. The man screams and drops the gun to the floor. I kick it behind me and wrench open the door. The door opening knocks him off-balance and he falls backward into the snow. I take a step forward but then I hear Doreen's voice in my head. *Close it, idiot! Or at least get the gun first!*

I step back, slam the door, and lock it. Then I turn to look for the gun, but it's too dark. I sink to my knees and feel around on the floor, groping in Dulcie's bed and through the piles of lint and old socks and half-chewed dog bones under the dryer. Finally, my hand closes on cold steel. I feel along the barrel gingerly for the safety and find that it's off.

The bastard was ready to shoot.

Leaving it off, I get to my feet but stay half crouched below the window. He could have another gun. I peer out the window.

He's gone.

Which means he could be trying the front door. Did I lock it? Doreen's always after me to, but living out here at the end of the road, surrounded by woods, I hardly ever bother. *What's to steal?* I'd ask Doreen.

Your life, she'd say.

Who'd want that? I'd quip back.

But now there are two more lives in this house. I head for the front door—and trip over Dulcie. I reach out to brace myself but the gun's in my hand and I end up banging poor Dulcie's head. She whimpers and I feel terrible. I could have shot us both. I thumb on the safety and keep going more cautiously, left hand out, feet feeling for obstacles. I know the way well enough, but there are piles of donation bags in the hall and boots lying by the door.

This is what comes of bad housekeeping, my mother's voice says in my head.

"Fuck off!" I shout out loud as I throw the bolt on the front door.

"Who are you talking to?"

The voice right behind me nearly makes me jump out of my skin. I wheel around, right arm extended, left hand bracing my grip, dominant foot back, body angled to protect my own vital organs (who knew I even still cared about them!). I'm aiming into the dark, though, and for a moment I wonder if I really heard anything at all. Haven't I been listening to the voices in my head for years? Didn't I just hear Caleb's voice in a tin can?

But then the voice comes again. "What the fuck? Are you trying to kill me?"

Of course she can see me. Now I'm the one standing in the dying gray light. "Alice," I say.

"Who the hell else would it be? What happened? I heard someone scream. It sounded like—"

"A man," I say. "A man was coming through the kitchen door. I stabbed him and took his gun but he's still out there."

"A man? What did he look like?"

"I didn't get a good look at him . . . why? Were you expecting someone?"

"What? No! I just thought it might be someone *you* knew."

I'm about to snap back that I don't know any housebreakers but then I realize that I probably do. Instead I ask where Oren is.

"Hiding," she says. "Upstairs, I think."

"Shit. We have to find him. I need to get my phone from

the kitchen and then we'll go upstairs and . . ." And then what? We tell victims of domestic abuse who are in their houses with their abusers that if they can't get out they should lock and barricade themselves into a safe room with their children. The only room that locks is down here. But I don't tell Alice that. "Stay right here. Watch the door and listen for breaking glass. If you hear glass breaking run upstairs and hide under one of the beds."

I walk past her toward the kitchen but she grabs my arm. "I'm coming with you," she says. Her hand is clammy and trembling. Her breathing sounds shallow. Like a person having a panic attack.

"Fine. Just try not to trip me up. This is no time for me to break a hip."

She hangs on to me like a barnacle all the way to the kitchen. I feel my way to the kitchen table and retrieve the flashlights I pulled out earlier. I pocket one and hand the other to Alice. "Don't turn it on yet," I say as I feel around on the counter for the phone. "I don't want him to know where we are."

"You couldn't see his face at all?"

"Not really. He had a baseball cap on under a hood." The baseball hat jogs a memory: Camo from the Stewart's handing Atefeh a MAKE AMERICA GREAT AGAIN hat. The asshole whose groin I doused with hot coffee. Who was driving a jacked-up plow truck with fake antlers on the hood, just like the plow truck that nearly ran me over as I was going into Sanctuary earlier today. I'd been too busy looking for Oren to notice, but now I'm sure it was the same truck. He might have waited for us to come out of Sanctuary and followed us back to the house.

"How tall was he?" Alice asks.

"Why?" I ask. The phone's not on the kitchen counter and I remember it was still in my hand when I reached for the knife on top of the dryer. I must have dropped it there. I approach the back door warily, checking the window to see if the intruder is out there, but it's too dark to tell. It's full night now.

"Did he have a goatee?" Alice asks.

"A goatee? Honestly, I have no—" My hand closes on the phone. I thumb the home button and the screen lights up. "Thank God!" I say, and then realize that the lit screen might be visible from the outside. I turn my back to the door and bump into Alice. She's so close that I can smell her coppery fear-soaked breath. In the light of the phone screen her face looks gaunt and haggard. Why did I ever think she was in her twenties? She must be thirty-five at least, and those years have not been kind to her.

I touch the phone icon and tap in 911. As it's ringing the low battery alert comes on. Shit. It was plugged in only long enough to get a tiny charge before the power went off. But maybe it will be enough. The police operator answers on the third ring.

"911. What's your emer—"

The screen goes black. "Fuck!" I swear, shaking the phone as if that will bring it to life.

"Mattie," Alice says. "There's something I have to tell you."

"Not now, Alice," I snap, years of reflective listening training going out the window. "We have to get upstairs. Find Oren. Block ourselves in my bedroom. We've got two guns and the police will trace that call. The chief of police is my—" I'd been about to say *my friend,* but that really isn't true anymore. Frank Barnes hasn't so much as smiled at me since the night Caleb and my parents died. Still, Frank's too upstanding a guy to let personal feelings come between him and his duty. "He'll head out here when he sees I tried to call. We just have to stay safe until he gets here. This asshole—I think I know who he is—is just a redneck blowhard. I pissed him off at the Stewart's last night and he came out here to teach me a lesson. He's probably nursing his injured paw and crawling back to the nearest bar, where he'll tell the regulars that he put the fear of God into a couple of pussy-hat-wearing feminists."

I'm not sure I believe any of what I'm saying. Secretly I am hoping that dumbass Jason has crawled off to freeze to death in the barn, but as soon as that thought appears in my head I picture Caleb in the barn and I have to brace myself against the dryer.

Alice grabs my arm to hold me up. She lowers her face so it's inches from mine. "It's not some dumbass redneck you pissed off at the Stewart's," she spits out. "It's Davis. He's alive and he's come to get me and Oren. And he won't stop until we're all dead."

CHAPTER TWENTY-ONE

Alice

MATTIE DOESN'T SAY anything right away and it's too dark to see her face. I can picture it, though, the same sour disapproval I've seen in a dozen caseworkers, foster parents, and teachers over the years. People who put their trust in me and were then disappointed when I wasn't able to live up to the pretty picture they'd made in their heads. The young teachers and social workers were the worst. They'd get the idea that they were reaching the poor foster kid and then you'd make one little mistake—missing curfew, lifting a lip gloss from Walmart, punching the dickwad who called you white trash—and their pretty picture of themselves as your savior blew up in their faces. It wasn't you they were mad at; it was themselves for being stupid enough to trust you.

When Mattie does speak, her voice is flat with rage. "You told me Davis was dead."

"No," I point out, "*you* told me that he was dead."

"They found a body at his house."

"Yeah, well, it wasn't Davis, it was Scott."

"Who is Scott?"

"Oren's caseworker," I say, "and a nice guy. I called him to tell him not to worry about us." Yes, I'm leaving out the idea of running away with Scott. Mattie doesn't have to know all my business. "When I called Scott's cell phone, Davis picked up. So I figure Scott must have gone by to check on us and Davis killed him. That must be the body the cops found."

Mattie doesn't say anything right away. She must be deciding whether she believes me. It's creepy standing here talking in the dark, like being in a confessional. One of my foster parents, Maria Tomaselli, was Catholic and took us kids to church every Sunday trying to convert us. I hid in the confessional one week and wrote some comments about the Virgin Mary and Jesus in Sharpie on the walls. Maria gave up trying to convert me after that; she'd made up her mind I was going to hell.

"Did you ask Davis to come get you?" Mattie squeezes out the words like toothpaste from a spent tube. "Did you tell him where you are?"

"No! What kind of an idiot do you think I am! Like I'd endanger my boy—"

"I know Oren's not your son."

This takes me by surprise—and it hurts too. She says it like she knows every dirty secret I've ever had. Like she knows me inside and out. But she doesn't know the first thing about me.

"You assumed he was my son and I just went along with you. He's still *my boy*. I've put up with Davis's shit for two years because I couldn't stand to leave Oren with him or let Oren end up in the system. I love that kid."

I brace myself for her to challenge that but she doesn't. "Where did you call from?"

"The CVS pharmacy phone. I don't know if it has caller ID—"

"It does," Mattie says. "Shit. Why didn't you tell me? We could have told the police."

"I'd've lost Oren. I've got no claim to him. And . . . I've got a record. Little shit . . . shoplifting, pot . . . but I'd never get custody of him. You know where he'd end up."

She doesn't argue with this. Instead she turns on her flashlight and shines it right in my eyes, blinding me. "I know you took drugs from my bedroom." Her voice is cold and hard. "Have you taken it all?"

I fish out two Oxy from my pocket and hand them over. "I only took one of the Valium to calm down," I tell her. "I've been under a lot of stress lately."

I don't mean it as a joke but she laughs. When she lowers the flashlight I can see her face. It's wet and shiny; she's cried all through my story without making a sound. "Okay," she says, wiping her face with her shirtsleeve. "We're not going to solve anything by standing here jawing. Let's go up and find Oren and then hunker down. Do you have any idea where he is?"

"I heard him in your brother's room. I thought he was under the bed but then when I looked he wasn't there. Though I did find this." I hand her the R2-D2. She turns it over and reads the sticky note. Even in the weird glow of the flashlight I can tell her face has gone pale. "What?" I ask, for a second more afraid of what the note means to Mattie than the fact that Davis is prowling outside the house.

"I'll explain on the way up," she says, stroking the plastic robot with her thumb as if it were a holy relic. "I think I know where Oren is."

AS I FOLLOW Mattie up the stairs she explains in a hushed whisper something she calls "the game."

"Caleb loved to play hide-and-seek. It was his favorite game and he didn't get to play a lot of games. My parents . . . they were old by the time Caleb showed up—a change-of-life baby, some people called him. A mistake, others said."

"That's mean," I say.

"People are mean. I expect you've learned that, Alice. Caleb didn't have many friends. My mother didn't like for him to bring other kids home—too much mess, she said—or to go to the neighbors' houses. When I was growing up my father would read to me, teach me about the stars and trees and birds, but by the time Caleb came along he had less patience." She pauses and I suspect there's more to the story that she's leaving out, but I don't press her. There's plenty I'd want to leave out of my story too.

"So I played with him. In the summer we would play hide-and-seek for hours out in the fields and woods. He got so good at it that he scared me sometimes, disappearing for hours. I made him agree to a place he'd always come back to if I couldn't find him in an hour—home base, we called it—and he started leaving clues there. At first they were pretty simple, like 'I'm with the pips' for the apple orchard, but after we saw the first *Star Wars* movie he started mapping out whole adventures for the characters."

"Oren did that too," I say. "I think it was easier pretending to be a rebel Jedi hiding from Darth Vader than a scared little boy hiding from his asshole father."

We've reached the door to Caleb's room. It's closed, though I don't remember closing it. Mattie turns to me, the flashlight lighting up her face like a fright mask. Despite the scary shadows on her face her eyes look kinder than they have since I pulled Oren's arm. "Of course it was. The game got more complicated the summer Caleb was ten. I was away at graduate school. When I came back I knew right away that things were . . . *different*. My mother, who'd always been a compulsive cleaner, had gotten crazy. She'd mop the kitchen floor and then forget she'd just cleaned it and start all over again. She was always yelling at Caleb not to track in mud, not to make too much noise, not to move things around—"

"Not to move things around?" I ask, thinking of Oren's poltergeist.

"She was imagining it," Mattie says with a sigh. "She was in the early stages of Alzheimer's. I tried to talk to my father about her but he was too busy with his own worries. Some of his past cases were being reviewed by the state . . ." She pauses again and I guess this is something else she's leaving out. I let her. I'm getting impatient with this story; I want to find Oren.

"And . . . ?" I prompt.

"So he was holed up in his study poring over his files all day and late into the night. He told me my mother was just high-strung and Caleb was just going through a phase. *The thing is not to coddle the boy.*"

Mattie's voice lowers on this last part and I shiver. It doesn't even sound like her. It sounds like some hard-ass judge.

"I tried to keep Caleb busy and out of their way. The third *Star Wars* movie had just come out." Her voice softens. "I took him to see it three times. Each time we came back the game became more complicated—there was a whole plot having to do with Han Solo on Endor with the Ewoks . . . well, you can imagine. That's when he hid Yoda down in the hollow behind Stewart's."

It takes me half a second to realize what she's saying and then I feel as cold as if we were still standing in that frozen hollow. "Like the one Oren found? You think it was the same Yoda? But how . . . ?"

"I don't know," Mattie says. "Maybe it's just that two boys in the same situation think the same." She sounds unsure but goes on. "Caleb was straying farther and farther from home. I was afraid that he was going to run away. We started playing in the house more. That's when he found the house inside the house."

"That's what Oren wrote in his note. What does it mean?"

Instead of answering me Mattie opens the door. Even though the electricity's out, the room has a muted glow: a Milky Way of plastic glow-in-the-dark stars across the ceiling, walls, and even the floor, hundreds of them. Mattie walks into the center of the room, her face tilted up to the ceiling, turning around in a slow circle as if she's as weirded out by the spectacle as I am. I kneel and check under the bed, just in case, but Oren's not there. When I get up I find Mattie running her hand along a pattern of stars on the wall.

"That's the same pattern that's on all the windows," I say. "Does it mean something?"

"It's the constellation Virgo," she says, her voice small and far away.

"Was that Caleb's zodiac sign?"

"No," Mattie says, "it stands for Justice. It's a story from mythology that my father liked to tell." She's still tracing the pattern of stars with her fingertips. Then she looks down at her feet. There are stars there too, but the pattern is interrupted by an old rag rug. She picks it up and flings it aside. There's the pattern again, pointing toward the floor under the bed.

"Wow, Caleb really went to town with these stick-on stars," I say, just to be saying something. It creeps me out that the stars point under the bed.

Mattie shakes her head. "These ones on the floor weren't here before."

"But then who . . . ," I begin, but then I stop at a sound from downstairs. Mattie hears it too. Breaking glass.

"Come on." Mattie pushes me to the floor and begins scrambling under the bed. It's crazy; we'll never both fit under there. There's got to be a better place to hide.

"Where the hell are we going?" I demand as Mattie pushes me against the far wall under the bed.

"To the house inside the house," she says as the wall gives way and I begin to fall.

CHAPTER TWENTY-TWO

Mattie

I'D FORGOTTEN ABOUT the drop. It's been thirty-four years since I used the sliding panel under Caleb's bed that leads to the closed-off back stairs. Before the stairs were blocked off I asked my father what the panel was for and he told me it was a laundry chute to make it easier for the housemaid to collect laundry from upstairs. There would have been a wicker hamper underneath it. Now there's a three-foot drop to hardwood floor.

I hear Alice's aggrieved curses as she hits the floor. I scramble down to put my hand over her mouth and shush her. "Do you want to give away where we are?" I hiss. I feel her head shake no. When she's still, I reach up and slide the panel shut as slowly and carefully as I can. Then I crouch next to Alice and listen.

The breaking glass sounded like it came from directly under Caleb's room, which means it came from my father's study. Even after all these years I feel a shock at the violation of the sanctity of that space. *Sancta sanctorum,* Frank, an ex–altar boy, jokingly called it when we snuck up the back stairs, past the now blocked-off door that led to the study.

The intruder is in the study. Thank God I took the gun out of the desk drawer. And thank God the study door locks from the outside . . .

Assuming I remembered to lock it. *Did I?* I'd been upset about seeing that pattern in the dust. Could I have forgotten to lock the door from the outside, like I forgot to let Dulcie in? I strain my memory, but while I remember dropping the key in the crystal bowl, I don't remember locking the study door. At least I have a gun. I reach to feel its comforting cold bulk in my pocket, but before I can touch it Alice grabs my hand.

"What *is* this place?" she whispers. Her voice sounds much younger.

It's creepy, Frank had said when I showed it to him.

"It's just the back staircase," I whisper. "My parents had it blocked off when I was fourteen."

"Why?" Alice whispers back.

I sigh. This is not a story I want to tell, but at least it might take Alice's mind off her murderous ex (*Could it be?* I wonder. *Did Davis have time to get here from New Jersey?*) rifling through my father's study. "I used to use the stairs to sneak out at night—and then I got in trouble and was sent away."

"Where to?" She's not letting anything go.

"To juvenile detention," I reply, glad it's too dark to see

Alice's expression. This is not something I often tell people. Doreen once said I should *own* what happened to me, that I was a survivor of the antiquated juvenile corrections system and that by sharing my story I would empower other survivors.

That was the only time I ever told Doreen to fuck off. No matter how *enlightened* people think they are (*woke*, the interns call it), they look at you differently when they know you were in JD. But I don't have to see how Alice is looking at me. Her voice is awed when she asks, "JD? A judge's daughter?"

"Yeah, I know, ironic, huh? But my father had this idea that if he went easy on me people would call him a hypocrite. He had a reputation as a judge who was tough on juvenile delinquents. He thought the world was going to hell in a handbasket because parents were too permissive and kids didn't have to face up to the consequences of their actions. So when I got picked up for making out in a parked car—"

"That's a crime?"

"'Public indecency,' my father decreed." *Slutting around,* my mother called it. "He thought he had to treat me the same as any other miscreant. I got sent to the New York Training School for Girls in Hudson."

Alice is silent for a moment. "I've never heard of that place," she says at last.

"They shut it down in 1975, two years after I finished my time there. It . . . It wasn't a very nice place." And just like that the black hole we're sitting in becomes the windowless basement cell used for solitary confinement, Hudson's preferred method of punishment. I can hear even now the *drip, drip, drip* from the leaky faucet in the hall and the tread of the guard's footsteps on the stairs.

"Shit," Alice says in a tone of commiseration.

"Yeah," I agree. "When I came home the back stairs were boarded up. My mother said it was because of the new baby—Caleb—that she was afraid of him falling down the stairs, but I knew it was a message to me. There'd be no more sneaking out at night." It had felt, when I came back, like a piece of me was gone too, like that rebellious girl who would sneak out to meet Frank Barnes down in the hollow had been erased. I had thought I might find her again when I saw Frank, but Frank had been sent straight from boot camp to a military school, and then he joined the army. Although I'd caught glimpses of him on holidays, it was another ten years before I really talked to him again.

"Wow," Alice says, "what a weird-assed thing to do."

I almost laugh. Weird-assed, indeed. It's like we're two teenagers on a sleepover, cuddled in a closet, telling each other ghost stories. "Yeah, but then Caleb found the sliding door underneath his bed the summer he was ten. *The house inside the house,* he called it. I didn't know what he was talking about at first. I'd *forgotten* about the stairs. But then he took me here and I thought, yeah, this is what he needs: a house inside the house, another place with a different family where he could be a normal little boy without my parents carping at him every minute. It became our place."

I listen for a moment and hear a step and the creak of casters—my father's chair being moved. The intruder's still in the study. Then I turn on the flashlight, aiming it at the ceiling. It's still here: a night sky and a million stars and tiny spaceships hanging from invisible fishing lines. A galaxy far, far away that I made for Caleb a lifetime ago. I don't know what I thought would have happened to it—I've barely let myself think of it in the decades since Caleb's death—but it feels like a miracle that it has survived.

I hear a clunk from the study below us. We have to find Oren. I sweep the beam of my flashlight across the landing from the stairs that lead up to the attic to the ones that lead down to the first floor and basement. The light comes to rest on a figure standing on the newel post of the downward stairs. It's Princess Leia, holding her hands up, as she does in the first movie when she appears as a hologram begging for help from Obi-Wan Kenobi, only here she's holding a Post-it note. Alice grabs it and shines the flashlight on it.

"You're our only hope, Obi-Wan Kenobi," it reads. "Return to Dagobah for more information."

"Dagobah is the planet Yoda lives on," Alice says.

"When we were playing in the house, Dagobah meant the basement. There's a crawl space there that reminded Caleb of the cave Yoda lives in."

"Can we get to the basement from here?" Alice asks. I notice that she doesn't question why Oren would know something that Caleb knew. Earlier she accused me of bringing Oren back here so that he could communicate with Caleb, and she wasn't wrong. But the idea that he is actually doing that now is not something I want to dwell on.

"Maybe. My parents didn't wall that door up, they just stacked boxes in front of it. I moved them just enough so I could get by when Caleb and I started using the stairs again and I haven't moved them since." I sense Alice staring at me, but if she thinks it's odd that I haven't touched the boxes in my basement for thirty-four years she refrains from commenting, so I go on. "The stairs go by the study, though, so we'll have to be really, really quiet. And we'd better turn off our flashlights."

I turn off my flashlight and Alice follows suit. When we're plunged into darkness, for a moment I can't move. Once Caleb found these stairs again I used them regularly to sneak out. At twenty-five, home from graduate school, I shouldn't have *had* to sneak out, but my parents never trusted me after I got back from Hudson. It was as if, having consigned me to that hellhole, they blamed me for what happened to me there, I was tainted. And the worst thing was that a part of me agreed with them. When I ran into Frank again—back from military school and two years in the army—I sensed that same whiff of damage in him.

I told Caleb I'd come back for him the next summer, when I'd gotten my MSW and could get a job. My mother was carping and shrewish, so consumed by her own anxieties that she had to control everything—and everyone—around her. I knew she squelched every boyish desire in Caleb's heart, but he had such a big heart I thought it would remain intact. My father was strict, but his punishments were always impartial and cold. No dinner. Extra chores. Time-outs. Carefully calibrated punishments that left you feeling ashamed.

I thought that Caleb could survive them both for another year. At least that's what I told myself. Really, I wanted that year to myself. I wanted to answer that siren cry of the train whistle calling me to New York City. *That's nothing to be ashamed of,* Doreen tells me. *You wanted what any young woman would want. And you did come back.*

I could have come back after college.

And worked at Stewart's? You wanted a good job so you could take care of him. You were going to take him with you once you graduated.

I hadn't counted on my father's own sense of shame.

I feel Alice's breath on the back of my neck and her hand on my elbow, ready to be led into the darkness. Trusting me. As Oren has. As Caleb did.

And then I see something glowing faintly on the first step. I look closer and see that it's a plastic Day-Glo star. There's one on each step going down, a trail to follow. *A lifeline,* like the one we'd used in Lava to navigate the treacherous terrain of our own home.

It unfreezes me now. Only, as I step forward, I can't help thinking that a *lifeline* tossed by a ghost might be anything but.

CHAPTER TWENTY-THREE

Alice

WALKING DOWN THESE dark stairs feels like the scariest thing I've ever had to do. Scarier than the time I ran away from my last foster home and had to sleep in a bus station two nights in a row. Scarier than the stint I did at Pine Crest JD, the *nice* JD, which wasn't that bad but still felt like shit.

This is worse because I know Davis is here. I don't care if Mattie thinks it's her redneck Stewart's guy; I know it's Davis. I can feel him, like a cold draft rising up through the cracks in the floorboards, that prickle I get at the base of my skull when I'm around someone really bad. *Cray-dar,* one of the girls I met in lockdown called it: creep-radar.

When we go past the boarded-up door that Mattie said leads to her father's study, I feel like there are a million bugs crawling over my body. It's not Davis's face I picture, though, it's that smug sonofabitch judge from the newspaper story. Mattie's father. What kind of an asshole sends his own daughter to lockdown? That's what's off about this house.

One of the things about my foster mom Lisa was that she was really sensitive. The least noise would make her jump. *Do you have to walk so loud? Can you not make the whole house shake? Can you lower your voice? Can you only use the toilet before nine P.M. and after nine A.M.? Do you have to toss and turn and make the bed creak?*

Tamara, a big girl from Yonkers, said, *She'd like for us to crawl inside the walls and stay there.*

The image of us all stuck behind the walls—literally *stuck* in the walls—haunted me, woke me up in the middle of the night because I'd dreamed I was smothering in plaster. And now it feels like we're inside the walls of this old house, where the mice crawl and the ghosts dwell. That's what Oren felt when he stopped on the path outside the house. He felt Caleb's ghost.

Oren, who always knows things, like what town to buy the bus tickets for, and who can make things disappear, like the poltergeist. Oren's been talking to dead Caleb and now he's leading us down these dark stairs to the basement, where it's cold and damp as a grave. I stumble at the thought, and when I reach out to steady myself I feel cold rough stone and something slithers over my hand. I bat it away and trip down the last few steps, banging off something soft and squishy and landing on my hands and knees on the floor—only it's not even *floor*, it's dirt. I can smell it. It smells like worms. It smells like a grave. Of course, that's what the ghost wants, to drag us down into its grave. I can feel a scream clawing its way up my throat when a hand clamps over my mouth.

"Alice!" The voice is in my ear, hoarse and rough. It doesn't sound like Mattie, but then her big capable hands are on my shoulders and she's shushing me like a mother would hush a scared child, and I just collapse into her and cry as quietly as I can and Mattie sits by me in the dirt with her arms around me until I'm good and done.

"It's just the basement," she says, "see?" She turns on the flashlight and moves the light over the dirt floor, rough stone walls, and beams that look like they were hewn out of whole trees. Boxes are stacked in front of the stairs we just came down so that you wouldn't even know the stairs were there. There's another long flight that probably goes up to the kitchen and a shorter flight of stone steps leading to slanted doors that look like they came from a movie set in Kansas. Metal shelves with junk and cloudy-looking jars line the far side of the room, and a huge hulking furnace lurks in an alcove that looks like it was carved out of the rock face. I remember Mattie said she replaced the old one after it killed her family, but still, there's something scary about it. As I stare at it something moves in the shadows behind it. Something *boy* shaped.

I get up and march over there, shining my flashlight into the alcove. It's more like a cave than an alcove, and it goes farther back than my flashlight reaches.

"Oren?" I call. "Come out of there right now!"

"Did you see him in there?" Mattie asks, adding her

flashlight beam to mine. "There's a crawl space back there where Caleb got stuck once."

The last thing I want to hear about right now is Mattie's dead brother—or anything called a *crawl* space—but that would be mean to say. I can see Mattie measuring the distance between the wall and the furnace, but the truth is she's too wide in the beam to clear the narrow space.

"I'll go," I say, pushing past her. I flatten myself against the stone wall, imagining centipedes and spiders crawling into my hair, and inch my way past the hulking machine. It's not really that hot; it must have turned off when the electricity went out. Still, I find I don't want to touch it. It's greasy and dirty and somehow just . . . *bad*.

"Thanks a lot, Oren," I mutter. I hear a muffled sound that could be giggling—or sobbing. *Damn*. If Oren's really gotten himself stuck in here he must be scared shitless. "It's okay, sweetie," I say, backtracking. "It's just a smelly old basement. I'm coming to get you out."

Once I'm past the furnace I can lift my arm and aim the flashlight into the back of the cave. Past the pipes and wires, toward the bottom of the wall, there's an opening maybe two feet high. The crawl space Mattie mentioned, only you'd have to be a midget to crawl in there. I shine the flashlight into it and the beam catches the glint of eyes. Big, wide, scared little-boy eyes.

"Oh, baby," I say, crouching down, "how'd you get yourself into such a mess? Here, give me your hand."

He sobs. Shit. Oren never cries. I put down the flashlight

and flatten myself on the cold, wet ground, reaching into the dark. "Take my hand, baby."

His hand clasps mine. It's so cold it scares me. How long has he been lying here?

"I'm so sorry, baby," I say. "I'm sorry I yelled, I'm sorry I didn't get you away sooner. I promise it will be better from now on. I'm gonna take care of you."

He squeezes my hand and I feel something cold and hard press into my palm. And then his hand is gone. It's not like he's let go; it's like his flesh just melted away.

"Oren?" I scrabble closer to the hole and sweep my hands inside. There's nothing there. Could he have crawled in even deeper? I inch back, find the flashlight, and aim it into the hole. The light shines onto a stone wall two or three feet in. I crawl farther in, feeling every inch of the wall for an opening Oren could have slipped through, but there's no way out of this hole.

In fact, I'm not 100 percent sure I can get out.

Fighting off rising panic, I push my way back. Then I search the rest of the alcove for Oren, but he's not here.

Maybe I imagined him.

Or maybe that wasn't Oren.

Suddenly I can't stand another minute here. I squeeze myself past the furnace and into the basement.

"Did you find him?" Mattie asks. "Is he stuck back there?"

I don't know what to tell her. Instead I hold out my hand and open it, palm up. Mattie shines her flashlight on my hand and plucks up the cold hard thing he—*it?*—pressed into my grasp. I had been holding it so tightly that it's left a pattern imprinted on my flesh, some kind of complicated seal like you see on old buildings and stamped on official papers. It looks kind of familiar. It must be to Mattie too. She's looking at it like it's a puzzle piece.

"Where'd you get . . . ," she begins, but her words are drowned out by a loud grating noise coming from the slanted doors on the other side of the basement. We both turn our flashlights on them in time to see the doors fly open. Snow comes pouring in, then a man's booted legs appear.

Mattie grabs my hand, pushes me to the side of the stairs, and turns off her flashlight. I turn off mine too, but not before I see Mattie take a gun out of her sweater pocket. As the man comes down the stairs, shining his own flashlight in front of him, Mattie raises the gun over her head. She waits until he reaches the bottom step, then brings the gun down on his head with an audible crunch.

The man falls to his knees, arms flailing, flashlight flying. I hear a thump and a groan, and I thumb on my own flashlight to see Mattie sitting on top of the man, one knee pinning down his right shoulder while she struggles to pull his left arm behind his back.

"There's a roll of electrical tape on that shelf over there," she shouts at me.

I find the tape and try to unpeel it, but my hands are shaking too hard. The man is moaning and bucking under Mattie's weight. Any second now he could get free and come at me. And then what? When Davis hit me I froze. I'd crawl into a ball and pray for it to be over. But here's middle-aged soft-hearted Mattie fighting like a hellcat.

I force my hands to work and unpeel the dusty end and hand it to Mattie. She wrenches the intruder's hand back and uses, like, half the roll of tape to wrap both wrists together, then pulls out a knife from her sweater pocket to cut off the tape.

"Do you have an Uzi in there too?" I ask like a smart-ass, trying to sound less scared than I really am.

She barks a laugh and then eases her weight off the man. "Help me roll him over."

We shove him over like a sack of potatoes. His face is smeared with blood, but I see to my surprise that it's not Davis. "I could've sworn it was Davis in the study," I say.

"You weren't wrong, darling."

The voice—*his voice*—curdles my stomach. I look up and see Davis on the stairs at the other end of the basement. He's got a flashlight in one hand, a gun in the other, and a smug, satisfied look on his face.

CHAPTER TWENTY-FOUR

Mattie

I START TO reach for the gun, which I'd lain down on the floor, but I hear the click of a hammer being pulled back along with a soft *tsk*.

"I wouldn't do that, darling, unless you want me to put a bullet through your head." The man comes down the stairs, aiming the revolver straight at my forehead. I force myself to look away from him, glancing at Alice to see her staring at him with sheer hatred. Ah.

"Davis, I presume," I say, turning my attention to the man's face. He's slight, in his mid-thirties, with feathery brown hair and a wispy goatee, wearing jeans and an unbuttoned flannel shirt over a Nirvana T-shirt. He looks like half a dozen interns I've trained over the years.

"No shit," he snarls. Then he points the gun at Jason. "Who's this asshole?"

The asshole himself answers. "Hey, man, this nosy bitch got up in my face defending a towel-head at the Stewart's. She's one of those nosy social workers. I came out here to teach her a lesson."

"That so?" Davis asks, kneeling to pick up the other gun from the floor. He slides it into his back pocket, then pokes his gun in my face. "Is that what you get off on, bitch? Defending women from nasty men? Is that what you've been doing with my Allie? Cuddling her to your bosom?"

When he says *bosom* he moves the gun to my left breast. My skin crawls.

"Aw, you're blushing! Have I figured out your big secret? As if all you 'domestic abuse' sob sisters"—he makes air quotes with both hands—"weren't just dykes out for some damaged pussy."

He points the gun at Alice's groin and I can feel her tense beside me. He's groping us with his words, and he's had a lot of practice at it. But I've had practice dealing with this kind of man. "You sound like you've had experience with domestic violence services before," I say.

He tilts back his head, revealing a scrawny neck pitted with acne, and laughs. "If by 'domestic violence services' you mean the legion of feminazis who like to butt their fat asses into a man's business because they're jealous *they* don't have a man, then yes, I've encountered my share."

I'm tempted to point out the inconsistency in his characterization of social workers as lesbians being jealous of not having a man, but I hear Doreen's voice in my head suggesting I listen for the emotions beneath the words. "I can hear a lot of pain and loss in your voice," I say.

He's dead quiet for a moment, and I think maybe this could work. I've been trained to talk to people in crisis, after all. I just have to keep him talking until Frank gets here—

Then Davis swings back his arm and hits me on the side of the head with the butt of the gun. As I go over I hear Alice shriek and Jason snicker. A darkness swells in my head, black satin spreading over my eyes, and suddenly I'm in that basement cell at Hudson where they sent the bad girls for punishment. I can smell piss and mold and fear. I can hear the steps of the guard on the stairs, feel his arm on my arm—

No, please, I plead.

What's the problem, sweetheart? This is what you were sent here for. I read your file. Making out with your boyfriend in the backseat of his daddy's car. Little slut—

"No, please." It's not me pleading now; it's Alice. I can't make out all her words over the ringing in my ears but I hear the fear and desperation in her voice. It's my voice all those years ago, pleading with the guard not to hurt me. But it didn't work then and it won't work now. Men like that guard and Davis feed on the powerlessness of women and children because they need to feel better than someone else. Someone made them feel weak once, and the only way they can make that feeling go away is by hurting a weaker person.

I open my eyes and try to focus on a spot ten inches in front of me, which turns out to be Jason's ear. So he came out to teach me a lesson, did he? I bet he didn't bargain on getting involved in *this* shit storm.

Jason looks back at me, then flicks his gaze up and down rapidly. I follow his downward movement to his waist and glimpse a wood-grained handle protruding from his pocket. A knife. I give Jason a terse and tiny nod, then inch my hand steadily toward his pocket.

As the ringing in my ears abates I can make out more of what Davis is saying now, something about how Alice has alienated his son's affections and is a lying no-good cunt that he should never have taken in. Poor Alice is crying.

"You're right," Alice chokes out between sobs. "I made Oren come with me. It was all my idea. Just leave him alone."

Poor Alice. She thinks she can protect Oren if she sacrifices herself.

"Where is the little shit, anyway?" Davis demands.

Where indeed? I wonder as my fingers touch the knife handle in Jason's pocket. Hiding, I hope, in the old back stairs. Lucky I pushed back the boxes in front of them. Maybe he's gotten up to the attic. A smart little kid like Oren could make himself vanish up there. Caleb always could. When my father was on the warpath Caleb could vanish for days. I used to worry that he would starve to death before he came out.

I curl my fingers around the knife handle—and realize as I do that I've still got that button Alice handed me. I've been gripping it in my clenched fist so tightly that it sticks to my palm even as I grab the knife. There was a design on the button that had jarred some memory, but I can't think what now and it isn't important. Still, I keep the button in my hand as I slip the knife out of Jason's pocket and slide both knife and button into my own.

I hold my breath for a moment, afraid to look at Davis, praying that he didn't see me take the knife. But no, he's too busy berating Alice.

". . . and I should have known that a piece of foster-care ass would have no respect for blood. Did you think you could be Oren's mommy? That it didn't matter that he's *my* son?" Out of the corner of my eye I see Davis thump his chest with the same hand that's holding the gun. *"My son,"* he says again, pounding his chest. *"Mine."*

I've heard this before too, abusive men storming Sanctuary, demanding to know what we've done with *my* children, *my* wife, *my* family. I've stood my ground while they spit in my face. I've even felt a sliver of sympathy for them. They may have once loved that woman, those children, but something twisted inside them—some thread that got tangled in their own childhood, usually—and turned that love into a need to control. Now it's all unraveling.

When they're done yelling Doreen will step in and offer the men a cup of coffee. If they'll sit down with her she'll tell them about our anger management group. She'll talk about the steps that might lead them back to their families. Most of the men tell her to go fuck herself, but a few have sat down with her, and one or two have actually joined the group and recovered.

No one is irredeemable, Doreen likes to say. I wish she were here now. She'd know how to talk to Davis.

"Tell me where he is," Davis is yelling.

"Alice doesn't know where he is," I say, interrupting him.

Davis snaps his head around to me. "What did you say, bitch?"

"Oren is hiding," I say, trying to keep my voice even like Doreen would. "There are dozens of places in this house where a smart kid like Oren could hide. He won't come out as long as you're yelling. If he sees that you're calm, that we're all sitting around peaceably—say, in the kitchen—he might come out."

Davis cocks his head to one side as if he's considering what I've said. "Oh, really? What if I yell real loud like this: HEY, OREN!" He presses the barrel of the gun to my temple. "I'M GOING TO SHOOT THIS BITCH IF YOU DON'T COME OUT RIGHT NOW."

"I don't think that will work," I say, praying it's true. Hoping Oren doesn't come out of hiding to keep Davis from shooting me. "That's only likely to make him more scared. But if we go upstairs to the kitchen—"

"What's in the kitchen you want so much?"

Nothing, I think, wishing I'd hidden the gun there. "Just a pot of chili, candles and oil lamps, a woodstove. This house will get pretty cold soon without the furnace working. We're all stuck here tonight. We could make a fire in the woodstove, heat up that chili, show Oren that everything's okay."

"Why, you make it sound real cozy," Davis croons.

The thought of sitting around the woodstove eating chili with this asshole turns my stomach, but I swallow my own bile. "The alternative is freezing to death," I say as flatly as I can.

"Hmm." Davis looks around the basement, taking in the cold furnace, the shelves, the boxes—his eyes go right past them, I'm relieved to see—and light on the still-open Bilco doors. "Well, that's not going to help any. Hey, asshole." He nudges Jason with the barrel of the gun. "Is that how you got in?"

Jason nods. "Yeah."

Davis strolls over to the Bilco doors, the gun dangling loosely from his hand, and reaches to pull them closed. If I could hit him over the head . . . I try to sit up, but my head swims. Jason hisses, "Cut my hands loose and I'll jump the sonofabitch."

Alice clutches my arm, digging her nails into my flesh. "He'll kill us," she rasps in my ear.

Davis turns back to us and grins. "Don't think I don't hear you guys whispering." He waves the gun at us. "Mattie, darling, are you telling me you just left these doors unlocked? That's plain careless. That shows an utter disregard for your own life, which I wouldn't mind so much except that you had my boy under your care. Now let's see . . . there must be a way to secure this entry . . ." He looks around and plucks a short board from a shelf, then shoves it between the handles on the Bilco doors, effectively sealing them from the inside. Satisfied, he walks back to us and points the gun at Alice.

"Help her up," he barks, directing the gun toward me. "And don't even think about trying anything, bitches, or I'll put a bullet in both your brains. We're going to do as our hostess suggests and have a cozy meal by the fire upstairs. Then we're going to have a little talk."

Alice helps me up. As I clutch her hand I press it against the knife in my pocket so she knows it's there. I see her eyes widen. Davis has shifted his gaze to Jason, though, so he doesn't notice.

"Should I help him up, too?" Alice asks.

He cocks his head, considering the man on the floor. "Nah," he says, "too much trouble." Then he shoots Jason in the head.

CHAPTER TWENTY-FIVE

Alice

BLOOD SPRAYS ON my shoes and over my legs, and a smell like copper pipes hits me in the back of the throat.

"Why'd you do that?" I cry.

I'm not sure if I'm going to throw up or pass out. Mattie squeezes my arm so hard that the pain helps keep me from doing either. I look at her and see that she's pale but her jaw is set and she's staring at Davis like he's a science experiment.

"Too much trouble to keep track of the three of you," Davis says, his mouth stretched into something between a grin and a snarl. "Besides"—he looks up, his eyes glittering like he's got a fever—"he was gonna mess with you. You two should be thanking me. And you can start by getting me something to eat and a nice cold beer. Woo-hee! Killing's thirsty work!"

My stomach turns. Davis looks like he does when he's playing World of Warcraft. The reek of blood hits my throat again and I gag.

"Let's get upstairs," Mattie says, propelling me forward. "There's nothing we can do for Jason."

"You sound almost sorry for him," Davis says as he follows us up, holding the gun to my back. "Maybe the idea of a man breaking into your house turns you on. Maybe *that's* why you leave all your doors unlocked. I mean, when *was* the last time you got laid?"

Mattie flinches and I instantly regret that I wondered the same thing when I went through her bedroom. The thought that living with Davis for two years has made me anything like him sickens me almost as much as seeing what happened to Jason. Only Mattie's grip on my arm keeps me moving up the stairs.

Davis holds the flashlight so we can see our way but the beam is dim and flickering. At the top of the stairs he moves the beam over the darkened kitchen and I catch a flicker of movement in the doorway leading to the front door. My heart stops at the thought that it could be Oren, but Davis keeps moving his flashlight over the kitchen counters so he must not have seen what I did.

"We need to get a fire going in the woodstove," Mattie says. "It's right over there." She points at the corner opposite to where I saw the movement. Maybe she saw it too and wants to make sure Davis doesn't.

"Okay," Davis says. "Here's the plan. Allie and I are going to sit down here at the kitchen table while you get that stove going and warm us up something to eat." He pulls out one chair with his foot and pushes me toward it, then sits in the one next to it. As soon as I'm seated he presses the cold barrel of the gun to my forehead. "If you do anything stupid I'll blow her brains out. Understand?"

Mattie turns to Davis and looks him straight in the eyes. Her face looks awful in the beam of the flashlight—haggard and old—but she doesn't look afraid. She looks pissed. "Yes, I understand," she says. "I just need to get those matches on the table by your elbow."

Davis switches the beam to the table to find the matches. As he looks away from Mattie she reaches behind her to the counter and slips something into her pocket. Another knife, I'm betting. Now she's got two.

"What the fuck is this?"

For a second I think Davis has seen what Mattie did, but when I look at him I see he's training the flashlight on a plastic figurine standing beside the matches on the kitchen table. It's an Ewok with a Post-it note stuck to it.

"Oren left that there before," I say, even though I am sure that it wasn't there before. "He was playing a game."

Davis rips the note off the Ewok and reads it aloud. "'Don't worry. The rebel alliance is on the way to help. May the Force be with you!'" He crumples the note up and throws it on the floor, his mouth twisted with disgust. "More of that *Star Wars* fantasy shit you've been encouraging him to believe. It's time the boy grew up and learned the way the world really works. DO YOU HEAR THAT, OREN? THERE'S NO REBEL ALLIANCE ON THE WAY SO YOU MIGHT AS WELL COME OUT AND KEEP YOUR OLD MAN

COMPANY." He pauses, waiting for an answer, then tosses the matches at Mattie. "Get that stove going."

Mattie catches the matches handily and turns toward the stove, but Davis barks, "Wait, light these lamps first so I can see what you're doing over there."

I can see by the slump in her shoulders that Mattie is disappointed. I bet she'd been counting on being able to work in the dark. But she comes back to the table and lights the three kerosene lamps that she'd put there earlier. They're real old-fashioned lamps that cast a surprising amount of light. One's a square hurricane lamp with metal reflectors that sends out a beam like a lighthouse.

"Take that one over to the stove," Davis says, pointing at the hurricane lamp, "and put it on the top so I can see what you're doing over there."

Mattie gives Davis a look like he's a simpleton but quickly washes that expression off her face. "I'm not sure it's a good idea to leave kerosene on top of a lit woodstove," she says tentatively. She's treading carefully around Davis's temper, as I have learned to do over the last two years, and though it makes me feel sick to watch her do it—and to realize how second nature it's become to me—it works. Although a muscle twitches in Davis's eye, he waves her away as if such details are beneath him.

"Yeah, whatever, you women always worry about shit like that."

I catch the hint of a smile before Mattie turns away with the lantern. She places it carefully on a counter two feet from the woodstove, then kneels beside the basket of wood and begins putting logs, paper, and kindling into the stove. Travis and Lisa had a woodstove and it was always a bitch to light, but Mattie's got a real nice fire going in a few minutes.

"I could get the chili from the stove," I offer, itching to move around.

"That's nice of you, Allie," Davis says, "but I feel better with only one of you gals up and about."

"I'll get it," Mattie says, standing up and brushing wood shavings from her pants. "Is that okay with you, Davis? Can I go to the stove and get the chili?"

"Knock yourself out," Davis says, grinning. He's enjoying ordering around one woman while I sit captive beside him. He leans back, tipping the chair off its front two legs, resting his hand with the gun on the table.

"So," Mattie says as she puts the chili on top of the woodstove and stirs it. "You certainly made good time getting here."

"Ha!" Davis barks. "I was already on the Thruway when I got Allie's call. I figured she'd head upstate. She was always yammering about the crap foster homes she lived in up here, so I figured she must have some connections. When I got into town I spotted that charity place on Main Street right off the bat and figured she'd have gone there. I went in, pretending to be shopping at the free store, and overheard a couple of college kids talking about Mattie Lane taking a DV case home. Did you know you can google a person and find their address on the internet?" He taps his forehead. "Smart, huh?"

Mattie nods. "I can certainly see where Oren gets his

brains. He's such a bright, sweet boy. I hated to see him land in a shelter."

"You're right there," Davis says, thumping his chest with his hand. He's left the gun lying on the table. "He sure as hell didn't get his smarts from his idiot meth-head mother, who didn't have enough brains to keep herself from OD'ing."

"Oren mentioned his mother was away a lot. Rehab, I guessed. It must have been tough being left with a kid on your own like that."

"Tough?" Davis slaps the table, the two front legs of his chair hitting the floor, the gun jumping a few inches in my direction. "You don't know the half of it. Your lot were no help. When I signed up for the food bank I got a lot of nosy questions about bruises on Oren's arms, like kids aren't always getting themselves scraped up."

"That must have been painful," Mattie says gently, "to feel suspected of hurting your own child when you were only trying to do your best by him."

"No shit, Sherlock!" Davis says, leaning back again. "You social worker types, you don't trust men. A single mother, you're all over her trying to help, but a single dad? You look at him like he's a pervert."

"I always tell my volunteers and interns to check their biases at the door, to give everyone who comes to us the benefit of the doubt. But it can be hard—seeing all the things we do—not to sometimes suspect the worst in people."

"I get that," Davis says, nodding his head. "Hey, you got any beer?"

Mattie turns from the stove and smiles. "I think I've got a couple of Coors stashed in the back of the fridge."

"No kidding? I would have figured you for a white wine kind of gal."

"Nah," Mattie says, walking to the refrigerator and opening it. It's dark inside and I'm hoping that she has a gun stashed there with all the bottles she's rattling around. "I like a cold beer in summer and a snort of whiskey in winter. Here—" She pulls out a bottle and brings it into the light of the table, twisting the cap open and handing the bottle to Davis. While Davis leans forward to take it from her, Mattie cuts her eyes over to where the gun lies on the table and then to me. "I bet that chili's real hot now," she says to Davis, still looking at me. "Are you ready for a bowl?"

"Damn yes," he says, leaning back in his chair, the front legs coming off the floor again. I always tell Oren not to do that because the chair could slip out from underneath him.

I look back at Mattie. She's ladling chili into a bowl, steam rising up from it. It *is* hot. She's going to throw the chili in Davis's face to give me a chance to grab the gun. As she turns from the stove I nod at her to let her know I understand and that I'm on board.

"You know, Mattie," Davis says as she approaches. "You're not so bad—"

I lay my hand on the table and tense, ready to grab the gun.

"—it's too bad your father was such a corrupt asshole."

"What?" I say, and then curse myself for saying anything.

Davis looks at me and then at my hand. He rocks forward

and snatches up the gun. "Your new friend didn't tell you about that, Allie?" he says. "Her father was a corrupt judge. I found out while I was poking around his office before. He was being investigated for taking kickbacks to put juvies in a private detention center owned by one of his cronies." Davis laughs. "Ironic, huh? He could have been one of the judges who locked you up, Allie. Only he killed himself and his family before the scandal could come out."

"That's not true," I say, turning to Mattie, but I can see on her face right away that it is.

Davis laughs. "You were always too naive, Allie." He waves the gun at Mattie. "Let's eat and then we'll go have a look at those papers in your daddy's study. Wait'll you see, Allie. I think you'll be surprised at what your new friend has been hiding from you."

CHAPTER TWENTY-SIX

Mattie

STUPID. STUPID TO care what this asshole has to say about my father. Stupid to care about my father after all these years. After the things he did.

And we were so close. Alice definitely got my signal. All I had to do was throw the chili in Davis's face and she'd have gotten the gun. Now we're all sitting around the table eating chili—well, Davis is eating while the bowls in front of me and Alice go cold—and Alice is looking at me as if *I'm* the enemy.

They'll drag his name through the mud and yours and Caleb's along with it. It will bring up all that old business about your time at Hudson. That's how people will see you, Mattie, like you're tainted by your father's deeds. Do you want that?

No, I hadn't, and I don't now. I'd rather Davis shot me right now and got it over with, but I've got Alice and Oren to think about, and anything that uses up time until Frank gets here is useful. "Would you like another bowl?" I ask after Davis has finished his second and is on his third beer. "Another beer?"

"Nah. I'd better keep my wits about me. Don't think I don't see you two ladies giving each other the side-eye. I had kinda hoped Oren would've joined us by now, though. HOW ABOUT IT, SON? JOIN US FOR SOME CHILI?"

Davis's booming voice echoes in the house, which feels bigger and emptier outside the circle of our lamplight. Is Oren even still here? I hope he hasn't tried to go outside. I think of Caleb's frozen body and reflexively check the window that faces the barn, but the snow has mounded so high on the sill that I can't see anything except that it's still snowing.

"Expecting someone?" Davis asks.

"No one's getting out here," I say, shaking my head. "Or out of here, for that matter. We could be snowed in for days. Where did you leave your car?"

"Never you mind," he snaps.

I shrug. "I was just wondering what your exit plan was. Do you have four-wheel drive? A plow?"

"What would I need those for?"

"To get out before the police come checking on me. I'm friends with the chief of police. He'll come out once the snow stops tomorrow to see if I need help digging out." This last part is true even though Frank and I haven't exactly been *friends* for years; he still checks up on me after snowstorms and hurricanes. "Jason's truck has a plow. You might want to check his pocket for keys. Do you know how to operate a plow?"

"Of course I do!" he says in an angry voice that tells me he absolutely doesn't. "I'm surprised you do."

I shrug. "Living out in the woods all alone like I do, you pick up these things."

"Well, then you can help drive when we're ready to go. And we'll worry about that key later." He smiles slyly. "I think you're just trying to put off our little trip down memory lane in your daddy's study. But I suspect Allie here is looking forward to it, aren't you, Allie?"

Alice shrugs. "Why should I care? I already know her folks died here in a gas leak." She takes out a bit of newsprint from her jeans pocket and unfolds it on the table. As Davis leans forward to read it I recognize my father's picture. Seeing his face makes me go cold all over, as if he were here, sitting in judgment of us all.

"This doesn't say nothing about him being under investigation," Davis says. "You got it hushed up, eh? Figures. Rich judge's daughter living in a big fancy house, you probably had your daddy's cronies sweep all the nastiness under the rug."

I raise one eyebrow. "Does the state of this house look like I have a lot of money?"

"That's true," Alice says. "Everything's falling apart here. Even the clothes she's wearing have holes in them. I don't think she's got two dimes to rub together, Davis."

Davis gives Alice a condescending smirk. "That just shows how you don't understand rich people, Allie. Least not the snooty old-money kind. They *love* to look like they don't care. Like your buddy Scott, the way he dressed in raggedy jeans and faded old T-shirts." Alice blanches at the mention of Scott. "And this bitch . . . well, one look through her daddy's papers will show you how rich he was. He owned half the real estate in town, not to mention farmland all over the county and interest in some surprising ventures. She probably has bags of money stowed away—and she's gonna give us some to keep quiet about her daddy's secrets." Davis tilts back the last of his beer while Alice looks at me as if she's considering how much I'm worth. As if she's considering which side she's on. Then Davis slams the empty beer bottle to the table. "Let's go have a look, Allie. You might've made our fortune by landing here!"

DAVIS GIVES ME the hurricane lamp to hold and has me walk ahead to the study while he follows behind, his arm linked with Alice's, the gun pointing at my back. I could crash the lamp to the floor and start a fire, but I can't risk that with Oren hidden somewhere. If I were sure of Alice's cooperation, I could kill the wick, plunging us into darkness, and whack Davis with it, but I'm no longer so sure she's on my side.

When I shine the light on the study door, I see it's closed. "That's funny," Davis says. "I left it open."

"It's a drafty old house," I say. "Doors swing shut on their own all the time. Sometimes they swing shut when there's no draft at all."

"Are you saying a *ghost* closed the door?" he says with heavy irony that fails to hide the tremor in his voice.

"There *is* something creepy going on in this house," Alice says. "I saw something down in that crawl space."

Did she? I wonder as Davis snaps, "Shut up, Allie. You're always imagining shit like that, like the poltergeist you and Oren dreamed up to mess with me."

I look back at Alice to see that she's white around the mouth. She's genuinely scared and not just of Davis. What *did* she see in the crawl space?

"Well, there must be a fucking key, Mattie." Davis jabs me in the back with the gun. "Where the hell is it?"

I consider for a moment pretending not to have the key, but I have a feeling that Davis is about to snap. He *really* doesn't like the idea of a ghost. There might be a way to use that to our advantage, and if it's ghosts I need, the best place to look is my father's study.

"It's over here on the sideboard." I swing the hurricane lamp toward the cut-glass bowl, which refracts the light into a kaleidoscope of prisms that dance over the wall and ceiling. It's an unnerving effect and Alice gasps.

"Yeah, yeah," Davis says, his voice high and nervous, "that's a good trick. Cut it out and get the key."

I obey, shifting the beam so that it doesn't touch the glass as I withdraw the key with a shaking hand. For a moment I thought I'd seen something forming in the play of light too. When I put the key in the lock, something occurs to me. If the door slammed shut after Davis it shouldn't be locked. It's the kind of lock that needs to be turned with a key on either side of the door. But it *is* locked.

As I turn the key to unlock the door I feel an icy chill. I pause in the doorway, reluctant to cross the threshold, but Davis gives me a nudge with the barrel of his gun. I hold the lamp up, suddenly terrified that I'll see my father sitting at the desk . . . but what I see is the broken window. Of course. This is how Davis got into the house in the first place. "We'll freeze to death in here with that broken window," I say.

"Draw the curtain over it and light that kerosene heater I noticed when I was in here earlier," Davis says. "Here, I even brought the kerosene." He draws a bottle out of his jacket pocket and gives it to me. While I pour kerosene into the heater, he nudges Alice into one of the straight-backed chairs in front of the desk. Again I think of how easy it would be to start a fire. Throw some kerosene on Davis, light him up. Burn the whole place down to the ground. But that would leave Alice, Oren, and me out in the snow, and we don't even know where Oren is. If he's holed up in the attic he could get trapped in the burning house.

When I've adjusted the flame on the heater I turn around. Davis is ensconced in my father's chair behind the desk, his gun lying on the blotter in front of him. It makes me sick to see him sitting there, but whether it's because of the insult to my father's memory or that Davis is beginning to remind me of my father, I'm not sure.

"Have a seat, Mattie." Davis gestures to the other straight-backed chair. "The show's about to begin."

I do not want to sit in that chair. It is where I sat when my father called me in, and I have not sat there again in all the years since my family died. "I don't mind standing," I say.

"SIT DOWN!" Davis bellows, pointing the gun at me.

I sit. Instantly I become the frightened little girl who's done something wrong. When I wasn't in trouble, my father would pat his knee and beckon me to sit on his lap while he read to me or showed me the constellations in the star globe. I knew I was in trouble when he motioned to the chair as if seating a witness in the dock.

I notice that I've folded my hands in my lap, the way I was supposed to when I awaited my father's judgment. I am digging my nails into my palms as I used to. I pry my hands apart and spread them on my knees and look at Davis. His face is framed by the figurines of Lady Justice and Lady Liberty that stand on either side of the pen set, just as my father's face used to be when I sat here.

"You two look like you've been called into the principal's office for . . . hmm . . . let me see . . ." He strokes his goatee. "Oooh, I know! Diddling each other in the little girls' room. Well, I'm gonna have to think of an appropriate punishment for that. But first, let's look at these files I found in your daddy's drawers . . ." He slaps his knee. "Ha! Get it? Your daddy's drawers?" When neither of us laughs he frowns. "You're right. This is a very serious business." He picks up a file. "I was just looking for some credit card numbers, loose cash, et cetera, and of course the first place I think to look is the locked drawer in the desk. Luckily the key to it was sitting right there in that little statue." He wags his finger at me. "You really ought to be more careful of your valuables, Mattie. I mean, sure, they look like just a bunch of old papers—I was kinda disappointed at first—but then I recognized the gold seal on them from my own judicial dealings with the great state of New York." He turns the file folder around to show us the front. It's stamped with the great seal of New York: Lady Liberty and Lady Justice holding up a shield containing mountains and a river, an eagle on top. The same image that is depicted in my father's pen set, the same image—

I look over at Alice and see she's leaning forward, her brow furrowed. I wonder if she's put two and two together. The great seal of New York is the image on the button she found in the crawl space. I slip my hand in my pocket and rub the rough metal surface—

"Hands where I can see 'em!" Davis barks.

I take my hand out and lay both hands flat on the desk.

"At first I thought, snore, what could be more boring than a bunch of old court cases—and they *are* old. They date all the way back to the early seventies. They're all juvie cases, all tried by your father, the Honorable Matthew T. Lane, and guess what? Your daddy found every one of them guilty!"

"He adjudicated them delinquent," I automatically correct. "There's no guilty verdict in juvenile court."

Davis sits back and makes an O with his mouth. "Well, la-di-da, look who knows her legalese. Why didn't you follow your daddy's footsteps into the law?"

"I didn't have the best experience with the legal system," I say.

Davis grins. "No, you didn't! Your own father *adjudicated* you a delinquent for . . . let me see . . ." He picks up another file. "Public indecency, apparently for making out with one Frank Barnes in a stolen car."

"Isn't that the name of that cop?" Alice asks.

"What cop?" Davis asks.

"The one Mattie's friends with."

"The plot thickens," Davis says gleefully. Digging through my family's secrets has banished all thoughts of ghosts. The only ghosts here are ghosts of my benighted childhood.

"I told Alice all this before," I say, affecting boredom. "Yes, Frank's father, the town chief of police, caught Frank and me making out in the backseat of his dad's Dodge Dart. Frank got sent to Camp Maplewood—a boot camp—for six months and I got three months at the Hudson Training School."

"I thought you said you were away for a year," Alice says.

"I—I got more time for bad behavior," I say. "So yeah, I was a bad, bad girl and my father was a draconian hard-ass—"

"Who sent all his juvies to a place called Pine Crest Child Care after 1975," Davis supplies. "Why didn't he keep sending them to Hudson?"

"Because Hudson closed down in 1975. My father led the fight to have it closed down."

"Because of what happened to you there."

"In part."

"Oh, I think in large part, Mattie. It says here"—he plucks a loose sheet of paper off the desk—"that you were raped by a guard there."

I don't answer. I am gripping the edge of the desk to keep from shaking, but it's making the desk shake instead. Lady Justice's scales tremble and chime.

"Is that true, Mattie?" Alice asks in a small voice.

"Yes," I say. "My father hadn't counted on that consequence of my adjudication. Ironic, huh? They sent me away to teach me a lesson for making out with a boy and I get raped by a thirty-four-year-old guard."

"Your father had the place closed down. The guard was sentenced to ten to twenty. The next year Pine Crest Child Care opened up—a brand-spanking-new juvenile facility! I'm surprised he didn't name it for you, Mattie. You must have felt proud!"

"Hey," Alice says, "I was at Pine Crest. It's—"

"Not as bad as Hudson," I say, "but that's not saying much."

"No, but your daddy sure thought it was great. He sent every one of his *adjudications* there . . . almost as if he had a financial interest in the place . . . oh wait . . ." Davis whips out a piece of paper from another pile. I'd be impressed with how he's put the whole story together if I didn't know how all the papers had been stacked in that bottom drawer. I've made it easy for him. "Look, he did! Pine Crest was built on land your family owned. Your father held a ten percent share of the facility, so every time he sent some kid there he made a pretty penny."

"It's like that 'kids for cash' scandal in Pennsylvania," Alice says, staring at me.

"Exactly," Davis crows. "Only Judge Lane never got caught—at least he hadn't gotten caught. This here letter, though, from the federal prosecutor, says that they were gonna be looking into some irregularities and unorthodox connections between Judge Lane's adjudications and his financial interests in Pine Crest. It's here with all the other files." Davis waves his hand at the stacks arrayed on the desk. "And here's another thing I noticed." He holds up another page, this one splattered with bloodstains. I know what's on this one. It's my father's suicide note. It was on his desk when I found him.

"Forgive me," he'd written, "but justice must be served."

"Your daddy shot himself, didn't he, Mattie? Because he knew the feds were coming for him."

"I thought your family all died from carbon monoxide poisoning," Alice says, giving me a suspicious look.

"He tampered with the pipes on the furnace so that the house would fill with gas," I tell Alice. I don't care about explaining to Davis but Alice deserves the truth. She's too young to have been one of those kids my father sent to Pine Crest for a minor offense, but if she had ever been in my father's courtroom that's what would have happened to her. "I think he thought that the shame of the scandal would be too much for us to live with. He may have been right about my mother; she was in the early stages of Alzheimer's and would have been truly lost without him. I can even forgive him for including me in his plans. He thought I was *ruined* after what happened to me at Hudson. He blamed himself—that's why he contributed to having Pine Crest built—but I once overheard him saying to my mother that it would have been better if I had been murdered. He said being raped had turned me into a promiscuous slut."

"Why *didn't* you die that night?" Alice asks.

"I wasn't here. I was, true to my promiscuous nature, out with a guy. Frank Barnes, to be precise. Only we had a fight and I came back early. I came in through the basement and up the back stairs. I didn't realize that there was gas in the house until I got to Caleb's room. I could barely rouse him. I dragged him down the front stairs and met my father at the bottom." I pause, as breathless as I'd been in that headlong flight from my home all those years ago. "He was coming out of this room, a bandanna over his mouth, waving his gun. I turned and pushed Caleb out the front door—I told him to run—and I was right behind him in the doorway when I heard a gunshot. Then everything went black. When I came to, Frank was here. He'd found me lying in the doorway, outside in the air enough that I didn't asphyxiate, but inside enough so I didn't freeze to death. The bullet had only grazed my scalp, knocking me out but not causing any real injury. Caleb . . ." I gulp air that tastes like blood and gasoline, the smells I've carried with me since that night. "Caleb wasn't so lucky. Frank's father found him in the barn, his head caved in. My father must have chased him out there and killed him. Then he came back in, stepped over my body, presumably thinking I was dead, went into his study, and shot himself."

I look away from Alice to Davis. "He was sitting where you are now, blood splattered all over the papers on his desk, those papers you've got out now, and even over that window . . ." As I look up at the window my voice freezes. Part of the window has been covered by the drapes to keep the cold and snow out, but the uncovered part is frosted by mist and covered with the same splatter marks I saw that night when I made Frank and his father show me what had happened.

No one has to know he went like this, Hank Barnes had said to me. *You don't want the world to see him like this. They'll drag his name through the mud and yours and Caleb's along with it. It will bring up all that old business about your time at Hudson. That's how people will see you, Mattie, like you're tainted by your father's deeds. Do you want that?*

No, I had told him.

Then let me help you put this behind you. The medical examiner is a good friend of mine and your father's. He'll say they all died of carbon monoxide poisoning. It's what your father wanted. After all, the person who is guilty has been punished. I think your father would agree that justice has been served.

That's what the splatter pattern on the window looks like. The constellation of Virgo. Justice. The same pattern that has appeared on every window in the house, in the stars in Caleb's room, written in the dust on my father's desk. If justice has been served, then why is Caleb still demanding it? Is it because I hid the truth?

As if in answer to my unvoiced question I see a figure rise up on the other side of the frosted glass—a specter coalescing out of swirling snow. But it's not Caleb; it's Frank Barnes. He has a gun in one hand; his other hand is clenched in a fist. When he's sure that I see him he holds one finger up. This is a signal we had when we used to play war games in the woods with Caleb. He's counting to five. I'm supposed to do something on the count of five. But what? Out of the corner of my eye I see that Alice is leaning across the desk looking at some paper Davis is showing her. That's why she doesn't see Frank—who's put up a second finger and is pointing the gun at Davis. *Oh.* I nod, and Frank puts up a third finger. I brace my left foot on the ground and pivot slightly toward Alice while keeping Frank in my peripheral vision. Four fingers. I check that there's nothing behind Alice that will strike her head. Then as Frank begins to lift a fifth finger I spring forward and tackle Alice to the ground at the same second that the window explodes.

CHAPTER TWENTY-SEVEN

Alice

DAVIS IS SHOWING me a stamped certificate of some kind when Mattie tackles me to the ground. For a moment I think it's because she doesn't want me to see what's on the certificate—it's got one of those stamps on it with the two Greek ladies—but then I hear a gunshot and glass explodes over our heads. There's a thump behind the desk, and when I open my eyes I see Davis lying on the floor, blood covering his chest. *Thank God*, I think, *thank God he's finally dead*.

But then his arm moves. The gun he'd been holding on us was on top of the desk, but I remember that it's not the only gun he has. "He's going for the gun in his back pocket," I hiss in Mattie's ear as I struggle to get out from under her.

Mattie rolls off me and hisses back: "Run! Find Oren. Look in the attic." She scrambles under the desk, trying to reach the gun before Davis does.

I feel like a coward leaving her but I need to find Oren

and I want to get away from Davis. As I run from the study I hear another shot and another explosion of glass. I don't wait to see who's shot; I sprint up the front stairs and into Caleb's room, dive under the bed, and scramble through the panel to the back stairs. The attic, Mattie said, so I grope around until I find stairs that go up, wishing I had a flashlight. Anything could be on these stairs. Spiders. Mice. *Ghosts.*

One particular ghost. A little boy whose own father killed him thirty-four years ago. Caleb Francis Lane. It was his birth certificate that Davis had been showing me—

Something brushes against my hand. Spiderwebs, I tell myself, but then the spiderweb grows fingers that intertwine themselves with mine. Small fingers, ten-year-old boy fingers. The same cold hand that clasped mine in the crawl space and gave me the button. Caleb Francis Lane, born May 10, 1973, at St. Alban's Hospital, and he wants to tell me something. Just like Oren wanted to tell me his secrets through the tin can phone that day.

Part of me wants to wrench my hand away. But I don't. I let this ghost boy lead me up the stairs, navigating the dark far better than I could.

At the top of the stairs I can tell we're in a lofty space because I can hear the snow pattering on the roof high above my head. As my eyes adjust I start to make out a glow too, swirling through the dark as if the snow has gotten in and turned into glitter. I turn to share the wonder of it with the boy at my side but my hand is empty. And then I have the sense that he is *everywhere.* That he is the glow that moves through the dark and the heart of the light coming from the center of the attic.

I walk across the wide wooden planks toward the source of the light. It's a lit snow globe revolving slowly on its base, playing a faint tinny lullaby. "Twinkle, Twinkle, Little Star," I realize as I get closer. In a circle around the globe is a battalion of toys: Ewoks and Wookiees, but also dinosaurs and Beanie Babies. They're standing guard over the boy who sleeps, curled up in a Tauntaun sleeping bag, inside the circle.

I kneel and brush the dark curly hair from his warm forehead. He opens his eyes. "Alice," he says, yawning. "You found me."

"Of course I found you, buddy," I say, wrapping my arms around him and drawing him into my lap. "We're a team, aren't we? And you left good clues."

Oren nods, squeezes me once tightly, then wriggles out of my arms. "Some of those were Caleb's idea. Look"—he digs in a box next to the sleeping bag—"these were his baby things."

He takes out a pair of hand-knitted baby booties and a tiny baby hat. Then a blanket with the initials CFL embroidered on it. When he shakes out the blanket a picture falls out. It's an old faded Polaroid of a woman in a hospital bed holding a baby. No, not a woman. A girl. A teenage girl. I peer closer at the picture. Even though she's so much younger in the picture, even though I've only known her for hardly longer than a day, I recognize her. It's Mattie. Fifteen-year-old Mattie holding baby Caleb. Caleb Francis Lane, born May 10, 1973, mother—

That's what the certificate Davis was showing me said. Mother: Mattea Celeste Lane. Father: Unknown. Mattie, who was raped at the Hudson Training School, got pregnant. And *had* the baby. What monster would make a fifteen-year-old rape victim *have* the baby?

Judge Matthew T. Lane, that's who. The same monster who sent kids away to juvie for kickbacks from the JD he sent them to. He probably thought he was teaching Mattie a lesson. She'd fooled around with a boy and look what it had led to.

Poor Mattie. I look at the girl in the picture. She was hardly more than a child herself and yet her face is glowing. She loved that baby. Caleb. I think of the picture on her night table and the way she looked when she talked about him dying. She isn't mourning a lost brother; she's mourning a lost son.

"Is this what Caleb wanted us to know?" I ask Oren. "That he was Mattie's son?"

Oren wrinkles his brow the way he does when he's tackling a tough math problem. "I think there's something else. I found this." He holds out a button, identical to the one I found in the basement. I hold it under the light of the snow globe and examine it. It's worn and corroded, so it's hard to make out the pattern on it. Some kind of crest, like the fancy buttons on blazers. Scott had a blazer like that, only he said he was wearing it *ironically*. This has a crest with an eagle on top and two figures of women in drapes—

Just like the seal on the judge's folders and the birth certificate. It's the seal of New York State.

"Who would wear buttons with the seal of New York State on them?" I ask.

"Policemen," Oren says without hesitation. "New York State policemen. Like that policeman Mattie was talking to."

"Huh," I say, turning the button around in my hand. "So why would there be a policeman's button down in the crawl space behind the furnace—"

Suddenly a terrible thought occurs to me.

"Oren," I say. "I have to ask you a question and I really, really, really need you to tell me the truth. I promise I won't be mad at you no matter what the answer. Mattie's life might depend on it."

"I understand," Oren says with a solemn nod that makes him look like he's grown years older since we arrived at this house. "I'll tell the truth. I promise."

I hold up the button. "Did you put a button like this in the crawl space behind the furnace?"

"No," he says, shaking his head. "I haven't been in the basement. I was too scared to go down there."

"Shit," I say, forgetting that I promised myself to watch my language around Oren. "We have to get downstairs right now."

CHAPTER TWENTY-EIGHT

Mattie

THE GUN—THE ONE Davis took off Jason—has slid underneath the bookcase and Davis is crawling toward it. There's another explosion of glass and a concussive thud as half the desk shatters in a spray of woodchips and paper. Sawdust rains down on my head.

I crawl under the desk, hoping that Frank will stop shooting. I hear glass breaking but no gunshot; Frank must be clearing enough glass to get inside. I wriggle toward the bookcase beside Davis. The floor is slick with his blood, which, disgusting as it sounds, makes me go faster. I reach under the bookcase at the same time he does, our hands touching over the cold metal of the gun, and before he can grab it away from me I slip my other hand in my pocket, take out the knife, and jab it into his arm, aiming for the open bullet wound.

Davis lets out a howl that barely sounds human and lets go

of the gun. I grab it and pull it out from under the bookcase. Something comes with it that scrapes and skitters across the floor but I don't have time to worry about that. I roll away from Davis, out from under the desk, and come up in a crouch, bracing the gun with two hands. I take the safety off and point it at Davis. "All I can reach from this angle is your groin," I say, "so you can either lie still or lose your balls."

"I'd listen to her," Frank says as he steps across the sill and picks up Davis's gun from the desk. He points his own gun at Davis's head. "I've been calling her a ballbuster for years and I wasn't being metaphorical."

I smile in spite of myself.

"The cunt stabbed me right in my wound!"

Frank kicks Davis in the stomach. "Don't use that language around a lady," he says as Davis screams and rolls into a ball. "Or I'll stick this gun up your ass."

"Do you want me to get tape to bind his hands?" I ask. "There's some in the dining room."

"Yeah," Frank says to me. Then to Davis: "Roll over, asshole, hands behind your back."

"Oh man, don't tie them behind my back. That will hurt like a mother—"

Frank lands another kick in Davis's side. I turn and go for the tape. The sooner we've got Davis bound the better. For us—and maybe for Davis too. I've glimpsed this violent side of Frank once or twice before. I blame the boot camp my father sent him to, and then the military school his father sent him to after that. He's never really been the same since.

I grab the roll of packing tape from the dining room and turn back to the study. Frank has hauled Davis into my father's chair. His arms are wrenched behind his back, which really does look painful, and his face has gone chalk white. I secure his hands with the packing tape and then his torso to the chair. I have to put down the gun, but I'm careful to put it on top of the bookcase, next to the hurricane lamp, far away from Davis.

"Get his feet too," Frank tells me.

When we've got him secured, Frank spins the chair around and jabs the gun into the middle of Davis's chest. "What the fuck were you thinking, asshole?"

"I was only trying to get my son back, man. My crazy-ass girlfriend kidnapped him. And this cu—woman was hiding them. That can't be legal, man, can it?"

"He also killed a man downstairs," I offer. "That guy Jason who was bothering Atefeh at Stewart's the other night. He followed us here and Davis shot him *after* we tied him up."

Frank looks at me and shakes his head. "Damn, Mattie, you sure as hell know how to make enemies. Anyone else you pissed off I should know about?"

I take a deep breath. Frank's gruff ribbing has calmed my racing heart. "I don't think our Republican congressman is too fond of me after my last email to his office, but since he can't even be bothered to show up at our town halls, I don't think he'll be making an appearance here."

Frank smiles—the first real smile he's given me in thirty-four years—and, God help me, I feel the stirring of an unaccustomed hope. Doreen always says that out of our darkest moments come our greatest gifts. I've always thought that was bullshit, but if Frank and I can come out of this night . . . *friends,* well then it won't have been a total loss.

Frank's smile vanishes when he looks down at the desk. The gunfire has scattered some of the files and papers to the floor but there's still a few stacks on the desk. He picks up one of the files and gives it a puzzled look. "What's all this?"

I think about the last thing that Davis was showing Alice and feel a quiver of dread. I am not ready for Frank to see *that.* "Davis nosed around in here and found some files that were locked in the bottom drawer . . ." I look down at the files, but I don't see the birth certificate anywhere on the desk. "The files my father was looking at the night he died. Davis thought he could blackmail me by threatening to expose him. As if I care who knows about that now. Sometimes . . ." I look up at Frank and find that he's staring at me. "Sometimes I think it would have been better if we'd come clean about it all back then."

"Oh, Mattie," he says, hanging his head. "What's the use of going over all that? We did what we thought best. We were only trying to protect you. You need to let it go—you need"—he gestures at all the papers—"to get rid of all this. I can't believe you held on to it all."

He's right; I never have let it go. Ever since that night I've blamed myself for what happened to Caleb. And although it had made sense when Frank's father said they could make my family's death look like an accident, it had felt dirty. *I* had felt dirty. "I thought . . . I thought that someday I might be able to make amends to all these kids"—I wave at the papers on the desk and those that have spilled over the floor—"all the kids my father sent away."

"Haven't you done that by building Sanctuary?" Frank says. "And by starting the home for at-risk youth? The battered women's shelter? All financed by your parents' estate."

"It's not enough. Those kids' lives were ruined. Look at what it did to us."

"Actually, I think getting sent to boot camp was the best thing that ever happened to me," Frank says, anger sharpening his voice. "It wiped clean all my illusions. I saw the world for what it really was. And as for all those kids your father sent to Pine Crest, hell, most of them were thugs who were better off for the experience. I know because my father arrested most of them—"

A low chuckle from Davis stops Frank cold. I think we'd both forgotten he was there. "What are you laughing at, asshole?" Frank demands.

"Oh, not you, buddy, *her*. She doesn't know, does she?"

"Know what?" I ask, and then mentally kick myself for playing into his game.

"His father wasn't the arresting officer on *most* of the cases in that stack. He was the arresting officer on *all* of them. I noticed it right away. He was probably in on the whole thing."

Frank's jaw is clenched and his eyes are narrowing, looking at me as if I'm the dangerous criminal. I take a step toward him to reassure him and my foot lands on something . . . a metal button, which I see, when I kneel down and pick it up, has the same pattern as the one Alice found in the basement, the seal of New York State. Did it fall out of my pocket? But when I check, the other button is still there.

I glance up from the button to Frank, and my eye catches on his uniform. On the buttons. New York State police officer buttons emblazoned with the state seal. Well, sure. Frank's father sat in this office a thousand times and could have lost a button any of those times—

But how did he lose one in the crawl space behind the furnace?

"Frank? Is that true? Was your father involved in putting those kids away at Pine Crest?"

"And what if he was?" Frank snaps, all the softness gone from his voice now. "Those kids needed a firm hand. I see it all the time now—kids getting away with too much, their parents going too easy on them. Your father knew that, but he was too high-minded to understand what it took to make a place like Pine Crest work. When he found out a few details that weren't up to his standards he was going to turn my father in. Can you blame my father for wanting to stop him?"

"*Stop him?*" I ask, appalled. "By killing him? What about my mother? What about Caleb?"

"My father said they would be all right. He planned to come by and rescue Caleb and your mother, but then you came home. You were supposed to be with me but then we fought and you came back here. When you came down the stairs with Caleb, your father revived and came out of the study, and Caleb ran and saw my father."

I replay the scene in my head: my father stumbling out of his study, waving his gun . . . not at me and Caleb, but at Hank Barnes standing in the doorway behind me. "I heard a shot . . ."

"Your father fired at my dad. You were turning. If you had seen my dad we would have had to kill you too, so I hit you over the head."

I feel like I've been hit over the head now. "You *let* your father kill Caleb?"

"I didn't know that's what he was going to do until it was done. What could I do about it then, Mattie? If I said anything my father would have killed you too. I kept quiet to save you. All these years . . . I could barely look you in the eye because of Caleb, but I knew that I had saved you."

"Aw," Davis says, "that's really kind of sweet . . ."

"If you don't shut the fuck up," Frank says, pointing the gun at Davis, "I will shut you up."

He's just trying to scare him, I think. The Frank I know wouldn't shoot an unarmed man. But then the Frank I knew wouldn't have gone along with covering up Caleb's death.

"Like father like son, eh?" Davis says.

Maybe, I think as I see Frank's finger tighten on the trigger, *I never knew him at all.*

Davis's head jerks back and seems to vanish in a red cloud. I hear a scream and turn to find Alice and Oren, openmouthed and wide-eyed, standing in the doorway.

"Run," I tell them.

CHAPTER TWENTY-NINE

Alice

I GRAB OREN and turn. Behind me I hear a scream and then a gunshot, and a bullet thuds into the wood sideboard two feet to our left. I push Oren toward the foyer, not looking back even when I hear a door slam behind us.

Oren wrenches open the front door and a gust of snow blows into the house. I try to stop him—we should stay in the house, hide in the basement or the attic—but he's already outside, barreling down the steps and into the snow. I am afraid we will both die out here like the boy in that story Lisa told us, but what choice do I have? I fling myself down the porch steps, landing in an open patch of ice at the bottom, stumbling to my knees.

When I look up I'm held by a sense of wonder. In front of me is the path Oren shoveled earlier today, impossibly free of snow. The howling wind must have blown the snow up into drifts that tower on either side, so that the path is like a tunnel carved out of ice. But what's truly remarkable is that it's *lit up*. There are little hollows scooped out of the ice where plastic figures stand—Han Solo, Princess Leia, Luke Skywalker, Chewbacca—all the *Star Wars* heroes glowing as if they were lit by candles. But there are no candles. The light seems to be coming from the snow itself, from the ice walls and the swirling crystals.

I remember the feeling I had in the attic that Caleb was in the glittering snow, and I'm certain that he is here now, lighting the path that Oren shoveled to the barn. In fact, I can just make out a figure on the path ahead of me, flickering in and out of focus as the wind scours the snow. It doubles, turns into one, and doubles again until there are two boys on the path. Caleb is leading Oren to the barn.

I used to dream that the frozen boy came knocking at my window. I would look outside and there he'd be, his white face shining like a second moon, his eyes dark as the surrounding night, his lips moving in a whisper only I could hear. All I had to do was open the window and take his hand, and we would fly away like Peter Pan and Wendy. He would take me to my *real* home, to my *real* mother.

But in the dream I also knew that he was dead and that if I went with him I would be dead too. So I wouldn't open the window, no matter how long he knocked or how many ice tears he shed. I'd wake up still hearing that knocking in my chest, the tears on my face chilling in the gray morning light.

Now Oren has taken the frozen boy's hand and is following him into the barn. *Take me instead,* I want to call out, but the wind would only whip my words to the sky. The path is already closing around me, snow drifting across the shoveled tunnel. I put my head down and push against the wind. *Take me, take me,* I whisper under my breath, *I'm ready.*

I fight my way to the barn door, which gapes open like a rotten tooth. I catch the whiff of iron I'd smelled earlier and know it now for what it is: the stench of death. As I see Oren go inside I brace myself for one last push against the wind, but the wind shifts, comes around behind me, and pushes me forward, so that I fly through that black hole, like I always knew I would if I took the frozen boy's hand. *It's easy to fly,* he whispered to me in my dreams, *all you have to do is let go.*

I land in the dark. There's no magical glow here, no Peter Pan pixie dust, just the smothering dark and the smell of death pressing in all around me. "Oren?" I whisper, afraid to shout in this place, afraid of what might answer back.

There's only a creak, and then another, somewhere in front of me, and then a rustle high above my head. For a moment I imagine that floating boy, grown wings, roosting in the rafters above my head, but then I remember the loft. Oren has climbed up the ladder to the loft, which is the best place to hide, especially if we can take up the ladder.

"Oren," I whisper again, this time a little louder, "I'm coming." I put my hands out and walk forward, trying to remember the layout of the barn. There was a path in the middle that was relatively clear, and the ladder was at the end of it. I should be able to find it if I walk straight ahead.

I shuffle forward, hands out, testing the terrain with my feet. Newspapers rustle underneath my steps, the brittle old pages whispering like gossips' tongues. What had that article said?

"Chief Henry Barnes discovered the body . . ."

But he was on the scene much earlier. That's what the button behind the furnace meant, that's what Mattie found out. Her cop friend's father killed her father, her mother—and then he followed Caleb out here to the barn and killed him too. I can smell blood here, getting stronger with every step I take—

My hand grazes something hard and cold. I push it away and it groans and screeches and swings back at me, hard cold iron slamming into my chest. It knocks the wind out of me but I manage to grab it and it judders in my hand, the sound traveling up and across the barn. How could I have forgotten that awful iron hook hanging from the ceiling by heavy chains? Mattie said it was how they hauled hay into the loft, but holding it now I can smell blood coming off it. This is where the smell comes from.

I leave the hook swinging behind me and keep walking toward the loft, holding my hands out until I find the ladder. Thank God Oren has left it down for me. I climb up, each step sounding loud as a gunshot in the snow-covered barn. When I reach the top I feel a hand on mine. I nearly flinch away and fall backward, but the hand is warm and so is the breath whispering in my ear.

"We have to lift up the ladder before he comes. Quick!"

I scramble into the loft and pull at the top rung of the ladder. I feel Oren's hands beside mine, but it's too heavy . . . and then another pair of hands is beside ours and the ladder lifts up. We slide it across the loft floor, stirring old hay and dust, the smell welcome after the reek of iron and blood.

"Oren?" I whisper, needing to know it's Oren here with me and not that other boy.

"Shh," Oren says, pushing me down flat on the floor. "He's here."

Does he mean Caleb? But then I hear a noise coming from across the barn, a footstep in the doorway. A flashlight beam slices the dark, lighting up a hulking figure of a man in the doorway. It's that policeman. When he sweeps the barn with the flashlight the light catches on all those brass buttons and the dull glint of a gun. Why is he here and not Mattie? Does that mean that Mattie is dead, that he's killed her? That we're all alone with this murderer?

The light travels across the barn, pausing on the hook, which is still swaying on its chain. Then the light moves swiftly upward toward the loft. I flatten myself down harder to the floor and reach out my right hand to squeeze Oren's warm hand—and my left to hold the bone-cold hand of the other boy.

CHAPTER THIRTY

Mattie

AS I TURN back to Frank I am praying that I will find that the last few minutes have been a product of my clearly deteriorating mind. Frank, my childhood best friend and first sweetheart, upstanding citizen and protector of justice in the village of Delphi, has not just blown out the brains of an unarmed, restrained man, and therefore it is also not true that his father murdered my family and he helped cover it up.

But as I turn I am also taking the second knife out of my pocket.

Hope for the best, prepare for the worst, my mother used to say.

When did you ever hope for anything good? my father, weary of her eternal pessimism, would quip back.

In this case the pessimists have it. Frank is aiming the gun at me, a sad but firm set to his face. I throw the knife at his right arm, a trick he taught me, and his shot goes wide, striking the sideboard as I run into the dining room. I slam the door behind me and am reaching for the key in my pocket when a second bullet rips through the door. I turn the lock, pocket the key, and run. Behind me I hear the rattle of the doorknob and then a thud as Frank throws himself at the door. *Good luck with that,* I think. My father had that door made from a four-inch-thick slab of oak, cut from a tree that had been planted before the Revolutionary War, and fitted with tempered steel hinges. He was a man who liked his privacy, my father.

A shot blows a hole in the lock, followed by a splintering thud. I run out into the foyer and see the open door, snow swirling in, footsteps in the snow on the porch. Alice and Oren have fled to the barn. I have an overwhelming urge to follow them—as I tried to follow Caleb that night—

When Frank hit me over the head. That's what blacked me out, not a graze from my father's bullet. Frank had been here. He knew what his father was planning. He'd known as we argued at the hollow.

Another blow to the door sends me up the stairs to get the gun from my bedroom. As I run up I remember the argument we'd had that night. It had started when he accused me of avoiding him all that Christmas break. He was right; I had been avoiding him. But not for the reason he thought.

It's your parents, isn't it? They disapprove of me.

Again, there was truth in that. My mother disapproved simply because the Barnes family was not in the same *class* as the Lanes. *The Barnes men are graspers,* my father had said one night at dinner, and my mother had chimed in, *That Hank Barnes is always hanging on to your coattails, Matthew.*

Because they were colluding on taking kickbacks from Pine Crest? Or because Hank Barnes was making sure my father didn't suspect *he* was?

"Forgive me, but justice must be served."

That wasn't my father's suicide note; it was part of a letter he'd sent to Hank Barnes.

What does it matter? I think as I reach my room. Either way, the end result was Caleb's death. He looks back at me now from the photograph on the night table. When he was born, Sister Martine put him in my arms. She told me I didn't have to go along with what my parents were planning.

What else can I do? I asked her. *I'd have to give him up to strangers otherwise.*

She had nodded and then said, *Your father thinks he is doing the right thing, the* just *thing, raising your son as his own, and he may be right. But justice isn't the same as love.*

I told her I knew that.

Then she showed me Caleb's birth certificate and where she'd written in my name. *No matter what,* she told me, *you're his mother. Don't ever forget that.*

I told her I never would.

When she asked me if she should write down a name for the father, I told her no. She thought it was because I didn't want to put my rapist's name down. I let her believe that.

I slide my hand under the mattress and pull out the gun,

just as I hear a violent crash from downstairs. I freeze, listening for footsteps, then take the safety off and walk carefully across the floor, avoiding the loose floorboards. Too bad I don't avoid Dulcie's paw. She whines as I crush it beneath my foot and I crouch quickly down to soothe her. Did Frank hear? Downstairs I hear his footsteps halt at the bottom of the stairs.

"Mattie," he calls, his voice soft and tentative. I haven't heard him say my name like that for thirty-four years. It's how he said my name that night we met at the hollow.

Mattie, he'd said when he saw me come down the path, his face lit up in the moonlight, *you came.* In that moment he looked like the boy he'd been before, and all I'd wanted was *that* boy back again. That summer, the summer Caleb was ten, we'd both been in Delphi for the first time since we were both sent away, and for a little while it was like we were fourteen and sixteen again. We'd spent the hot days swimming in the hollow and playing games in the woods with Caleb. Caleb had brought out the boy in Frank again, the boy who'd coaxed and sweet-talked me into the back of his father's car. I'd gladly given myself to him when I was fourteen and again when I was twenty-five. I could tell that boy about Caleb. I could tell him we could raise Caleb with Caleb's little sister.

I knew the baby I was carrying was a girl. I'd known since two weeks before Christmas, but I'd been afraid to see Frank because I didn't know what I wanted to do. Keep the baby? Give it up the way I'd given up Caleb, only worse, to strangers? I didn't even know if that *would* be worse than watching Caleb grow up under my mother's critical harping and my father's hard sense of justice. He was even harder on Caleb than he'd been on me. Maybe because he was a boy, or because he thought he was the child of a rapist. Would he have been easier on him if he'd known I was already pregnant when I was raped? That Caleb was Frank's? Maybe. But he wouldn't have been easier on Frank.

Maybe, though, it would have made a difference to Frank. Maybe he would have grown up differently if he'd known Caleb was his.

The night I went to meet Frank at the hollow I thought I could fix things. He'd called me and asked me to meet him. That had to mean he still cared. And when I saw that lit-up look on his face, and heard the soft way he said my name, I was ready to tell him everything. Frank had already taken his police exam and been hired as a deputy by the town. I would have my MSW in the spring and I knew that I could get a job at the youth center in Kingston where I'd interned. We could manage. And if my parents fought me on Caleb I had that birth certificate. I'd fight them until he was mine. I would never leave him again.

It may have been that determination that Frank saw on my face as I came into the moonlit hollow. He might have read it as defiance and Frank never did well with defiance. It awoke something *contrary* within him. I could see his face harden against me.

I didn't think you were coming, he said.

Of course I came, I should have said, *I love you.*

But I have always had a streak of the contrary myself. (*You'd argue that the sky was gray on a sunlit day,* my mother would say. *My little lawyer,* my father would call me with pride—until I argued with *him.*)

I said I would, I told Frank instead. *Did you think I'd break my word?*

You've been avoiding me since you got home from college. It's your father, isn't it? I know he disapproves of me.

I'm not a child anymore, I said, irked that he thought I was that weak-willed. *I don't have to do what he says. I'm getting my MSW in the spring.*

I only meant that I could get a job and support myself— and our child—but my going away to college and then graduate school had been a sore point. Two years at Ulster Community had been good enough for him.

I suppose you've found a new boyfriend there. A college boy—

That's right, Frank. He gave me his letter sweater and everything. Honest to God, I'm sick of the attitude around here that anything that doesn't come from this godforsaken backwater is suspect. God forbid anyone take advantage of New York City—

Then why don't you go back there?

I will. Maybe I'll go right now—

As I turned to go he reached out for me, but I could already feel tears stinging my eyes and I didn't want him to see me cry. If he did I would end up telling him I was pregnant. And then he would "do the right thing" and it was suddenly clear to me that we weren't right for each other. We couldn't go five minutes without bickering. We'd end up like my parents, fighting like cats and dogs every day of our lives. What good would that do Caleb? What chance would it give the baby I was carrying?

I wrenched my arm out of his grip and ran out of the hollow. I ran all the way home, through the woods so I wouldn't meet him on the road. I saw his truck pass by, looking for me—

To stop me from coming back while his father killed my family, I realize now. When he didn't find me, he must have driven ahead to warn his father. Maybe he really did plan to save Caleb and me, but when it came to a choice between my knowing what his father was doing and saving Caleb, he hit me over the head. How could he have been sure he wouldn't kill me?

Clearly he's ready to kill me now. But he hasn't come up the stairs yet. I listen for his footsteps, back braced against the wall, gun gripped in both hands. But I don't hear any footsteps at all. All I hear is the wind.

Coming from the open front door. He's not coming after me; he's gone after Alice and Oren in the barn.

CHAPTER THIRTY-ONE

Alice

I KNOW YOU'RE up there . . . Alice, isn't it? And Oren? There's no need to hide, you know. Davis is dead. Maybe I shouldn't have shot him, but you and I both know that even with two murders there was always a chance he'd get off. Our judicial system isn't what it should be. A lot of these bleeding-heart judges let men like that go. You should know that, Alice. That's why you had to run in the first place.

"I don't blame you for running and no one else will either. Nothing that's happened here has to affect you. Tomorrow I'll file a report that Davis followed you up here and tried to kill you and the boy, and I killed him to protect you. You can go home and file for custody of Oren. Mattie will help you; she's good at that kind of thing."

He pauses. He's a few feet in front of the hook, holding the flashlight beam on it as if he's afraid to walk by it in the dark.

"She's a good woman," he says, as if the silence had suggested otherwise, "but she's . . . not entirely right in the head. She's never been, not really, not since she was sent away to Hudson. It changed her. Those places do . . . well, *you* know that, Alice. I read your record . . . Oh, I know what you're thinking, juvenile records are sealed. But my father taught me how to read between the lines, the gaps between foster homes, the petty crimes after you turned eighteen. I'm betting you spent time in Pleasantville . . . or Pine Crest. So you know what it's like being locked up when you're just a kid for doing something stupid that a million other kids do and get away with. The way they treat you in there—the lice shampoos and cavity searches—your body not your own anymore, your mind not yours either. For some of us, withstanding that makes us stronger, but for others . . . it breaks them. It broke Mattie. My father told me she was raped. She could never trust anyone after that, especially not men. We tried . . . the summer she came home . . . we tried . . ."

He's let the flashlight drop down by his side, creating a circle of light that surrounds him like a pool. His face, uplit, has softened, like Mattie's did when she showed me the hollow and talked about teenagers making out there. That must be where they met. He's thinking about it now and it's made him look like a boy—not a man who just killed a man. Not a man who would hurt us.

"I thought she had recovered. I thought she trusted me. I was going to tell her that night what my father was planning to do. And I was going to tell her that I was *glad*." He looks defiant now. Like a boy still, but a boy who is ready to pick a fight. "Her father and mother deserved to die for what they did to her—to *us*. She would be free without them. Caleb would be better off without them . . ." His voice trails off as a flicker of doubt crosses his face, a furrow in his brow. ". . . I never, ever meant for Caleb to die," he says fiercely. "I loved him . . ."

"Like he was your own."

He spins around and aims the flashlight at the doorway. Mattie is standing there. She's holding a gun in her hand but it hangs by her side. His gun hangs at his side too.

"My father told me about what happened to you at Hudson . . . about the guard. He told me Caleb was yours . . . because of the rape."

Mattie shakes her head. "I was already pregnant when I was raped. Caleb was yours."

I can't see Frank's face but I can see his shoulders flinch as if she struck him. His voice cuts like steel through the dark barn. "You should have told me."

Mattie's voice is tired. "You were gone for ten years, Frank. The few times you came home, you didn't want to have anything to do with me."

"I couldn't face you." His voice cracks. He's still angry but now it's clear he's angry at himself. "What happened to you happened because of me."

Mattie's face crumples like a piece of old paper. "Oh, Frank, we were *kids*. None of it was our fault. It was my father and your father."

"I thought he'd made you hate me," Frank says. "When you came home that Christmas you avoided me."

Mattie hesitates. "I did, but only because I was afraid. I had something to tell you and I didn't know how you were going to react."

"You didn't trust me," Frank says bitterly. I don't have to see the change from soft to hard in his face; I see it mirrored in Mattie's.

"I didn't trust myself," she says. "I didn't know my own mind yet—what *I* wanted—and I had to know before I saw you. It wasn't just about you and me. It was Caleb and . . ." There's a pleading look on Mattie's face, so naked that I want to look away.

"And who?" Frank demands. "Who else mattered?"

"Our daughter," Mattie says. "I was pregnant. Again. Four months pregnant. I was afraid that once you knew I'd have to do what you wanted—keep it, end it. I needed to know what I wanted first."

Frank's back is tense as a board. "But you never gave me a chance to weigh in."

"We fought. And then when I got back to the house . . . well, you know what happened. After, I wanted to tell you but you had left town."

"So you ended it," he says, his voice flat.

Mattie bristles. "As would have been my right—"

"Are you going to give me a pro-choice speech *now*?"

"—but as it happens, I didn't. I went to St. Alban's and had the baby, a little girl. Then I gave her up for adoption."

"*Without* letting me know?" Frank demands.

"Without letting you know," she says, looking contrite. "Which I can see now was wrong."

"Oh, can you? That's very big of you, Mattea Lane. You were always . . . *fair*. I suppose you get that from your father. You get more and more like him, you know, as you get older. The same sanctimonious holier-than-thou superiority. Do you know that he pretended to my father that he didn't know what was going on? All the cases my dad brought before him—scumbag druggies, trailer park meth heads, snotty professors' kids—all those kids your father happily sent to Pine Crest Child Care, which was built on his land and which paid out dividends to your mother—"

"To my mother?" I can hear the surprise in Mattie's voice as well as distaste.

"And mine," Frank says impatiently. "That's how it worked. The director of Pine Crest paid money into an account in both our mothers' names. Your father pretended he didn't know. He pretended he never inquired into his wife's family's money, that he left all that to his accountant. What willful blindness! As if he was Justice with a blindfold over his eyes. When what did it matter? It was all in trust for you anyway."

"But my mother had Alzheimer's," Mattie says. "She wouldn't have known what she was doing."

"You tell yourself that, Mattie Lane," he barks at her, his voice rising with pure anger now. "Your mother liked living in a big, fancy house and lording it over all the other women in the village. Do you think a judge's salary was enough for that? She was happy to take the extra money and your father was happy to keep sending kids to Pine Crest. It was only when he thought the feds might be onto the scheme that he threatened to turn my father in."

"Oh, Frank," Mattie says with a sound somewhere between a laugh and a sob, "my father spent a lifetime *not* paying attention to my mother. And as for sending those kids to Pine Crest, I think he honestly thought it was the best thing for them." She wipes her face. "Don't you see? We're both victims of what our fathers told us."

I'd almost forgotten about Frank's gun, so I startle when he raises his arm and points it at Mattie. "I'm no one's victim." His voice is so cold that I shiver and clutch Oren's hand tight. My other hand, I realize, is empty.

"No," Mattie says, bending her knees until she can place her gun on the floor. "You're not a victim; you're a survivor. You're not your father and I'm not my father either. I don't need to see you in jail for what you did with your father or what you did to Davis. I just need to see Alice and Oren survive this night and go on their way. Then you can do to me what you like."

"Always the martyr," Frank says. "Do you think I haven't seen what you do? All the good works, living like a church mouse, sacrificing yourself for your derelicts and battered women, drug addicts and runaways. All so you can feel *good* about yourself, so you can lord it over the rest of us."

A muscle twitches in Mattie's jaw. I'm ashamed to think that this is what I thought about her only twenty-four hours ago.

"You're right," she says with a defiant tilt of her chin. "I'm a pathetic, vain old woman who likes people to think well of her. I'd never want it to come out that my father took money to send kids away. I agreed to your father's terms easily enough thirty-four years ago; I'll agree to yours now."

Frank steps forward, jamming the gun in Mattie's face. I hear a metal *click* that could be the sound of him cocking back the trigger. "And why should I trust a fucking word you say after all the lies you've told me?" he spits out.

"Because," Mattie says without a blink or a cringe, holding her ground while keeping her voice impossibly gentle, "look at the life I've built on *not* trusting."

A tremor goes through his whole body and I think, yes, she's got him. But then he shakes it off like a dog shaking water off its fur and he cocks the trigger—really cocks the trigger, I realize; that sound I heard earlier must have been something else. In fact, I hear it again now, coming from over our heads. I look up, but there's not enough light to see. I can smell oil and metal, though, and hear the ancient, rusted pulley moving the hook, which judders and groans like an animal being led to slaughter, and then, impossibly, it swings back.

Mattie screams and tries to pull Frank out of the way, but he resists her, turning to face—

I have one last glimpse of his face as he turns and then he drops the flashlight and I am spared what happens next.

A horrible *thunk* and Mattie's scream and the smell of blood and iron. Even though it's too dark to see I close my eyes and clutch Oren to me. Frank must have seen Caleb in that last moment, or why else would his face have opened like he was looking into the face of the person he loved most in all the world?

CHAPTER THIRTY-TWO

Mattie

FRANK IS TURNING back to me when the hook hits him and he falls into my arms. I catch him like I can save him, but I heard that blow to his head and know I can't. Still, I let him down gently to the ground, where the flashlight lies and shows me his face. There is still a flicker of life in his eyes—and the oddest expression. Not horror. Not surprise. But something I haven't seen on Frank's face since the night we got caught in his father's car. Love.

"Oh, Frank!" I cry. There's so much I want to tell him, so much I want to explain, but his eyes are already clouding over and his weight settles heavier into my arms. He's gone.

But what is left is that boy he once was. The hard lines of the man he became fall away. His jaw softens, the scowl lines around his eyes vanish. I'm looking down at the boy who coaxed me into his daddy's car forty-five years ago.

When he pulled up in the Stewart's parking lot in his

father's cruiser, I told him he was crazy. *Your father is the police chief, Frank Barnes, and this is government property.*

Stop being the judge's daughter for five minutes, Mattie Lane, and get in. It's too goddamned cold for the hollow tonight.

He was right about that. There'd been a sudden cold snap the way it happened sometimes in the Catskills, banishing summer in one fell swoop. The air smelled like woodsmoke and apples. School would start in a week, and then there'd be no nights at the hollow anymore. I'd be stuck inside with my carping mother and judgmental father and the cold that was between them.

Frank's smile, though, made me feel warm. I got in the car. *Where are we going?* I asked as he peeled out of the Stewart's lot.

A surprise, he told me.

We drove up into the mountains on an old lumber road, one I'd never been on. Frank had to stop and get out to unhook a chain strung across the road. NO TRESPASSING, a sign on it said. STATE LAND.

You've just added trespassing to your crimes, young man, I said.

I plan to plead insanity. You've driven me crazy, Mattie Lane.

I punched him in the arm and told him that was the corniest thing I'd ever heard. But I couldn't stop smiling the whole way up that rutted unpaved road. It felt like we were the only two people in the world, alone on that road with the trees arching over us as if they were shielding us from the rest of the world.

And then suddenly the road opened up. Frank braked and we came to a squealing stop just feet away from a sheer drop. In front of us lay a dark expanse like the void of outer space. Then Frank killed the headlights and that void filled with a million stars. It felt like we were in a spaceship gazing out on the far reaches of the universe. It felt like we were the first two people to step foot on the continent. It felt like Frank Barnes had just handed me my own private galaxy.

I knew when I saw it I had to show it to you, Frank said. *It's like—*

The best present anyone has ever given me, I said.

Frank didn't say anything for a minute and when he did his voice was hoarse. *I wanted you to remember this . . . in case my father makes good on his threat to send me to military school—*

He won't! I'll make my dad convince him not to.

But just in case. If we're apart I want you to look at the stars and think about me. I know how much you love your constellations.

No more than I love you, Frank Barnes. And then I kissed him, before I could feel embarrassed for telling a boy I loved him. Before he could feel awkward and think that he was supposed to say it too.

But I didn't need to worry. *I love you too, Matt,* he said.

Somehow we ended up in the backseat. All summer we'd been exploring the fringes of this feeling, the boundaries of skin and clothes and lips. But up here among the stars it didn't feel like there were any boundaries. He slid his hand under my bra and I unclasped it. I started unbuttoning his shirt and he pulled it over his head, shedding a button on the cracked vinyl seats. But when I touched the metal button on his jeans he stopped me and leaned back.

We don't have to, he said. *You're two years younger than me. I can wait.*

Who said I could? I asked, drawing him back down to me.

I have always felt grateful that Chief Barnes found us *after.* We were dressed again and climbing back into the front seat. And I've never regretted what we did that night. Not even after what it brought down on both of us. How could I regret that Frank was my first? How could I regret Caleb?

The only thing I regret, looking down at the face of that boy, is that I never had the courage to make Frank see that. And now I never will.

I gently close Frank's eyes. Then I lift my head to call out to Alice and Oren.

There is a boy standing in front of me.

At first I think it's Oren, but this boy's hair is light like Caleb's. But it isn't Caleb either. This boy is six years older than Caleb will ever be. It's Frank, aged sixteen, looking exactly as he had that last night, wearing the same Led Zeppelin T-shirt under a flannel shirt that's missing the button that came off when he tore it over his head.

I cover my mouth with one hand and reach for him with the other. He holds out his hand too, but not for me. A wash of cold moves through me but it's not a bad cold. This is the cold of the water in the hollow and the first cold snap at the end of the summer. It smells like woodsmoke and apples. I can even see a bit of smoke curling around me, forming into another boy, who reaches for Frank's hand and then turns to look at me.

Caleb smiles at me and then turns to Frank. They smile at each other, my two lost boys. They turn away from me, then, but Caleb looks over his shoulder one last time and mouths two words.

Bye, Matt.

They walk toward the open barn door, where the snow is swirling around like a million stars. They step into that spinning galaxy and become part of it, their shapes dissolving into shining atoms, each atom a star in a new constellation that someone, looking up into the night sky, might see and make up a story about: a story about a father and son and mistaken identities and missed chances and vengeance so terrible that they were pursued by terrible furies and a goddess had to step in and say, *Enough!* In the play my father told me about that goddess renamed the furies of vengeance the Kindly Ones. That's what they'd call that constellation. But I'd call it Forgiveness.

CHAPTER THIRTY-THREE

Alice

IT TAKES OREN and me a few minutes to put the ladder back in place and climb down, and then hand in hand we walk gingerly toward Mattie. I press Oren to my side, shielding his face, not wanting him to see the wreck of the man's face. But when I look down I see that Frank Barnes must have been turning back toward Mattie when the hook struck him. His face is intact, and whatever happened to the back of his skull is concealed in Mattie's lap. When I look at Mattie's face I find another surprise: she looks strangely peaceful. She is looking out the barn door, and though I aim my flashlight there, I see nothing but swirling snow.

When I turn back Mattie has settled Frank's head down on the barn floor. As soon as she is free, Oren rushes to her and throws his arms around her. Mattie holds him to her, patting his back. "There, there," she says, "it's all right. All the monsters are gone. We've defeated them, haven't we?

The rebel alliance has won." Over Oren's shoulder she looks into my eyes and mouths a silent question: *Who?*

Who what? I wonder, and then I realize she means who operated the pulley—Oren or me? How can I tell her it was neither of us? I point to myself. Me. I'm the one who did it.

Good, she mouths back, then holds her hand out to me. I think she means for me to help her up but she pulls me down instead and folds me into her arms. The moment I sink into her warm, soft flesh, I begin to sob. She holds me tight.

I'm not sure how long we stay like that. I want to stay in Mattie's arms forever, but when I feel her shiver I pull back. "We need to get back to the house," I say, "before we freeze to death out here."

"Good point," Mattie says. "Oren, be a good boy and help your mom help me up. I'm afraid these old bones have gotten a chill sitting here."

Oren pops up right away and takes Mattie's left hand while I take her right. She grunts and groans as we pull her up, but I have a feeling some of that is for show so that Oren feels good about helping her. Once she's on her feet she's steady, and the arm she puts around my shoulders is strong. *Your mom,* she'd said to Oren, even though she knows that isn't true. But it felt good.

At the barn door we find a wall of snow up to my thighs. Whatever force scoured the path before is gone. We'll have to tunnel our way back to the house. I think of that boy who froze to death two feet from home. "Maybe we should stay in the barn," I say to Mattie. "Start a fire to keep warm."

Mattie chuckles. "And burn the whole thing down? Besides, I'm not sure there are any matches out here . . ." Her voice falters. "Do you see headlights or am I imagining things?"

At first I think the stress of the night has finally unhinged her, but then I see them too, two lights piercing the snow-filled gloom. As I squint at them I hear a roaring sound.

"It's a snow plow!" Oren cries.

"What the hell?" I say. "Who's showing up now? Should we hide?"

"I honestly think we've run out of people who wish me ill," Mattie says. "So unless you've got anyone else on your tail . . ."

"No," I say, "no one I can think of."

So we stand in the barn door, waving at the lights like shipwrecked sailors as the plow shovels a path toward us. When it's cleared a lane from the barn to the house it backs up and a silhouette gets out: a tall, rangy man in a hooded parka. I shine my flashlight at him but the hood hides his face until he reaches us and pushes it back.

"Wayne?" Mattie says. "Wayne Marshall?"

The man, who's got thick gray hair and lines around his eyes, smiles. "I didn't know you knew my last name, Ms. Lane. Are you people all right? Whatcha doing out in the barn on a night like tonight? I was heading up to the house when I saw your flashlight beam."

"What are you doing here?" Mattie asks. Her voice is flat. I can't tell if this is a friend or not, and I tighten my grip on Oren's arm.

"Well, that's kind of embarrassing," he says, ducking

his head and rubbing his neck. "Looking for my dumbass brother-in-law, basically. Have you seen him?"

"What made you think he was here?" Mattie asks. I notice she's not answering his question. I bet that's something she learned at the hotline.

"Well . . . my sister asked me to track him down. He'd been mouthing off about you . . . and she has this gizmo on her phone that shows his location."

"How'd she know this was where I live?" Mattie asks.

"Wow," Wayne says, rocking back on his heels. "Anyone ever tell you you'd make a fine lawyer?"

"Yes," Mattie says curtly. "Answer the question, please."

"She didn't," Wayne admits, "but when she told me the location I knew it was where you lived. I grew up in this town. Everyone knew where old Judge Lane's house was. I headed right out here, but I passed three cars that had gone off the road that I had to winch out. City folk, mostly." He shrugs, like, *What can you say?* "So here I am. Is Jason here? Has he done something stupid?"

"I'm afraid so, Wayne, but it's a long story and this woman and child are cold. Let's get back to the house."

As we walk I hear Mattie talking in a low voice to Wayne. I can't make out everything that she's saying, but from the bits I do I gather she's filling him in on the events of the night. By the time we get to the house she's gotten to the part where we tied Jason up in the basement.

Wayne whistles. "What an idiot! I can't tell you how sorry

I am. I've been telling my sister for years to leave him. Is that where he is now? I hope he's trussed like a turkey and feeling every ache."

"Let's get the woodstove going and I'll tell you the rest of the story. Alice, why don't you put that chili back on the stove and fill the kettle. Let's get something warm in Oren and get those wet clothes off both of you. There's plenty of clothes in the parlor. I'm going to go down in the basement with Wayne for a moment."

She's talking fast, rattling off chores like Lisa used to do, only her voice is kinder. "Do you want me to come with you?" I ask.

She looks up, surprised. "I'll be fine," she says. "I think Wayne is a good guy. You came out here in a blizzard to find your dumbass brother-in-law before he did something stupid, didn't you, Wayne? That makes you a good guy in my book, so I'm sorry that I've got some bad news for you."

Their voices fade as they go down the stairs. I put some wood in the woodstove and make Oren sit down in front of it. I peel off his damp *Star Wars* sweatshirt and for once he doesn't complain. Mattie's old dog comes lumbering into the kitchen and huddles up next to Oren. I leave him there rubbing the dog's ears and hurry into the parlor, grabbing clothes as fast as I can, not wanting to leave Oren alone for long.

When I get back Oren is staring at the basement door. "That man is sad," he says. "I heard him crying."

"Oh," I say, "that's too bad." I don't know what else to say, so I busy myself putting the chili pot and kettle on the stove, washing bowls and spoons. When the water boils I make four cups of hot chocolate and take one to Oren. He's still staring at the basement door.

"Mattie will be all right," I say, wondering if I should check on her.

"It's not that . . . I can hear them talking. She's trying to make Wayne feel better."

I listen, but I can only hear the faintest murmur. Maybe Oren just has super-powerful hearing . . . or super-powerful sensitivity. I look at him closely. He looks small and miserable in the too-big hand-me-down clothes I've brought him. "What is it, buddy?" I ask. "You can tell me."

"It's . . . I wonder . . . is it okay to feel bad for someone who was bad?"

It takes me a second to understand what he's asking, and then I sink straight to the floor, kneeling in front of him. I put my hands on either side of his head and turn him to face me. "Of course it is, sweetie. We all of us have good and bad inside. And the bad parts . . . well, likely they got there through something bad that happened to that person. That's not an excuse not to try to be your best . . . but it can help you to understand and forgive the people who are mean to you. And as for your father . . ." I try to think of something good to say about Davis. I remember those crappy Happy Meal toys Oren would play with and recall that Davis would bring them home for him. I remember how proud he was of Oren when he first came up with the game. *The boy gets his smarts from me.* It was a self-centered kind of love, but still . . . "Your father loved you," I say firmly. "And it's okay to feel bad that he's gone."

Oren nods, a couple of tears sliding down his face, and then he falls into my arms and fits himself to my body. "Can I stay with you, Alice?" he asks after a few minutes.

"Of course, buddy," I say, hoping it's true. "I won't let anyone take you away."

MATTIE AND WAYNE come up a few minutes later. Wayne is wiping his eyes. "I'm only crying on account of my sister and her kids," he says to me, as if he needs to apologize for grieving.

"I get it," I tell him, handing him a cup of hot cocoa.

"It's okay," Oren says, patting Wayne's hand. "Everybody's got good and bad inside of them."

Wayne looks at Oren as if he'd just heard the Dalai Lama's voice come out of him. I'm amazed and ridiculously proud to hear my own words coming out of Oren's mouth.

While Wayne sits down next to Oren, I jump up to help Mattie fill bowls with chili. "We need to call the police on Wayne's cell phone," Mattie says in a low voice. "I'll tell them there are two bodies in the house and one in the barn. I imagine they'll be out here by morning. I plan to be forthright in what I tell them. Except for one thing."

She waits until I look up at her to continue. "What thing?" I ask.

She glances over to check that Wayne and Oren are busy talking. "You probably don't know that there's a switch by the barn door that operates the hay pulley—or that there's a generator out there in the barn that I fired up when we were out there earlier."

"I don't remember . . . ," I say, wondering what she's getting at. I'm pretty sure she did no such thing.

Mattie lifts one eyebrow. "I think if you search your memory you'll recall my saying that I just wanted to check that it was working. I left it running in case we needed it later. So when Chief Barnes pointed his firearm at me and made it clear he intended to kill me and then you and Oren, I switched on the hay pulley to disarm him."

"That's not what happened," I say.

"Do you want to explain to the police what *did* happen?" she asks me. "Neither you nor Oren have any idea how to operate that pulley. And if you say you did it . . . well, I don't want to add any complications to your custody suit for Oren. You do want to seek custody, I'm assuming."

I nod, unable to speak for a moment. Then I manage, "What about you?"

"I'll tell my story as best as I can and hope the judge and jury believe me. I've got a couple of lawyer friends . . . I'll be fine."

She looks away then to ladle the last bowl of chili. She's

not at all sure she'll be fine, but I don't think I can argue her out of it. And I *do* want to get custody of Oren. I want it more than I've ever wanted anything. The fact that Mattie is willing to risk her own welfare for me to get it makes me feel for the first time that I might be worthy of it.

CHAPTER THIRTY-FOUR

Mattie

WE SPEND THE waning hours of the night circled around the woodstove playing Texas Hold'em. At first I think we're all trying to act normal for Oren's sake. Alice keeps giving him more hot cocoa and cookies (so much for those dental bills),. Wayne engages him by talking about astronomy (and promising to let him come look through his telescope), and I cheat every once in a while for the pleasure of Oren catching me. But at some point I catch a satisfied smile on Oren's face and realize that here is a child who takes on the weight of the emotions around him by playing the peacemaker. I'd done it myself for my parents most of my life; the only time they didn't bicker between themselves was when they were united in their regard—or censure—for me. Winning first prize in the spelling bee and getting the highest grades in school worked for a while, but then so did getting called in by the principal for cutting class. I bet that poltergeist Davis mentioned is another way Oren shoulders that weight. There'll come a time when it's too heavy on him and I hope to be around to ease it a bit.

No one wants to go into any other room, so Wayne and I haul sleeping bags and camping mats into the kitchen. Alice and Oren curl up together, and Wayne and I share a pot of coffee, talking in whispers, as if Oren and Alice were our kids.

"You were in the class three years ahead of me," I say. "You played football and scored the tie-breaking touchdown of the last game your senior year."

"Guilty," he allows, blushing. "You were editor of the school newspaper and wrote an exposé of the money wasted in the school cafeteria. You couldn't wait to shake the dust of this town off your feet. Didn't you go to one of those fancy women's colleges? Wellesley? Vassar?"

"Barnard," I admit. "And it was an exposé on the food wasted that could be redirected to a food pantry. I made poor Mrs. Kaminsky, the head cafeteria manager, cry. I was kind of a shit."

"You were doing what you thought was right," he says. "And look—you've got your food pantry and shelter and crisis hotline. You've done a lot for this town and the county."

"Some people say Sanctuary just draws bums to the town," I say.

"Some people are assholes," he counters. "I've always been proud to have a place like Sanctuary in our town. I never miss the Cookie Walk."

I cringe. "I'm sorry I didn't recognize you when we met at Stewart's."

"No worries," he says, getting up to put a log in the stove. "You must see a couple dozen people a day."

This is true, but how have I missed this nice guy who contributes food and services regularly and was a classmate? What else—and *who* else—have I been missing all these years while I barricaded myself in this house and the work of Sanctuary? Sure, I've been "doing good," but how much of that was to appease my conscience for what my father did?

When I turn back to Wayne I see he has nodded off in his chair, coffee mug still in his hand. I take the mug from him and bring it and all the other dishes to the sink. It's stopped snowing and the sky is lightening. I feel a pressure against my leg and for a moment I think about feeling that two nights ago and wondering if it was Caleb. But when I look down I find that it's only Dulcie, looking up at me expectantly to be let out.

I guide her through the thicket of sleeping bodies and open the back door. There's almost too much snow, but the overhang has kept enough off that I'm able to clear a pie-shaped wedge. While Dulcie lumbers a couple of feet into the deep snow and finds a place to pee, I stand on the stoop and watch the sunrise. It tinges the snow a creamy orange, so much like the Creamsicle bar I used to get from the Good Humor man that it makes me hungry. The sky above is a clear, radiant blue with a smattering of celestial bodies: Arcturus, Jupiter, Spica, and a waning crescent moon. Spica is the only star of the constellation visible, but I know Virgo is there. Justice.

I once asked my father the difference between justice and vengeance, and he told me the plot of a Greek play. Orestes has killed his own mother, Clytemnestra, because she killed his father, Agamemnon, which in turn was in revenge for him killing their daughter, Iphigenia.

Talk about a dysfunctional family! Doreen had exclaimed when I told her the plot of the play during one long, quiet shift.

The problem is that with his mother's blood on his hands, Orestes is pursued by the Furies, the snake-haired, bat-winged agents of vengeance who hound their victims to a painful death. He flees first to the sanctuary of Apollo at Delphi, where Apollo tells him to go on to Athens. There Athena has Orestes tried for his crime by a jury of Athenian citizens.

This is the birth of law, my father told me, *triumphing over the old blood rules of vengeance.*

The jury is split, but Athena casts a deciding vote for Orestes. The Furies don't take it well. They rage against the Athenians and their city until Athena offers them an alternative: if they break the cycle of blood vengeance they will be worshipped by the Athenians under a new name: the Eumenides . . . or the Kindly Ones.

So basically she turned them into good furies by using positive reinforcement, Doreen said. *Athena would have made a great third-grade teacher.*

I smile, feeling like Doreen is standing here with me. Wait until she hears this story! Then I hear police sirens coming up the hill and remember I have others to tell my story to first. I can only hope my listeners are as well disposed as the old gods.

THEY TAKE US all into town to the police station to take our statements. I remind the officer—Tracy Bennerfield, who was in the third grade with Caleb—that they need to alert the Department of Child Welfare to be present on Oren's behalf. Tracy bristles and says that she *knows* that, but I see her nudge her fellow officer to remember to make the call.

I can tell it's not sitting well with anyone that a fellow officer has been killed. It's going to sit even less well when I tell them the whole story. How likely are they to believe that Frank, an upstanding member of the community and one of their own, was willing to kill to cover up his father's crime? I ask to use one of their phones to call Anita Esteban, who says she'll be there in twenty minutes. Then I call Doreen. There's no answer, but she's probably sleeping off a late shift.

Anita's at the station within fifteen minutes. I tell my story to her and I can see her eyes widen, but then she puts her hand on mine and says, "You're the most honest person I know, Mattie. I believe you. But I gotta tell you, those officers aren't going to like it."

"I know," I say, squeezing her hand. "Can you represent

Alice too—and make sure Oren is looked after? I'd like to reach Doreen to keep an eye on Oren."

I try Doreen again, but she still doesn't answer.

I tell my story to the officer on duty and he asks me a dozen questions to trip me up, but I keep repeating only the same facts: Frank Barnes shot Davis. He aimed his firearm at me. I escaped and armed myself. I followed him out to the barn, where he held me at gunpoint and told me what really happened to my family thirty-four years ago. When I saw he meant to shoot me—and no doubt Oren and Alice too—I switched on the hay pulley to distract him. I meant only to disarm him but the hook hit him so hard it killed him.

When I've repeated the same facts a dozen times Anita accuses the deputy of harassment and asks if I'm going to be charged with anything.

"Not now," the officer answers, indicating with a glare that he's not done with me.

I sign my statement and learn that Oren has been claimed by Child Welfare and taken to a residence. No one will tell me which one. Alice is half crazed with panic; Wayne is trying to calm her down. "Doreen will find out where they've taken him," I tell her. "Let's go over to Sanctuary."

At Sanctuary I find Alana and the Bard intern both wide-eyed and jittery, like they've been up all night drinking Red Bulls and cramming for an exam. "Thank God!" they both exclaim when they see me. "No one else showed up for their shifts, so we stayed on."

"We lost power but we got the generator going!" Bard tells us.

"We took in a dozen people stranded by the storm," Alana says. "I know we're not supposed to let people stay overnight, but what could we do?"

"We made frozen pizzas for everyone—"

"And directed the highway department to rescue people who were stranded on the road—"

"And organized a shoveling brigade this morning!"

They are giddy with their success. The place looks like a wreck. "Good job," I tell them as I plug in my phone to charge it. I don't mention that they gave away our location to Davis. I'll leave that lecture on confidentiality for another day. After all, I've broken a lot of rules myself. "But didn't Doreen come in?"

"She never showed up," Alana says. "We figured she was snowed in. I've called her a dozen times."

A ripple of unease passes through me. Doreen lives two blocks away in a second-floor apartment. Her landlord is a fit ex-fireman who gets out his snowblower at the first flakes. There's no way she's still snowed in.

My phone beeps to life. There's Doreen's message to me from last night.

Called Dept. of Child Welfare. Alice isn't Oren's mother. Not even stepmother. She's the next-door neighbor who babysits. The father has had custody since the mother OD'd. Oren's caseworker expressed concerns over Oren's welfare but there was no evidence, etc. etc. Anyway, thought you should know. Call if you need me.

It's the "etc. etc." that gets me. All the times Doreen tried to convince a caseworker that her son, Gavin, wasn't doing well at his father's and they told her that there was no evidence of abuse so they couldn't do anything . . .

"Etc. etc."

I can hear her weariness even in the text. And then there's the last line: "Call if you need me."

I hadn't called. Would she have assumed I lost power, or think I didn't need her?

I'll stick around as long as you need me, Doreen had said when I talked her down from killing herself.

Reflect back the invitations the person has given you, Doreen teaches in her suicide awareness training sessions.

Doreen had been upset by the call from Alice. I'd meant to talk it through with her but I never had. She asked if she could come stay with us last night. She hadn't wanted to be alone. She left a message asking if I needed her . . .

And the answer had been no.

"Call an ambulance and send it to Doreen's address," I bark at Alana and Bard as I rush out of the building.

I run the two blocks, dodging shovelers and snowblowers. How could I have been so blind? So deaf? Doreen had been telling me that she was struggling. I knew that Oren would remind her of Gavin. And yet I still let her go home alone to sit out the storm with her own bad thoughts.

The three-story Victorian house where Doreen lives is cheerful against the snow. The front path is neatly cleared. Assorted wind chimes peal on the outdoor staircase that goes up to Doreen's door. These stairs have been cleared too, and a note from her landlord has been left on her door telling her that garbage pickup has been delayed because of the storm.

I knock, but when I don't get an answer I kneel and move a Buddha statue aside to get her spare key. As I let myself in I hear the ambulance pull up downstairs. I'm going to feel really stupid if I'm wrong. Doreen will never let me live it down—

The only light in the apartment comes from a lava lamp in the corner of the living room—a gag gift the volunteers gave Doreen once because she is such a hippie. It bathes the room in purple, then red, then green, painting the bare white walls and the futon couch in lurid colors. The colors do nothing to disguise the fact that this is a lonely place. Why haven't I ever asked Doreen to come live with me in my great big lonely house? *Because you were too in love with your own solitude, wallowing in your guilt and pride. Mattie Lane, the judge's daughter, in her big house on the hill.*

Doreen is lying on the futon under an afghan. There's a bottle of whiskey and three pill bottles on the coffee table.

It feels like falling to reach the couch. I'm shaking so

badly that I can't tell if she has a pulse. I try to remember CPR training, but all I can hear is Doreen's voice saying, *Call if you need me, call if you need me.*

"I need you," I scream into Doreen's slack face. "I need you, goddamn it!"

And then the EMTs are there. They push me aside and start to work on Doreen. "I've got a pulse," one says. They load Doreen onto a stretcher, strap an oxygen mask to her face. I have just a second before they take her away.

I squeeze her hand and her eyes flutter open. "I'm sorry," I say. "I should have come sooner. I should have listened better. I should have—"

Doreen waves a limp hand in the air, and I know what she would say if she could. We always tell our volunteers not to beat themselves up over what they could have done differently on a call. *Learn from your mistakes. Move on.*

"Okay," I tell Doreen as she's taken from me. "I'll do better next time. Just give me that next time."

CHAPTER THIRTY-FIVE

Alice

AT FIRST I think they've all forgotten me. A social worker comes and takes Oren, and I'm put in an ugly room with uncomfortable plastic chairs, dreary paint, and a stale odor of burned coffee and sweat. I feel like I've spent my whole life in rooms like this one, waiting for one hearing or another, waiting to find out where I'll be moved next, like I'm a piece on a playing board. Not even an interesting piece, like the hat or dog in Monopoly, but one of those broken chips you use when the original pieces get lost. I'm not one of the original pieces that come with the game.

Then a young Latina woman comes in and brings a whole different climate with her. The click of her heels on the linoleum seems to wake up the room and her smart red suit overcomes the dreary paint job. She takes my hand in both of hers and tells me her name is Anita Esteban and that

Mattie's told her all about me and she's going to take care of everything.

"Where's Oren?" I ask.

"Child Welfare is placing him in a temporary residence." Her phone buzzes and she holds one finger up, looks down at the screen, then smiles. "Okay, this is good news, just give me a second." She goes out again, talking fast into her phone, leaving me with the dreary paint and stale air, and I feel deflated. Oren's already been swept up by the system. I'm not his mother. I have no claim on him. I've got a record. We're just two pieces caught in the cogs of a machine, being moved farther and farther apart—

But then Anita Esteban comes back in smiling. "Good news. Oren's been placed at Horizon House, which is an at-risk youth center run at St. Alban's—"

"The convent?" I say sharply. "He won't like that. He was scared by that building."

"Hmm," Anita says. "It can look a little daunting from the outside, but it's a good place. The best part is that in the other wing of the building they run a women's shelter, and I got you in there. That is, if you want it. You could see Oren—"

"Yes," I say, "that's perfect. But what about Mattie?"

"She had to run out because of an emergency with her friend, but she sent me to take care of you." Anita smiles at me. "Don't worry. Mattie saved my life. That's what she does. There are hundreds of people in this county who owe their lives to her. We're all going to help her and you and the boy. Okay?" She takes both my hands and looks into my eyes. "The first thing I'm going to do is get you in a better room. This place stinks. You okay with that?"

I nod because my throat is closed up and I'm afraid I'll start bawling if I speak. I feel like I've just gotten a Get Out of Jail Free card and landed on the big ladder that takes you to the top in Chutes and Ladders. I feel like I'm part of the game.

IN THE DAYS that follow, Mattie marshals an army of lawyers and social workers on Oren's and my behalf. She does all this even though her friend Doreen is in the hospital recovering from a failed suicide attempt. She does all this even though her own case is looking difficult. No one seems to mind that it's the week before Christmas or that everyone is still digging out from the blizzard. Whoever Mattie calls shows up to help. A man from DSS visits to help me fill out paperwork for Section 8 housing. Alana, the volunteer I was so mean to, brings a basketful of clothes for me. An old woman from Saugerties shows up to alter them for me. While she sews she tells me her story.

"My husband was mean as dirt and hit me and our kids regularly. I blamed it on the work he did—he was a guard at a juvenile detention center—and I blamed it on myself for not knowing how to stop him. Then he got fired because he raped a girl at the facility where he worked. I was grateful when he went to prison—and I was grateful when he killed himself two years in. But then I found out that we wouldn't get his pension. I'd like to say things got better, but the next ten years were a struggle. I drank. I hit my kids. I would have lost them, but this social worker showed up at my hearing and recommended me for a counseling group at Sanctuary. I thought I'd just go along with it to get my kids back . . . but then I started hearing the stories of other women who'd been through the things I'd been through and worse. I told the group one day that my dream was to open a quilt shop. The next day I found all these sewing supplies on my doorstep and Mattie Lane called to say that the Rotary Club was going to give me a business loan to open a quilt shop. It changed my life. It wasn't just the handout that did it, it was . . ." Her voice falters.

"Someone believing in you," I said.

"Yes," she agreed. Then she put down her needle and thread and leaned forward. "You're not on your own here, Alice. There are people here who believe in you."

Only after she left did I put it all together. A guard who raped a teenager at a juvenile detention center. Mattie. Mattie had found the wife of her rapist and had helped her put her life back together.

And that old woman was right; I wasn't on my own at St. Alban's and it's not a bad place. The nuns are kind and quiet. The other women are kind and loud. We have our own common room and kitchen. We cook dinner together and watch movies and talk late into the night. It's what I imagine college must be like.

The best part is that I see Oren every day. He looks well fed and happy. He's also got new clothes, including a brand-new *Star Wars* sweatshirt that I suspect Mattie got for him.

Mattie comes every night. She brings bags of groceries, toiletries, and clothes—not just for me but for all the women and children at St. Alban's. All the nuns and volunteers know her, and she gets to break whatever rules she wants, like getting Oren permission to come over to the women's wing to watch movies at night. She brings all the DVDs of the *Star Wars* movies and we have a marathon.

Mattie tells me that Doreen has a friend at Children's Court working on my petition for custody. It may take a while but they think they will prevail in the end.

"Is Doreen okay?" I ask.

Mattie nods, her face tightening. "She will be. It helps her to have your case to work on." Then she tells me her plans for me. She's got a friend who runs a B and B in Mount Tremper, on the outskirts of Delphi, who needs a housekeeper. The job comes with a cottage out back. It's not much, but it's a place that Social Services will deem suitable for Oren to live. She's got another friend at Ulster Community College who can talk to me about going back to school. She's even got a friend (*Well, Wayne actually,* she says, blushing) who has an old car I can use.

Anita Esteban was right. Mattie has hundreds of friends and she's calling on them all for my sake.

"What about your case?" I ask.

She sighs and I think it's going to be bad news. "When

the police searched Frank's house and computer they found evidence that he's been taking money from Pine Crest for delivering young people to a judge in Albany who always sends them to Pine Crest. That kind of backs up my story, so Anita's hopeful I won't be charged."

"You don't sound happy about that," I say.

She turns to me, her violet eyes shining in the reflection of the television set. "How could I have not seen what had happened to Frank?"

It takes me a second to realize she's really asking. That she wants my opinion. I look at her, at this woman who has spent a lifetime helping the most powerless and helpless people, who has built a safety net wide enough to catch me and Oren in our most vulnerable moment, and I know what to say. "You see the best in people, Mattie. You see what they once were and could be again if only someone would give them a chance. Look at what you've seen in me."

Mattie smiles, transforming her face into that beautiful teenager in the Polaroid photograph. She puts her arm around me. "Oh, that was easy, Alice. With you I see a woman who got stuck in a bad situation to save a little boy. I see a mother who loves her son. I'd have to be a lot older and blinder not to see that."

Then she wipes a tear away and turns back to the set, her arm still around me.

That night when I'm putting Oren to bed (another privilege Mattie has sweet-talked the nuns into giving me), he says to me, "I was wrong about this being a bad place. The bad things that happened here were a long time ago. Everyone here now is really nice. Mattie's friend Wayne said he's going to bring his telescope one night. They're both coming tomorrow to take us to the Cookie Walk. We're going to carry lanterns and walk through the village and eat as many cookies as we want. You'll come, won't you?"

I tell him I wouldn't miss it for the world. I don't ask him about the bad things that happened here a long time ago or how he knows about them. Instead I go the next day at four o'clock—the best time to catch her, Mattie has told me—to Sister Martine to ask her instead.

"I guess you could say that bad things did happen here," she tells me. We're in her office having tea and "biscuits," which turn out to be cookies. "St. Alban's ran a home for 'wayward girls,' as they were called then, from the 1890s through the 1970s. I came here in the 1960s and the first thing I did was read all the files. It was hair-raising, let me tell you; the maternal and infant mortality rate was five times the contemporary national average. It was clear no one cared very much about those girls and their babies. 'It is perhaps a blessing,' one of my predecessors had written, 'that the poor doves go so quickly to their maker, considering what lives lie ahead of them.'"

"Wow," I say, "that's cold."

"As the ninth circle of Dante's Inferno," Sister Martine responds. "I tried to improve conditions. I enlisted local doctors and health care advocates, wrote many an angry letter to the bishop. But perhaps what helped the most was just changing attitudes toward out-of-wedlock pregnancy. Once it was no longer considered a shameful secret, something to be hidden away, many girls could stay in their own homes rather than come to a place like this. And then, of course, there was *Roe v. Wade* and girls had other options."

Sister Martine must see the shock on my face—a nun remarking favorably on abortion?—because she smiles. "I'm not saying it's the best option, but it certainly did decrease our numbers. So much so that the diocese threatened to shut us down. I pointed out, though, that there were many other ways to help women and children. And of course there were still girls—and women—who needed a safe place to come and have their babies."

"Mattie," I say. "She had Caleb here."

Sister Martine places her hands together in a prayer position and then interlaces her fingers as if she is holding something inside them. "I can't discuss any of my girls."

"I understand," I say, "only, I wondered . . ."

"Yes?" she prods when I hesitate. She opens her hands, palms up, and I have the feeling that I could spill whatever secret I wanted into those hands and it would be protected forever, the weight of it taken off my shoulders.

"I understand you can't give out anyone else's record, but what about a person's own record? The thing is . . . I think I was born here. My adoptive parents lived up here in Ellenville, so I wondered if *I* have a file and . . . would I be able to see it."

Sister Martine leans toward me, elbows on her desk, face

grave. "Well," she says, "as you may know, New York is a closed-records state, which is one of the reasons that if you were indeed born here I would not have been able to keep track of you."

I nod. "When my adoptive parents died I ended up in the foster system. I always thought—"

"That if your birth mother had known she would have come to rescue you?"

"Yes," I say, embarrassed that she's guessed my secret fantasy. I look up and see from the look of compassion on her face that she's guessed my other one. "It's not Mattie, is it? I'd hoped . . . when I learned she'd had a baby . . ." I stop, unable to go on, all the longing to *belong* to someone rising up, cutting off the air in my lungs.

"That you were her baby?" Sister Martine says so gently it sounds like a prayer.

I nod, unable to speak.

Sister Martine gets up, comes around the desk, and perches on the edge of it. She takes my hand. "Do you think Mattie Lane could love you and that boy any more than she already does if you were?"

I shake my head, letting loose a couple of tears. "No, but . . ."

"But nothing." Sister Martine clucks her tongue. "If you want to find your birth parents, I will help you. Mattie will help you. She and I found her own daughter a few years back. She's happily settled in Buffalo with a family of her own. She's never looked for her birth mother. *She doesn't need me*, Mattie said when I asked if she wanted to make contact.

But you *do*. And if you ask me, you're the daughter Mattie needs. Just as Oren needs you to be his mother."

I nod and dry my eyes. Sister Martine gives me a tissue and a glass of water. Then she reminds me that our friends are gathering on the hill to go into town for the Cookie Walk. I get up to go and find myself embraced in Sister Martine's strong, bony grip. "Go on," she says. "I'll be right behind you."

It occurs to me that Sister Martine needs a few minutes alone to collect herself. What must it feel like to watch a baby she handed over to the world sit in front of her all grown up? Does she wonder what she could have done differently to make my life easier? Will Mattie?

When I get outside I see it's almost dark, the sky a lovely clear violet, like Mattie's eyes. I see her standing on the hill with Oren and Wayne and Doreen. They're all holding lanterns; as I watch, Mattie starts lighting them. Atefeh, the woman from Stewart's, is there too, with her two kids. When all the lanterns are lit they make a pattern, like a constellation, against the sky. But it feels incomplete.

A few nights ago, when I was putting Oren to bed, he told me something he had read about in a book that Wayne gave him. He said that hundreds of years ago an astronomer had thought there might be stars we couldn't see. He'd been watching the way stars moved and thought there was an unseen force pulling them into one orbit or another. The astronomer called that force dark stars.

Watching the group, I picture the people who have made them the way they are: Mattie's parents, Frank, Davis,

Wayne's dumbass brother-in-law, Doreen's son, Atefeh's brother and husband. I picture the people who have shaped my life: my birth parents, my adoptive parents, Travis and Lisa, Davis, Mattie, Sister Martine. All the dark stars have brought us to this particular moment and this particular pattern. We may not see them, but they're always here with us, pulling us out of orbit and bringing us back in.

Oren and Mattie lift their heads at the same moment and, seeing me, grin and wave as if pulled by the same force. I feel its tug too, and move forward to join them.

ACKNOWLEDGMENTS

I thought a lot about family and community during the writing of this book. I'm grateful for the community of support I've found at William Morrow, starting with the amazing Katherine Nintzel, the best editor I could have wished for, and Vedika Khanna, Camille Collins, Molly Waxman, Shailyn Tavella, Rachel Meyers, and everyone else who has made William Morrow such a welcoming home. I wouldn't have found that home without the faith and hard work of my agent, Robin Rue, and her assistant, Beth Miller. Writers House has been a true sanctuary.

As always, I'm grateful for my family for their love and support: my husband, Lee Slonimsky; my daughter, Maggie Vicknair; my stepdaughter, Nora Slonimsky; and her partner, Jeremy Levine. I am thankful to count so many friends as family. Thank you to Wendy Rossi Gold for reading everything from the beginning and Ethel Wesdorp for thinking up the title.

And lastly, I couldn't have written this book without the

good people of Family of Woodstock, most especially Tamara Cooper, Susan Carroll, Ron Van Warmer, Deanne-Harriet Hoffman, Alan Rovitzky, Gayle Jamison, Nancy Meyer, Micheil Cannistra, and Sharon DeVries. Thank you for showing me that there's no limit to how far we can extend the circle of family.

About the author

About the book

Insights,
Interviews
& More . . .

Read on

Meet Carol Goodman

CAROL GOODMAN is the critically acclaimed author of twenty novels, including *The Widow's House*, winner of the 2018 Mary Higgins Clark Award, and *The Seduction of Water*, which won the 2003 Hammett Prize. Her books have been translated into sixteen languages. She lives in the Hudson Valley with her family and teaches writing and literature at SUNY New Paltz and The New School. ❧

Franco Vogt

Finding Family

In the fall of 2016 I was teaching at SUNY New Paltz when a student came to my office to explain why she was behind in her work. I'd heard a lot of excuses in my years of teaching, but nothing quite like this. My student had fled an abusive marriage in the city and was living under an assumed name upstate with her two young children. She was struggling to make ends meet while also dealing with the post-traumatic stress of surviving domestic abuse. Of course I gave her an extension and asked what else I could do. She said that it had been helpful just to talk to me.

That didn't really seem like enough, though. I wanted to help her more, but I didn't know how. I asked some of my colleagues, and the English department secretary told me that there was a place called Family of Woodstock that gave assistance and counseling to survivors of domestic abuse. I looked up the organization and was impressed to learn of all the services it provided, from food pantries to domestic violence shelters to a crisis hotline. I was happy to have such a resource to tell my student about.

She'd beat me to it. The next time I spoke to her she told me someone else had told her about Family. She'd gone to its New Paltz branch and received help in obtaining Section 8 housing and finding a job. She was hopeful and optimistic. The people at Family had been wonderful.

I was hopeful for my student too and made a mental note to check out Family at the end of the semester. Listening to ▶

Finding Family *(continued)*

my student had struck a chord with me. Domestic abuse had been an issue in my own life. Years before, when I fled an abusive marriage, I had been fortunate enough to have family to go to, but I was well aware that many women did not have that resource. How wonderful that there was a place like Family for those women and children—and for men too. I told myself I should volunteer there—someday—when I had time.

I also thought, as I do whenever something truly touches me, that I might write something about a woman fleeing an abusive relationship who calls a crisis hotline. I began imagining a woman and a child on a bus driving through the snowy Catskills and another woman in an old house getting a call in the night. I started making notes for the book that would become *The Night Visitors*.

I'm not sure how long it would have taken me to volunteer at Family under normal circumstances. I was indeed busy, teaching three college classes, working on a new book, editing the previous book. But then something very *abnormal* happened: the 2016 election. When I awoke on November 9, 2016, I thought about how much more vulnerable so many people were about to become: immigrants, minorities, LGBTQ people, women. I wanted to do *something*. Which is when I remembered my intention to someday volunteer for Family. Maybe that someday had arrived. I could at least call and set the process in motion.

So I did. I called the hotline and a

volunteer told me I could come in and fill out an application for hotline training. The next session began in February. I told the volunteer that I'd fill out an application, but she must have picked up something in my voice, because she told me to hold on. When she came back she asked, "What are you doing right now?"

"Sitting here feeling crappy," I told her.

"Do you want to come in and help with a mailing?" she asked.

I told her I'd be right over.

I spent that day sealing newsletters with round stickers and chatting with a couple of lovely women. We didn't talk about the election because, as I was to learn, we don't talk politics at Family, since we serve everyone no matter what their political leanings. I watched volunteers bag up food from the food pantry and answer phone calls from strangers all across the country. Family is the oldest continuously running crisis hotline in the United States and handles all kinds of problems: its motto is "Any Problem Under the Sun." I signed myself and my daughter up to help serve food at Family's annual Thanksgiving dinner, and I registered for the hotline training, wondering how in the world I was going to fit that into my busy schedule but determined to do so.

In the months between that day and when I began volunteer training, I started *The Night Visitors;* by the time I began my shifts on the hotline I had finished most of the book. It may seem surprising that I wrote most of the book before I began working at Family, but I'm glad I did. The first thing I learned in my training is that everything you hear at Family— on the phone or in the building—and ▶

Finding Family *(continued)*

any personal confidences shared during training are completely confidential. I know that I never used anything that I heard at Family in this book because I'd written most of it before I started there. I did ask in my training if I could share procedural methods from the training and was told I could. So I was able to give my character Mattie some of the techniques I learned in training. Mattie knows how to brace her body for a physical blow and how to ask someone if she is thinking about suicide. I also learned, though, that much of what Mattie does goes against procedure, but by then I knew Mattie was the kind of woman who might throw out the rules when she had to.

The people I have met at Family inform the spirit of this book. Their dedication, selflessness, good humor, and kindness never cease to amaze me. They gave me hope in a year that seemed at times bleak and hopeless, when it seemed that the selfish and opportunistic had gained sway in the country. Family taught me that there are kindly ones willing to help the vulnerable and that family is not determined by biology—it's what we make from the people we help and are helped by. And in the end, that's what I wanted for my characters Mattie, Alice, and Oren—to find their family of choice. ༽

Reading Group Guide

1. Do you consider Frank a sympathetic character? Did his death change your opinion of him?

2. How does the hidden house layered within Mattie's house symbolize her relationship with Caleb and the rest of her family?

3. How does the book's wintry setting affect the events that take place? How does it constrain and aid the characters?

4. How did the alternating points of view between Alice and Mattie shape your impressions of both women?

5. How does the Greek mythology featured throughout the book inform the book's setting, characters, and events?

6. At the start of chapter thirteen, Oren decides Mattie is Princess Leia and Alice is Rey in their game of *Star Wars*. To what degree does this reflect Mattie and Alice's relationship? Are there other roles you would assign them or some of the other characters in the book?

7. Many characters are either running from the past or stuck in the past. In both cases, voices call to them from the past, whether it's Mattie's mom, Caleb, or Davis. How effectively does each of the characters deal with these voices? Are there voices from your past that echo in your ears? ▶

8. Forgiveness and vengeance are major themes in the book. How do they balance and counteract each other?

9. How does the book's ending subvert society's expectations of how families are supposed to look and the roles and responsibilities people are supposed to take on?

10. To what degree do you think Caleb's actions were driven by vengeance versus love?

11. Support between women plays a big role in the book, not only with Mattie and Alice but with Doreen, Atefeh, and Sister Martine as well. How does this contrast with the men in the book? How do you think this will affect Oren as he grows up? ⌒

An Excerpt from
The Other Mother

"Can you tell me when you first thought about hurting your child?"

"It was a few days after we'd come home from the hospital. I was carrying her down the stairs . . . there's a steep drop from the landing and when I looked over it I suddenly had this . . . *picture in my head* of myself lifting her over the banister and *dropping* her."

"And did you ever do anything like that? Deliberately drop her . . . or hurt her in any other way?"

"No! It was just a thought. I'd never hurt my baby . . . in fact, I did everything I could to make sure I didn't hurt her . . . to keep her safe."

"What exactly did you do to keep yourself from hurting her?"

. . .

"Ms. ■?"

. . .

"Ms. ■, what did you do to keep your child safe?"

Chapter One

She's crying again.

I don't know why I say *again*. Sometimes it seems as if she's done nothing but cry since she was born. As if she'd come into this world with a grudge.

"We're almost there, sweetie," I call to her in the backseat, but she only cries louder, as if she can recognize my reassurance for the lie it is. The truth is I don't know where we are or how far we are from our destination. The last time ▶

9

I looked at the map app on the new (cheap, pay-as-you-go) phone, it showed our location as a blue dot in a sea of endless green. As if we'd fallen off the map of the known world. When we crossed the river there was a sign that said WELCOME TO THE LAND OF RIP VAN WINKLE. I feel as if I've fallen asleep and woken to an unrecognizable world—only who sleeps with a crying six-month-old?

"Do you want your ba-ba?" I offer, even though she just finished a bottle half an hour ago. I root around in the diaper bag on the passenger seat but find only an empty bottle. Hadn't I made up two at the last gas station? Or had I been distracted by the woman in pressed corduroy trousers and Burberry jacket who'd eyed me microwaving a bottle with that Why-aren't-you-breastfeeding-don't-you-know-bottles-will-rot-your-baby's-teeth-and-lower-her-IQ look. She was holding the hand of a toddler who had an iPhone in his other hand, his eyes glued to the screen.

At least it won't rot her brain, I had it in mind to say but instead out popped, "Isn't it hard traveling with kids? We've been driving for hours! My husband's away on business and I'm relocating for a new job."

Burberry Jacket eyed me up and down as if she didn't think I looked very employable. In my ratty old sweatshirt, grimy jeans, greasy hair pulled back in a sloppy bun I suppose I didn't. I should have left it at that but I had to add, "— as an archivist at a private library."

Her eyes widened, either because she was impressed or thought I was crazy. The latter, most likely, from the way she clutched her electronics-besotted son closer to her. *Archivist*. How stupid could I get? She'd remember me. When she saw my picture in the paper—

It won't be in the paper, I told myself for the hundred and seventh time (I'd been counting) since we'd left. I'd made sure of that.

I drove away from the gas station repeating all the reasons I didn't have to worry: I'd ditched my old phone and bought a new one with cash. I didn't tell anyone except Laurel about the job and Laurel won't tell. I haven't passed a car in the last fifty miles. I'm in the middle of nowhere, just me and a crying baby—

She's stopped screaming. I'm not sure how long it's been since she stopped. Since Chloe was born I sometimes lose little bits of time like that. *Mommy brain*, Esta, the leader of the mothers' support group, called it. *It's a hormonal thing*. I angle the rearview mirror to see Chloe's face but the car is so dark I can't see her at all. I don't know how to find the dome light and there are no streetlights on this country road to illuminate the interior. It's so dark and quiet in the car it's almost as if she isn't there.

Of course she's there, don't be ridiculous, I tell myself, but already I can feel the thought taking root in my brain. *Bad thoughts*, my mother would say, *stick like burrs. You need something to make them go away*. A couple or six shots of whiskey is what she used. Sometimes when she got home late from her job at the bar I'd hear her muttering to herself, *Leave it!* like her brain was a dog who'd picked up a piece of garbage on the street.

Leave it! I'd tell myself on all the sleepless nights I lay awake imagining ▶

that Chloe had stopped breathing or that she had been stolen out of her crib. *If you keep going into her room, Daphne*, Peter would say, *she'll never learn to sleep on her own.*

Leave it! I say now. *She's in the car seat. She's just sleeping.* But I can't leave it. Instead I remember a Schuyler Bennett story that had been one of my favorites in college, the one called "The Changeling." Like many of her stories it was borrowed from an old piece of folklore. In it a woman who believes her own baby has been stolen by fairies carries the changeling through the woods to leave it on the fairy hill. She waits all night, listening to the sickly wail of the child, until at last at dawn she sees the fairies come and leave a healthy baby in its place. She lifts the plump but strangely quiet baby into her arms and carries it home. The baby seems to grow heavier and heavier in her arms until at last when she comes out of the woods she looks down and sees that what she carries is a log of wood and she knows that she has given up her own baby to the fairies and brought home a changeling instead.

Maybe you'd feel better, Peter had said, after skimming the story from the book on my night table, *if you didn't read such morbid stories.*

Now I can't shake the idea that when I reach the house I'll find an insensate lump of wood strapped into the car seat—or nothing at all. Maybe I left Chloe at the Quickie Mart. Maybe—the thought makes my mouth go dry—she was never in the car at all. I try to reassure myself by going over the details of leaving the house, carrying her out to the car . . . but all I can see is me sitting in the car, writing in my journal, getting ready to go in to get Chloe. I can see myself getting out of the car, going up the front path, but then the picture goes blurry, like a film out of focus. *Mommy brain*, like Esta said, *hormones*—but when the film comes back into focus I can see myself walking back down the path holding Chloe's car seat. I can see myself putting her in the back of the car. So it's ridiculous to think she's not in the car.

Still, I call her name. There's no response.

Because she's asleep, I tell myself, not because she's stopped breathing.

Leave it! I tell myself.

Once I get an idea in my head, though, it's very hard for me to let it go. *Intrusive thoughts*, Esta said, *get worse with stress*, and I've certainly been under a lot of stress these last few weeks. Hiding what I was doing from Peter, applying for the job with Schuyler Bennett without him knowing, then worrying that she would call and tell me she'd changed her mind, she didn't need an archivist after all. Hadn't it been too good to be true? The ad had appeared on the library job site as if it had been left there just for me. *Archivist wanted for author, must love books and be willing to relocate. Room and board included.* And when I found out it was Schuyler Bennett, one of my favorite authors, it really had seemed too good to be true—

Usually that's because it's not true. Peter's voice is so real in the car I almost believe that he's sitting in the passenger seat next to me. That he's been there all along. I can even hear what he'd say ▶

13

next. *You have to be realistic. No one's going to give you a job with your background—*

But then I see the sign. WELCOME TO CRANTHAM. POPULATION 4,300. A half a mile later there's a sign pointing to the village center. *After the sign for the village,* Schuyler Bennett had said, *you'll pass the entrance to the hospital. The turnoff for the house is a mile up on the right.*

I see why she mentioned the hospital. The entrance is the most noticeable landmark I've passed in an hour. Two brick pillars and a wrought iron arch with the name Crantham spelled out in large black iron letters. The Crantham Retreat for the Insane, it was called when Schuyler Bennett's father was the head doctor there in the fifties and sixties. Of course it's not called that anymore. Now it's the Crantham Psychiatric Center.

Don't worry, Schuyler Bennett had said when she mentioned the hospital's proximity to her house, *they take a very genteel class of patient there these days— celebrity rehabs, anorexic teenagers, overworked executives. You don't have to worry that any serial killers will get out and make their way over.*

I had laughed, knowing that was *exactly* what I'd be thinking about from then on.

The turn comes up so quickly, I almost miss it. The only sign is a mailbox with a number on it, no name.

I cherish my privacy, Schuyler Bennett had said. *I ask that you not divulge any details about the job to your social circle.*

Social circle? Ha! Who would I have told? The other mothers in the support group? I'd told Laurel, but she hadn't paid attention. No one knows where I am. As I make the turn into the narrow, unlit drive that climbs steeply upward it occurs to me that if I drove off the side of a cliff right now no one would know what had become of us.

Not that I would do that. I would never drive off a cliff, plunging Chloe and me to our fiery deaths.

Leave it! I tell myself.

We climb steeply up through deep pine woods, the trees so close they brush the roof of the car with a whispering sound. At the top of the drive is a stone house with a tower. It looks like the castle in a fairy tale—or in one of Schuyler Bennett's stories.

I pull into the gravel drive. A light has come on in the doorway and I can see the silhouette of a woman behind the glass. For a moment the outline, with its stooped back, looks like the cardboard cutout of a Halloween witch, but then as the woman comes out the door I see it's just that she has a limp and is leaning heavily to one side with a cane. She's much older than her last author picture but still I recognize her as Schuyler Bennett, come out herself to welcome us.

I turn quickly to check on Chloe. In the light from the door I can see her clearly, her face sticky with tears and formula, sound asleep in the car seat. After my morbid fantasy of her being gone I'm almost surprised to see her and for a moment she looks like a stranger. Then I feel a swell of relief followed by the familiar pang of guilt, as if imagining her gone were the same thing as *wanting* her gone.

I turn back around and roll down the window. Schuyler Bennett sticks a crooked hand in and says, "You must be Laurel." ▶

I can feel a hysterical response bubbling up to my lips: *Yes! That's who I must be! But all I say is "Yes, that's me."*

Daphne's Journal, June 11, 20—

It wasn't supposed to be like this.

That's what I said in group today and Esta said there are no *supposed-tos* here.

"*Supposed-to* is society telling us what motherhood should look like. Most of you are here because you didn't measure up to that *supposed-to*. We're here to say to hell with *supposed-to!*"

She actually pumped her fist and there was a smattering of applause and a chorus of *yeahs*—practically a cheering session for the sleep-deprived postpartum crowd. It all made me feel just exactly how I felt in third grade when I asked during a dental hygiene lesson if there was some other way besides brushing to remove the gooey white stuff that collected between my teeth and Miss Dubovsky led the class in a round of "Brush! Brush! Brush!" (She could have told me about flossing instead!)

Chastised. That's how it made me feel. Since this is my journal—Esta suggested we keep a journal in which to write down all the things we're afraid to say out loud—I may as well tell the truth. So there, Esta, your little motivational speech made me feel chastised.

But then one of the other mothers—the blond Valkyrie in $300 True Religion jeans who looks like she was doing Pilates *during* delivery—said, "I'm with Daphne here. I didn't think I'd be spending my baby's first few months feeling homicidal."

"Can you tell us whom you're feeling homicidal toward?" Esta asked, blinking at the Valkyrie. I noticed she hadn't fobbed *her* off with a slogan, but then the Valkyrie didn't look like she was used to being fobbed off.

The Valkyrie didn't answer right away. She crossed one long leg over the other and I noticed that her toenails were painted bright red. Who had time to get a pedicure with a baby at home?

There was a palpable tension in the room. So far all anyone had admitted to was feeling a little blue and maybe "even a little angry" at our progeny when they kept us up all night and spit up in our hair and cracked our nipples with their insistent hungry mouths. But then she smiled, cool as a cucumber, and said, "Right now I'm feeling homicidal towards whoever designed these fucking chairs."

We all moaned in sympathy. All our backs hurt. We could all agree on that.

AFTERWARD WHEN WE were all heading to our cars Valkyrie sidled up to me and said in such a casual aside I wasn't sure she was talking to me, "I was going to say I feel homicidal toward my husband for signing me up for this loony-tunes circus."

I hid my gasp with a laugh. "My husband signed me up too," I admitted in a conspiratorial whisper. "He's been so worried about me he even offered to babysit."

She snorted and rolled her eyes. "Please. Make him pay for a babysitter next time." She gestured to a young girl wheeling a white-bonneted Orbit stroller (the same one I'd seen advertised in *Parenting* for over $700) along the shaded edge of the ▶

parking lot. "That way we can have a playdate afterward."

"How old is your baby?" I asked, cucumber cool myself. *A playdate!* I wanted to jump up and down. Valkyrie wanted to have a playdate with me! I hadn't felt so excited since Todd Brill asked me out in the tenth grade.

"Four months and still screaming through the night, the little bitch."

This time I wasn't able to hide my gasp. I'd never heard anyone call her baby a bitch! I really didn't know what to say to that, but then she was already taking long-legged strides across the asphalt toward the keening cry of the baby, calling, "Here I am, here's Mommy—" And then, in an altogether different voice, to the babysitter, "Has she been crying this whole time? Why didn't you come get me?"

"She only started when she heard your voice," said the girl, a wide-eyed naïf who looked all of sixteen, looking nervously between me and her employer.

"Figures," my new friend said. Then she swooped the baby up in the air, surprising her mid-cry into silence, and making my stomach drop as she held the wiggling baby at arm's length over the hard pavement. "I'm Laurel, by the way, and this little imp"—she gave the startled baby a playful little shake—"is Chloë."

"That's so funny," I said, "my baby's Chloe too."

"Really," she said, arching one perfectly plucked eyebrow (*who has the time to pluck her eyebrows!*), "I guess we're fated to be friends then." ∽